# AIR FAY

## ROSA CARR

Crystal Peake Publisher

www.crystalpeake.co.uk

First edition published in February 2021 by Crystal Peake Publisher

Print I S B N  978-1-912948-34-5
eBook I S B N  978-1-912948-35-2





A catalogue copy of this book is available from the British Library.

Typeset by Crystal Peake Publisher
Cover designed by T K Palad

Visit www.crystalpeake.co.uk for any further information.

# AIR FAY

ROSA CARR

CRYSTAL PEAKE

# How reviews help our authors.

Readers choose books based on recommendations. Leaving an Amazon review is like telling your friends how much you enjoyed your latest read...

After 20-25 reviews, Amazon includes the author's books in 'also bought' and 'you might like' lists. This increases its visibility on the site and helps boost sales.

After 50-70 reviews, Amazon highlights the book for spotlight positions and its newsletter. A HUGE boost for an author.

Reviews help authors sell more books.

Leave your review here.

# PROLOGUE

*Night-time is the best chance to search the forest undetected,* thought the girl as she sneaked out of the house in the bright light of the full moon. Armed with a torch and an old map in a little book, she made her way to the path. She was filled with a righteous sense of duty to go through with this plan set down many decades ago.

Several hours later, however, she was exhausted and disappointed. She spun around on the spot to go back and caught a glimpse of yellow in the torchlight. Swinging the beam back, she saw the yellow rose bush that she had been desperately searching for.

Hurrying over to it, she paused to catch her breath and hide the book safely away.

Whispers floated through the trees, shattering the silence. As the first rays of the brilliantly red sunrise filled the sky, the whispers grew louder. For a moment, the chanting bounced among the trees. Abruptly, it ended, and reality shifted. The girl felt the ground beneath her tilt, and the boundaries of the human world shivered. With a jerk, she disappeared into nothingness.

As she tumbled between the junction of the worlds, her thoughts were a frantic stream of panic.

*This is not right!*

*What did she do to me?!*

That was the last thought she had before excruciating pain

overtook her senses.

Pain. Agony, unlike any other she'd ever experienced, pierced through every inch of her body. It was like a million tiny knives stabbing through her skin. A searing, ripping feeling exploded from the centre of her spine, causing her entire body to shudder. Her thoughts were a blur as the convulsions intensified. *What's happening? I need it to stop.*

She plunged through turbulent air. She felt as though she was being pulled from every direction. The most severe tugging seemed to originate in her back.

She had lost all bearings and didn't have a clue which way was upward. Not that it mattered anyway. She was in no fit state to think about directions.

There was a blinding yellow light, and then nothing.

# Chapter One
## AWAKENING

<u>Lareo</u> ♂

**B**linding yellow light shot through the sky, waking Lareo.

*Where am I?* he wondered in near panic. *Why am I in a forest?*

Without getting up, he looked around for the source of the light, but before he could react, sounds echoed through the forest- CRASH, CRUNCH, THUD...

Lareo got up and stared back and forth. His eyes scanned everything intently. He was simultaneously looking for the source of the disruption and trying to figure out how he'd ended up here.

It took him a few minutes to regain his bearings. Slowly his senses came back to him as he thought back to earlier in the morning.

Lareo stood in his chambers with his ear pressed to the door. He counted to ten. He heard the sound he had been waiting for; the footsteps of a passing guard. He counted another ten, then opened the door and slipped out. He knew the castle better than anyone living in it. And even better, he knew the Sentries' schedules.

Lareo had a bag on his shoulder with everything he would need. Or at least everything he thought he would need. It had taken some imagination, never having been out there long enough to know. He crept through the building as silently as the wind, thanking his training for some things.

He took a back way out, which was always unlocked, and gave him quick access to the forest.

Lareo breathed deeply. Already his nerves were calming down. He dashed across the open space and reached the boundary. He glanced around furtively, and then as quick as a bird, he darted over the wall.

He made it to the forest, but there was no time to rest; he had to get as much of a head start as he could. He began making his way through the trees with the moonlight filtering through to guide him. Dodging trees and plants as he went, he gained speed.

Slowly the moonbeams started to fade, and the sky lightened. Lareo was feeling the strain of the night's journey. Noticing the clearing up ahead, he slowed his pace. Without consciously deciding to do so, he stopped under a tree. Rummaging through his bag, he found a blanket to dump over the leaves he had gathered. He followed his blanket's path and collapsed on the makeshift bed.

The sun was shining brightly now, despite the strange yellow light from earlier. Something else had caught his attention. Bleary-eyed, he looked around. Did something fall? Shaking himself awake, he got up to investigate.

Lareo searched for a while and eventually caught sight of something reddish that stood out among the yellow roses around him. He came across someone lying deep amongst the rose bushes. Peering closely, he was relieved to see that the red stream wasn't blood, but the red hair fanned out of a girl who was lying spread-eagled on her stomach. Her chest rose and fell rhythmically with her breath, convincing him she was relatively unhurt. Her body began twitching as she woke up.

#

## Aria ♀

As she slowly awoke, she opened her eyes only to shut them again as light poured in immediately. It was then that the full weight of the pain returned, and she realised that every inch of her body was throbbing. Panicking, she kept her eyes shut, trying not to burst into tears.

Still keeping her eyes tightly closed, and fighting the pain, she began to get a sense of her surroundings. She was lying on something cushiony. Taking a deep breath, she could smell grass and open air, which helped calm her down. There was also a sweeter scent that she could not place. Gingerly, she moved her right hand, trying to get a sense of what was around her, and felt a cool moistness on something soft, yet spiky. In her left hand, she clutched something.

She opened her eyes tentatively. With the help of the sunbeams, she saw that lush grass cushioned her and that a ring of trees surrounded her. *Perhaps this is a forest of some kind?* she wondered. Before she could turn her head around to look properly, two feet appeared in her vision and, while her mind was trying to catch up, she felt two strong hands grip her arms and pull her to her feet. Excruciating pain hit almost every part of her body, and she howled in pain. The stranger, now satisfied that she was fully conscious, picked her up and walked a few steps. Placing her down gently on the ground, he plopped himself down lazily next to her.

Breathing deeply, while trying to ignore the pain, she took this opportunity to look at the stranger. She noted his thick, wavy hair. It was the colour of the sun and, being quite long, flopped across his piercing green eyes which mirrored the verdant grass around them. His body looked strong and well-built. He was wearing an emerald-green shirt and blue trousers, both of which shimmered like silk. Looking further along, she saw that his feet were bare. As she took in his general appearance, he shifted to reach for something, and, in doing so, she caught sight of his back.

Her breath caught in her throat. She looked at his shoulders, but wings obscured the rest of his back. *Wings!* Her mind screamed. Finally, able to draw breath, she let out an audible gasp which caused her rescuer to give her a puzzled glance.

Looking at this person with wings - *wings!* - she couldn't comprehend that. *Who is he? Where am I? Did he – my rescuer…* her train of thoughts halted. *Is he my rescuer? Did he do this to me?* She looked first to one side, then to the other; she could dart backwards if she had to.

He did not look at her except for a few glances. Looking at his awkward behaviour, she made another realisation: her clothes were in tatters. Her breathing became rapid and shallow. She tried to get up, but her body was still too painful to allow movement.

'Calm down! I'm not going to hurt you.'

'Where am I? What's going on?' At this, he looked even more confused, as if he could not understand her panic.

'This is the Rose Clearing,' he paused, and then added, 'in Aer-Faydom.' Judging from the look on your face, however, I take it you don't know what I mean. You must have hit your head pretty hard because everyone around here is part of this community,' he said. 'Did you come from outside the Faydom then?'

'I don't remember anything... I... something tells me I don't belong here. I mean, you have wings,' she paused to point at them, and then collected her thoughts, 'and that came as a shock to me... and... I... I'm... not used to seeing them.' This was not supposed to be a joke, but apparently the stranger found it hilarious.

'What... are... you... talking... about?' he said this slowly and deliberately, as if hoping she would suddenly know exactly what was going on. 'You also have wings, or hadn't you noticed?' he added as an afterthought. 'You are the same as me, a Fairy...'

Suddenly, she understood the pain in her back. She had not realised it before; it was not only a pain in her back, it was outside of her back, yet she could still feel it. She looked over her shoulder, and there, sure enough, she caught a glimpse of a pair of wings! They were similar to her rescuer's, yet somehow different to his; hers were purple, and his were blue. As if her panicking was not bad already, it got worse.

'Those... WHAT ARE THEY DOING THERE?! I... I shouldn't have them... I... don't...' she stammered while trying to turn and look at her wings.

At this point, she didn't know who looked more scared. His eyebrows shot up, and his eyes widened. Then he frowned in deep concentration. Strangely enough, his alarm seemed to have a calming effect on her agitation.

She squeezed her hands reflexively and felt something in her hand that she had forgotten all about in the apprehension of waking up. Taking advantage of this pause, she finally looked at it. It was a white square, as thin as a leaf and crumpled from being held. She spread it open and saw that there was a word written on it: 'Arianna.'

She stared at it for a few seconds and then glanced up to see him looking at it, distracted enough to regain his composure. He stated, 'Arianna? That's a weird name.'

'My name?'

'Don't you remember that either?'

She shook her head.

'Can I call you Aria instead? It means air. It's more appropriate as our element is Air.'

She was so confused that she stayed silent and deep in thought. She noticed he was smiling tentatively, as if waiting for her approval. She thought about it for a moment, and it seemed to make sense, so she half-smiled and then nodded. The sudden realisation hit her that she did not know his name.

'What's your name?'

'Oh, of course. I'm sorry, I forgot about that. I'm Lareo. Let me see that,' he pointed at the thing in her hand and then opened his hand. Aria passed it to him.

He looked at it puzzled, feeling it as he tried to make sense of what it was.

'This isn't a leaf, nor is it parchment. It is unlike anything I've ever seen before.'

He suddenly gasped and slowly came to a startling conclusion.

'This is human.'

'What?'

'This can only be human made. So that means you are a human and, somehow, you have been transformed into a Fairy!'

'What does 'human' mean?'

Lareo thought about it for a moment. 'They are another... type of... creature,' he said, tentatively trying to find the right words. 'From another place... or world. I'm not really sure, as their existence is mostly just a legend.'

'I... uh... is it possible that I'm one of these creatures?' Aria asked him uncertainly, hoping it was all a bad dream and she would wake up soon.

'Well, I think so. You don't seem to be an Elf, or a Goblin. So that's really the only thing I can think of. I've never personally seen it occur, but I've heard it said that it happened once, many centuries ago,' Lareo said, scratching his head, puzzled. 'I suppose we would have to talk to someone who has heard about this phenomenon.'

They pondered this in silence. Aria went over everything Lareo had just said, and none of it did anything to curb her unease. However, as much as she wished that it was all a terrible dream, something told her that it was not.

Peeking at her rescuer, Aria tried to figure him out; something was off, but she couldn't place it. The feeling of certainty she'd had earlier washed over her, and she accepted that Lareo was perfectly safe, although hiding something. But she shrugged it off; there were bigger things to worry about.

Unexpectedly, Lareo stood up and turned, giving her a clear view of his back. His wings were magnificent: blue, as she had noticed before, but now, looking more closely, she could see patterns mixing two shades of blue. There was a magic about them, because the patterns looked as though they were moving. There was solid muscle fanned out in intervals, and in between the flesh was the actual wing. Suddenly the movement stopped, and the wings seemed to shrink. No, not shrink, she thought. They were narrowing as if to close.

The next thing Aria knew, Lareo took his shirt off, allowing his wings to return to their usual striking size. He threw the shirt at her without looking. 'Here, put that on, then we can move from here and get you cleaned up.'

'What do you mean, cleaned up?' In all the confusion, she had not even looked down at herself properly, except for the glance telling her that her clothes were very torn. She looked now, and shock washed over her, and once more, forced her into silence. All over her were scratches and dirt. She looked up at him and all the emotions that she had been trying to control finally spilt over and she began to sob.

Lareo looked so startled that he stayed rooted to the spot, and as his senses came back to him, he turned. 'Now you start crying?' He laughed, attempting to cheer Aria up, but it only made things worse. 'I'm sorry I didn't mean that. Calm down. We'll get everything sorted out; I promise. Nothing hurt you badly. Those scratches are just from the rose thorns. I guess that when you were transformed into a Fairy, you fell and unluckily landed in the roses because you didn't know how to use your wings. But luckily your wings are undamaged. I also think it was the fall that wiped out your memory, not the transformation.'

This seemed to have worked because Aria managed to calm down and stop crying. 'I d-don't know how to p-put this on over m-my w-w-wings.'

Lareo smiled at this and picked up the shirt she was holding. Gently he closed one of her wings, which retracted and allowed one side of the shirt to slide on, and then he did the same to the other side. It was a slow process because he knew that she was hurting all over, and he didn't want to make it worse. When the shirt was on, he eased her up, making sure to balance her weight. The shirt fell as she stood up and reached halfway down her thighs. Looking up at him, she discovered that he was quite a bit taller than her. Then she looked past him and realised that she couldn't see the sky clearly through the thick trees.

With Lareo practically carrying Aria, they walked over beyond the rose bushes, and she saw a river which filled the silence with a bubbling, rushing sound. Next to it was a small campsite which had a bed made with a clump of leaves. Close by was a little shiny grey pot with an orangey-red liquid in it. There were also a couple of medium-sized bags. Before she could ask about it, she got an explanation.

'I was sleeping over there when I heard you fall. It took me a while to find exactly where you had landed. That's lava from the big lava reservoir. For heating things.' He didn't say more, and, from the look on his face, she didn't want to ask more about it.

They edged close to the river, and he set her down. Telling

her to clean herself up, he left to give her some privacy. Looking in the reflection of the water, she studied her overall appearance. Dark red hair gleamed in the sunlight, and sparkling turquoise eyes stared back at her, which, strangely enough, seemed to be the same colour as Lareo's wings.

Aria tentatively pulled one of her wings around her so that she could see it. It was smooth to touch. She could see the moving patterns, marvelling at the sight of them up close. The actual wing was indescribable. It was flexible yet durable. It felt like skin, but it was much sturdier. She could see they were a light purple colour with blue streaks running across them. And the palest yellow, that almost looked white, lined the outer edge. She released her wing gently into place.

Lareo came back from the camp carrying an old-looking shirt and a small pot. He began ripping the shirt into strips. When he finished, he took the small wooden container and came to sit down next to Aria. Without a word, he held out the pot as if to ask permission, and when she nodded, he started gently rubbing the contents onto her scratches.

Aria couldn't identify it, and when she asked about it, he said, 'It's a salve made from a plant called tea-tree, turned into a paste. It helps to heal cuts and grazes.'

When he had finished putting the salve on, he wrapped the strips of torn shirt around the bigger grazes.

By the time he had finished, the surrounding area had become darker. Turning to Aria, Lareo said, 'I don't have much food left. I was planning on being at my friend's house by now. Don't apologise; it's not your fault,' he added, as she began to apologise. 'Naturally, I only packed provisions for myself.'

'Where were you coming from?'

He did not answer her question, but instead got up and said that he would go to look for some more food. Aria felt hesitant distrust from him in response to her question. This confused her. How could she have read him so well if they had only just met? *Maybe I'm reading too much into things*, she thought. She put it out of her mind as she waited for him to come back.

Lareo returned sometime later with another cup filled with different kinds of berries and plants. He placed the cup down near the lava pot and then helped her move closer to it. Hunger gnawed at Aria's stomach as she smelled the food, and she wondered how she hadn't noticed it before. They ate in silence, and she was surprised to find that she liked everything he gave her. *Maybe he didn't like what I'd asked earlier?* she wondered and decided to apologise, anyway.

'I'm sorry if I upset you earlier.'

With that, he got up and walked away to make a bed for Aria, using a pile of large leaves that he had collected, and a spare blanket. Looking over, she saw that his bed, also made of leaves and a blanket, was already prepared. When Lareo had finished, he got up, walked over to her, lifted her gently and then placed her on the bed. A thought struck her: *How do I sleep without crumpling my wings?* As if he could read her mind, Lareo said, 'You can retract your wings. Watch mine.'

He turned around, and she watched in fascination as his wings closed again. This time she paid close attention and saw them slowly recede into his back. She moved closer and saw two bumps by his shoulder blades about half the size of her fist.

'You probably won't be able to do that yet. So, let's just wrap them in silk,' he said as he pulled some out of his bag.

When Lareo had finished helping Aria with her wings, he went over to his bags and took out a small pot with another herbal concoction. 'This is valerian,' he explained. 'It's a calmative and will help you sleep.' She drank it and was asleep before she realised it.

# Chapter Two
## FLYING AWAY

<u>Lareo</u> ♂

Lareo sat by the river the next morning, deep in thought about the day before. As he watched the sunbeams spreading through the forest and listened to the birds wake up with beautiful songs, he thought, *I haven't heard the birds singing in years. I used to sit with Brezan and his father when we were young, waiting in silence for the music to start.* Those had been good times, before everything changed for the worse.

*Now,* Lareo thought, *the situation is entirely different. I'm not in the courtyard at home where we used to sit, but rather, in the middle of the forest. I'm not sitting peacefully in the company of friends but thinking about my plan after my escape.*

He felt as though his life was starting anew now that he'd reached the forest. He wanted to be on the move, not cooped up inside... *definitely* not that... because he loathed being trapped indoors. The taste of freedom was a sweet one; he could feel the fresh air and the forest surround him, and he felt calmer than he had in years, although he was still very uncertain about things. In particular, he didn't know what to think of Aria. He had spent a lot of the night thinking about what had happened. Even now, he had trouble believing it.

*Human?* he thought. *HU-man... human?*

Lareo was confused by her appearance. He had always thought that humans were vicious monsters who relished destruction. But looking at Aria, she looked like any other Fairy, apart from her reaction to having wings. If she was what humans were like, then they can't possibly be as bad as he'd always thought. And it most certainly had nothing to do with how attractive she looked. *I don't like her in that way, of course,* he scolded himself.

Lareo put those ideas out of his mind and focused on what he was doing: gathering water. He was not using small pots that they could carry, but one large pot. He wasn't gathering water for them to take with them on the journey, but to stay there longer. Aria wandered over, looking disorientated and confused.

'Hello, Lareo,' she greeted.

'Aria,' Lareo nodded in reply. 'How are you feeling this morning?'

'I'm not as sore as yesterday,' she said, and then asked him about the large bowl.

He replied, 'I decided that we shouldn't move on until you get used to using your wings. We don't fly if we're inside, but we do fly everywhere we go when we're outdoors, and if others see that you can't fly, it will raise suspicion. As you're feeling better, I will start teaching you today.'

'I didn't even think of that. Why did you say you… I mean, uh, we don't fly inside?' she frowned.

'When we are indoors, we hardly ever use our wings as it takes up too much space. It becomes easier to knock things over. It's just good manners.' Smiling, he continued, 'We shall eat once I've finished. I found some roots that are good to eat when cooked.' As he said this, he went off to the lava pot.

Having put the lava away, he sat next to the spot where

it had been. When she reached him, she saw that he was concentrating on another jar in his hands. This one was grey and shiny. He had an area cleared out in front of him, with a shallow bowl in the same shiny grey. Slowly, a small glob of lava rose out of the jar and landed in the bowl.

'How...?' she trailed off, pointing vaguely at the area.

'Oh, um, I guess I should have explained that one beforehand,' he said sheepishly. 'We all have magic. We can make things move; do pretty much anything, except make fire or any other element.'

'Do I?'

'I don't know, we would need to find out, I guess,' he said uncertainly.

'You're putting the bowl into the lava?'

'It's made with a special Elf-made material. It doesn't burn, so it's safe to use with something hot like lava. But it keeps the heat in it. We can keep the food or whatever else hovering over it to cook.'

'Why can't you make fire?' she asked, puzzled.

'No one can create an element. We must use the lava. Everyone has access to the lava reservoir and can buy the elf jars and bowls. You only need a small amount per household because it is eternal.'

'Oh,' she said, nodding.

During breakfast, Lareo thought about the flying lesson. In fact, he had been awake thinking most of the night. It had come almost as a shock to him when he had realised that she was not able to fly. If she couldn't fly, someone would notice immediately. When he got up in the morning, he had come up with a plan. He needed to work out how flying *actually* took place. It was such an automatic thing that he couldn't even remember how he had learnt as a child.

He had started by flapping his wings. Then he had to tune in to that part of his body; it had taken a while to consciously find precisely the right spot in his back that controlled the movement, but eventually he had found it.

Concentrating hard, he took his mind into his body. He tracked the movement from the joining, out to the rest of the wings. He discovered that in this joint lay all the power. Therefore, he had to get Aria acquainted with this new spot, and the new appendages.

Once the flapping began, it was easy enough to work the wings: the beating became rhythmic, and the air flowing around them held the body up in the air. Then it was a matter of flying on the air currents and adjusting how much fluttering there was for direction.

After a rather tasty breakfast, they got started. Positioning himself behind Aria, Lareo started gently flexing her wings.

When she told Lareo that her wings hardly hurt, he was relieved. 'Good, that will make things easier. We'll start by getting you used to controlling them. It won't be easy, but slowly you will get the hang of it. Now concentrate on where I am touching. Once you acknowledge that feeling, I want you to try to move the surrounding area.'

She tried doing what he said. Concentrating on her back, Aria focused on the spot where he was touching. Feeling the connection to her wings, they became as commonplace, like her arms or legs. Although she was not used to having to control any part of her body consciously, she could feel a slight movement. Encouraged by this, Aria tried harder. After a short while of concentrating and attempting to make a few movements, she got the hang of it. Surprisingly, her wings started beating hard enough to raise her off the ground slightly for a few seconds.

'You're doing it, Aria! This is fantastic! Now we shall try using them to hold you up. We'll start from a low branch,' he said, leading her to a nearby tree. 'Right, this will do. Now climb up. All I want you to do is step off the branch while you flap your wings, like you have been doing. That should keep you up, at the very least. If not, I will be here to catch you.'

She did as he said, but she couldn't seem to do it properly. She kept falling instead of staying up. By lunchtime, she was hurting all over like the day before. They sat in silence and ate the roots left over from breakfast.

'I'll try again,' Aria said, once they'd finished.

Aria glared at the branch as she neared it. Closing her eyes and visualising what she had done before, she concentrated on finding the feeling in her wings. Once she had done that, she started moving them. It was only small twitches at first, which slowly got bigger until finally she could flap her wings vigorously. She took a deep breath and stepped off the branch.

'Lareo! I'm flying! I *actually* did it,' she exclaimed as she landed gently.

'Well done! That was perfect. Now I want you to try again, but instead of flying down, I want you to fly up. You're going against gravity so it will be harder, but I know you can do it.'

She did the same as before, but it took more power to lift herself. Her face was a mask of utter concentration. They kept practising all afternoon. Sometimes Lareo would stay on the ground in case she fell, and other times he flew up with her. They both preferred it when they flew side by side. Eventually, she could get her wings to move without concentrating so hard. They stopped practising when night began to fall.

Lareo prepared the rest of the roots from the morning meal that they had not finished.

'I think we should stay here one more day so you can get more practice flying.'

'That sounds good,' she said with a thoughtful look. She took a deep breath as if to brace herself and said, 'Yesterday you mentioned asking someone who might know what happened to me...,' she trailed off, giving him the chance to answer if he wanted to.

There was a long pause. He looked down at his chest where there was a beautiful blue stone on a chain. Aria looked at the stone with a frown but didn't say anything.

She looked up at him expectantly. Was it safe to answer her question? He looked down at his chain again. The lapis lazuli stone wasn't glowing. It hadn't glowed when he had approached her yesterday either. The stone never lied. She was being completely honest and was no threat to him. But her very nature worried him.

She was a human which complicated matters significantly. It had been quite a shock to figure that out the day before, and he was still coming to terms with it. He had heard stories about them, but only knew a few details about what they were and what their lives were like.

Looking at her again, she seemed normal to Lareo. Other

than the wings, to which she had reacted poorly, she hadn't mentioned anything else, so Lareo thought it safe to assume everything else about her was the same as he believed it to be. *This meant that humans aren't very different from Fairies or Elves,* he mused. He just couldn't get over this similarity; it was all he could think about now.

Looking at her, he could feel an innocent confusion radiating from her. *She genuinely doesn't know who or where she is. It doesn't make sense, but I need to help her. I don't know why, but I agree with the stone and feel compelled to trust her. I need to know more about her.*

*It's more than that. Since meeting her, I feel different.* Lareo hadn't had a moment to stop and think about what he had done since the chaos of yesterday. *That... trapped feeling... the feeling that I was being forced down a path that wasn't right... it's gone.* He marvelled at this realisation. *This feels right. This unknown path, as strange as that sounds, feels like I'm finally where I'm meant to be.*

He took a deep breath and answered, 'I suppose we'd have to talk to one of the Wise Leaders. They would be the only ones who know enough about everything to help us.'

'Who are the Wise Leaders?'

'They are the oldest in the community, and they gather all the magical knowledge. They are the second most revered after the Royal Family. Some of them teach,' he replied hesitantly.

'Do you think these Wise Leaders can turn me back and help me get my memory back? When can we go?' she asked excitedly.

'Hold your Griffins! We aren't going to rush anywhere just

yet. You could be in danger if it spread around that you were a human who had transformed,' he said. Then, realising she was confused, he continued, 'There are evil Fairies, and other creatures, that would use you for malevolent purposes. You know about the human world and their weapons, which could be used to wipe out the entire Fairy population. Even if you can't remember it for yourself, they have magical powers that they can use to extract those memories. So no, we aren't going to rush off anywhere.'

'So, I'll be going with you?' she asked hopefully.

He pondered about that. She would hold him up. He was already behind with his plan to get to safety. He couldn't waste any more time; the Sentries could catch up with him soon. She probably should go with him, though. No one else would protect her.

Sighing as he reached this conclusion, he said, 'Yes, I suppose that's the best plan. I'll be staying at the house of my friend; he won't be there, but his parents kindly offered to let me stay with them for a while. I'm sure they wouldn't mind having you there as well.'

This made her happy for some reason. *I suppose it's because I'm all she has*, he thought.

'You have a Royal Family?' she asked. This threw Lareo off. *She can't know the truth about me.*

'Yes, there are a few Royal Families. Ours live near our Wise Leaders,' he answered tensely. 'Let's get some sleep now.'

# Chapter Three
## ADAPTING

<u>Aria</u> ♀

With that abrupt end to the conversation, they headed over to their beds. After a while, Aria heard Lareo's breathing deepen. *Well, at least one of us can sleep*, she thought to herself as images of the day buzzed around in her head. *Flying was amazing! I can't wait to try it again! And what was with that odd gesture when I asked Lareo about someone who could help me? Why did he look at his necklace?* But then there were the not-so-pleasant aspects of evil creatures possibly trying to get her.

Maybe the disturbing thoughts still occupied her mind, as Aria suddenly felt her hairs stand on edge; she looked around for the source. Peering into the trees, she saw nothing but darkness. There were no gleaming eyes looking back at her. She looked over at Lareo and considered waking him up. But she decided not to; she was already a burden without adding her worries to his. Eventually she fell asleep, with dreams of flying next to Lareo.

The next morning, she woke up to a noise she couldn't place. It was a strange chirping musical sound. It seemed familiar, but before she could give more thought to it, Lareo greeted her.

'How did you sleep, Aria?' he asked gently.

'Well,' she replied happily; all notions of evil creatures and being watched were entirely out of her thoughts, and she felt a lot better today.

'We can have some food, and then you can practise flying some more if you would like to.' That was exactly what she had been hoping for.

Lareo started to prepare their breakfast as he heated some water in one pot. He had some nuts hovering over another bit of lava. He had his back to Aria while she sat nearby. His wings transfixed her. They were mesmerising. She studied them carefully as she couldn't see her own wings very well, and the idea of wings fascinated her.

As Aria had noticed earlier, Lareo's wings were blue, but not that of the sky (which she occasionally managed to glimpse between the trees), it was more of a turquoise blue. They were definitely more blue than green. *That's strange! It sounds absurd! How can a colour be more than one kind?* Throughout the turquoise, there were streaks of other colours: the faintest gold shimmer, barely visible; a pale yellow surrounding the outer edge of the wings; and streaks of purple through them. The colours weren't the only things that she saw. The faint patterns were visible up close. They were constantly moving, with a rhythm to it. It was as though the pattern stayed fixed and yet moved at the same time.

Aria then looked at the wings as a whole. They looked so thin and almost flimsy, with a transparency about them; she had felt her own wings, so she knew that they were strong. They were infinitely contradictory.

The one thing that she hadn't been able to see on her own wings was the supporting structure. She could see that they were like veins running through the wings, which were the same colour as the rest, only slightly darker. They looked much more substantial than the rest of the wings. She absentmindedly reached out and touched one of Lareo's.

Suddenly, Aria snapped to attention as Lareo stiffened and then turned around. She snatched her hand back, mortified.

'That's all right. I'm sure you're curious,' he said.

Aria smiled tentatively.

'Your wings are beautiful,' she said uncertainly. She wasn't sure if it was rude to talk about someone's wings.

'Thanks,' he smiled. 'All wings are beautiful.'

She nodded to encourage him to continue.

'There are magnificent combinations. The Royals have a bright, sparkling gold and the Wise Leaders retain their original colour but develop a silvery gleam to theirs,' he said, looking down at the stone on his chest again, and then glancing away. *What a bizarre habit.* Aria gave a mental shrug and overlooked the behaviour.

'We both have a very pale yellow on the edges,' she pointed out.

Lareo frowned and cocked his head at this. His wing moved around him, enveloping his one side. He looked at it closely, and his eyes widened.

His mouth gaped for a moment. 'That wasn't there before.'

His brow furrowed, and he stared into space, lost in thought. His expression cleared, and he said, 'Let's finish eating. We have lots to do.'

When their meal was over, they went back to the same branch. Before Aria could climb up, Lareo held her back.

'Aria, today, you are going to try taking off from the ground, not the branch,' he said. 'Taking off from the branch gave you a bit of a help because the fall made you airborne. If you can start flying from the ground, then our work is done.'

Aria took a deep breath. She got her wings moving without concentrating as hard as yesterday, but she wasn't rising. She flapped harder, and gradually she began to rise. After that first extra effort that was needed, she was flying better than yesterday.

Aria practised all morning. It took a while to get used to the extra effort needed to fly from the ground, but then, she could fly more instinctively. They stopped and went back to the camp where Aria collapsed in a heap on her makeshift bed. Lareo smiled at her as he wandered off into the forest in search of food.

While Aria waited for Lareo to return, she looked around her properly. Over the past couple of days, she had noticed bits and pieces about the forest, but she hadn't analysed it. *This is extraordinarily beautiful and tranquil.* Though the trees were dense, they weren't overcrowded, or overgrown with a lot of plants. They were thick enough to dim the light and cast a greenish haze but not block out the sun.

Among the trees in the distance, Aria noticed that she was surrounded by animals who were wandering around; however, nothing came near her. There were some medium-sized, brown-furred animals on spindly legs eating grass – she strained her mind for the word – *'deer'*. A small, fluffy grey animal with long ears hopped quickly through the bushes, – she paused for a moment – *'rabbit'*. The night before she had seen big golden eyes, and she wasn't entirely sure what they belonged to as it thankfully did not approach them.

Other small animals scuttled past. They were brown, had long bodies, and tiny paws with a big, full fluffy tail. The word sprang to mind: *'squirrel'*. *They are so cute, bouncing along.* She kept trying to spot more of them.

There were also all the sounds Aria heard. There was rustling at ground level, under the bushes. Tweeting and singing up in the high trees. There were the occasional growls and snarls from far away. At night there was a constant chirping. It was all strangely comforting, and yet it felt like a new experience.

Another interesting thing Aria had noticed was that the air was crisp and clean. It was cool but not cold; there was not much moisture hanging in the air. There was often a soft breeze flowing past. Closing her eyes, she focused on the air passing across her skin. The serenity broke when she heard footsteps coming from one side.

'Aria, I found some apple trees,' Lareo told her excitedly as he arrived back. 'I thought we could eat them for the next few days. However, I'll need your help with carrying these. There are too many for me to carry by myself. I hate to ask you to do something this big so soon after you have learnt to fly, but if we can get the apples, we'll have enough until we get to the village.'

'I'd love to,' she said excitedly.

They flew in the direction he had come from and soon found the apples. As they landed next to the apple trees, Aria couldn't believe how many colours of apples there were. She didn't have a clue how they would manage to carry them.

Lareo, however, had a plan. Pulling out a net from his bag and handing her one end, he explained, 'It's made of spun silk, like the smaller piece of silk I used to cover your wings.'

It was dark grey, similar to the bags at the campsite, and was a fine mesh which wouldn't let anything slip through.

'There is no way this silk is going to be able to carry all those apples,' Aria said to him in disbelief.

'It isn't ordinary silk; it is Elf-made. This is the same material that was used to make my bags. The Elves have a talent for creating objects and clothing. They intertwine different raw materials with their magic that makes them different to normal Fairy-made things.'

With that, they opened the net, put it down, and started putting the apples into it. When there were enough, they closed the net around the pile of apples. Aria concentrated like before. After a few attempts, she finally got her wings beating and slowly rose. Lareo waited for her to get up, then he handed her one end of the net and took the other end himself. Slowly, they lifted the apples together and flew back in the direction they had come from. Finally, their camp came into sight, and they landed. Aria once more collapsed onto her bed, but she was smiling from ear to ear.

'Let's get them ready for tomorrow's journey,' said Lareo.

'All right,' Aria said as she got up to help.

'We can alternate between them and any other fruit we find. I'm sorry about the food choices. In the village, they have more supplies and they also have vegetables to eat,' Lareo explained. 'We can cut some up now ready for the morning.'

Lareo took out a knife he kept on his hip and slashed into

some apples. Cutting them into pieces, he handed some to Aria.

'We'd better eat these quickly,' said Aria.

Lareo raised an eyebrow.

'Won't the fresh apples turn brown if we keep them out for too long?' she asked uncertainly.

'What?' he asked, with the same expression she had seen on his face on the first day.

'Apples turn brown if they're kept out too long, don't they? You're supposed to put lemon juice on them to keep them fresh,' Aria explained, confused as to why he did not know this. *Wasn't it common sense?* She thought.

'No, they don't. I have never in my life seen an apple change colour,' he said, exasperated. Then, suddenly, he gasped, and his eyes widened. 'Aria! You just had a human flashback. This is good! It means that you can get your memory back.' Lareo's sudden change of mood, from one extreme to the other, jarred Aria and she didn't register what he had said at first. As it dawned on her, she began to laugh. This was such good news. The sooner she remembered where she came from, the sooner she could go back.

They ate the apple pieces in good spirits. It had been a long and tiring day, indeed, but it had been a good one. They were talking as they ate, of nothing in particular but the highlights of the day. When they had finished, Aria barely had enough energy to drag herself to her bed. Sleep soon overtook her.

#

Aria woke up to that same strange chirping sound again. She had dreamed disturbing dreams of people lurking just beyond sight, as if they were behind a veil which masked their activities.

Slowly, Aria opened her eyes and shook the scary thoughts out of her head. From the corner of her eye, she saw Lareo packing up his camp. He had cut up some apples for breakfast, and there was yet another pot of something. When she sat up, he smiled and walked over.

'I found some honey that we can eat. It will help you regain your strength to fly. We can't follow the river for too long, as it's risky and not as covered. We'll go through the Aer-Forest, where the trees and foliage are dense enough to provide shelter and protection, but because of that, it's a bit more difficult to travel through. I would prefer not to stop too often so we can try to get to the village sooner.'

He poured the honey over the apple pieces, and they ate contentedly. Taking advantage of the good mood, Aria decided to ask some questions that were still bouncing around in her head.

'How old are the Wise Leaders?' she asked.

'Uh… the youngest is about 150 years old, I think,' he said, shrugging.

All Aria could do was stare at him in awe. If that was the age of the youngest of the eldest Fairies, how long did they live for? She asked as much.

'The oldest Elder I know of is about 500. But time doesn't move the same for us as it does for humans from what I understand. I believe our years last longer. When we die, we become part of the sky as stars. In that way, we give back to nature and don't just consume endlessly. Of course, we help nature while we are alive. We don't believe in harming the earth for our own gain. As I understand it, that is one of the differences between us and humans.'

Aria couldn't believe what she had heard. Though she knew nothing of other worlds, having spent only a few days in this one, she had come to appreciate and respect the nature around her. It had saved her life and helped to Heal her. Now that conversation had resumed, she wasn't going to let it slip away.

'Tell me about the forest and the Fairies living in it,' Aria prompted him.

'The Faydom is set into the mountain. If you follow this river upwards, it becomes narrower, and at the top there is a waterfall. On the far side of the waterfall is the Royal Castle. That's where the Royal Family lives. A high wall protects them. Inside the wall, the garden is decorated with the most beautiful flowers, and there is something magical about it. You can feel the magic in the air, almost as if it was put there to make the place even more beautiful.'

'Opposite the waterfall is the Wise Leaders' Tower. The tower is next to the mountaintop. They have a lot of protection around them because they tend to get paranoid in their old age and guard their precious treasures and secrets.'

'Following the river down the mountain, through the forest, there is the village where the ordinary Fairies live. Beyond the castle, there are strong defences against an outside threat. There aren't many visitors from elsewhere, because those defences are all around the forest and the village. The forest where we are now is between the tower and the village.'

Throughout this explanation, Aria imagined everything as he said it. It all sounded amazing to her. Something was missing in that explanation. 'What's the village like?'

He hesitated, then said, 'I think we should get more food. You will need your strength for today; we still have quite a bit of ground to cover.'

#

After eating and packing up, they gathered water for the trip and set off. Lareo was right; the flight through the forest was quite strenuous. They stopped occasionally, but Aria was coping well enough, which she could tell made Lareo happier. They stopped for a lunch of dried apples and added some nuts, which were a welcome addition to the meal. They rested for a while which gave them a chance to talk some more. 'How do you know the family you're going to?' Aria asked, hoping it wasn't wrong of her to broach the subject.

'I don't even remember. I practically grew up with their son and his father,' Lareo said rather shiftily. After a few minutes of silence, he said, 'I think once we get closer to the village, we must wait until nightfall. I don't think it would be a good idea to walk through while everyone is still around. Once we get to the house, we can work out a cover story for you.'

'That sounds fine. Are you just going to hide out in the house to avoid people gossiping?' she asked. This seemed to her to be an important question. Aria had been hoping that Lareo could show her around, as she wasn't keen to leave him and have to meet new people.

'No, I'm hoping I can get a disguise that can hide me well enough to allow me out into public. I'm not sure how though, because a Fairy's wings are particular. We'll have to see if it can be done when we get there. While we're talking about it, you will also need a disguise for your wings just in case,' he replied, looking slightly worried.

'What do you mean?' Aria was now confused again.

'It's the patterns and the combination of the colours; each individual has different patterns. I don't know if you noticed, but if you look closely, you can see the patterns and they look as if they are moving; that is a specific ancient Fairy-magic that we're all born with. I've already attempted to conceal the colour, which seemed to work well enough, but the problem comes with the pattern. If a well-trained eye looks at my wings, they will know who I am straight away. The problem is that it isn't easy to get a disguise. It takes powerful magic, but we should be fine.'

'What do you mean by colour?' she asked.

'The colours were supposed to represent the parents so the child could be identified. I think it was important when there was trouble so that children weren't lost. But the colours have been mixed over the centuries, so no one really keeps track any more. It may not be necessary to get a disguise, come to think of it...' he trailed off, talking more to himself than to Aria.

'How are we going to blend in if everyone realises that we don't come from here?' Aria began to get panicky again.

'Don't worry, I have thought of that. There indeed aren't many outsiders around here, but those seeking refuge have come in the past. Nomadic communities have always feared attack, but in the past few decades, it has got worse. Sometimes the attack is so bad that it leaves no survivors. People won't ask too many questions if the word spreads about us. We'll stay indoors for a few days to make it look like we're recovering from injuries. And luckily for us, my friend's mother is one of the most renowned Treaters around. She would be able to help us keep our cover.'

*Wow, he's actually put a lot of consideration into all of this*, Aria thought. *Lucky that it was him who rescued me.*

'What's a Treater?' she asked, confused.

'They are specially trained to Heal injuries,' Lareo explained. 'That will tie in with our cover story. And hopefully that will keep the gossip at bay, you know, discretion and all.' Lost in thought, he didn't even notice Aria's growing suspicion. 'If people don't look too closely at us, then anyone who might come looking for me won't get directions.'

As Aria considered this, another notion struck her. *What was he running away from, if he could come up with a cover story this elaborate? I hope he doesn't turn out to be some runaway criminal.*

Forcing a smile, she said, 'That all sounds great. Lucky for me that you found me, I would be completely lost.'

He smiled back, although his smile was a genuine one. *He looks so handsome when he smiles, pity he doesn't do it more often.* Shocked to find herself thinking this way, she shook herself to clear her head, and finished off her food. As Aria wondered more about it, she had the same feeling as before, which she couldn't explain to herself. She somehow knew that he was no threat to her. There was an air about him that made it very clear to her that Lareo was good.

They set off soon after this, which Aria was happy about. It gave her little time to dwell on anything except the forest which they were fighting their way through.

#

They had travelled a fair distance, when quite unexpectedly Lareo stopped. It took Aria a few moments to figure out what had occurred. In front of Lareo fluttered a bird, but it wasn't the only thing there. The bird was carrying a leaf. All she could do was stare, as she had so many times before. They landed, and the bird followed them. Lareo took the leaf, which had markings on it. As he read it, his face grew grave and ashen.

Suddenly he looked up and said grimly, 'Extra security has been put into place, today in fact. Apparently, something happened to a Royal, and they want the Castle Sentry in place. This is going to make things difficult for us because they will check everyone. The letter is from my friend's mother. It says that her husband is guarding the edge of the village. There is still time before that happens for us to do something. Once she finds us, we'll be fine because she can vouch for us. As a Treater, she can get us past on stretchers. They are used when people are injured and can't travel far. She said that we must send her a message, then she can come fetch us and one of us can pretend to be injured.'

'You said Sentry. What is that?'

'They are, um, guards or fighters that protect the Faydom.

They have different responsibilities.'

Aria nodded. She found this all fascinating, but she was also still caught up with the bird. She realised that she had known everything that she had come across, despite her memory loss. Aria did something without thinking, that seemed normal. But things that she had not come across yet, she did not know. She thought back and realised that birds chirp in the morning and that was what she had been hearing.

'What's on your mind?' Lareo asked.

'I just thought that I didn't remember what a bird was. I heard them chirping in the morning, but I couldn't place them until I saw this one. It made me realise that everything I know so far are only things we've come across. When I see things now, I automatically know what it is, but not with other things.'

'Don't worry too much about it. Everything will come right eventually. Whether by itself or with help, your memory will come back. Let me send a message back.'

From inside one of his bags, he took out yet another pot and a feather. 'We collect the feathers that fall out of the birds. Mostly we cut the points and use them for writing. But because the inside is hollow, they have a few other uses. To write we use ink made from crushed blackberries mixed with a few other plants and bark to give it a dark colour. We usually write on leaves. The Wise Leaders, however, make beautiful parchment from bark and other plants once they die or are damaged. We don't use it for messages because it takes too long to make, and it's a waste of precious trees. The Wise Leaders make it themselves and use it for important things like our history and their knowledge and wisdom, as it lasts longer.'

Lareo went back to the message. He carefully placed the pot on the ground and opened it; inside was a black liquid. He turned the leaf over and, taking the feather, he put the tip into the ink and then gently wrote a few words. Aria was amazed. When he had finished, he blew on it gently to dry it. Once he was sure it was dry, he folded it and gave it back to the bird.

'We should figure out which one of us should pretend to be injured,' he said, as they watched the bird fly out of sight.

'That's pretty obvious, isn't it?' she said, laughing.

It took him a few seconds to realise what Aria meant, and then he also started laughing.

'I hadn't even realised. You are right. That would be perfect because then I can carry you in case there are Sentries around.'

'Wait, I'm confused. You said that we're being picked up by the Treater lady?'

'Yes, we are, but she can't come yet. We have to make it to the Path. From there, there should be someone who can send for Lady Bia. She's my friend's mother, the Treater.'

'Are we on our way to that Path?'

'No, we have to do a lot of flying to make up ground. I hate to ask, but…'

'It's fine. I understand. We have to do it. Can I ask you a question?'

'Sure.'

'Why can't you Heal yourself? I mean, you have magic, can't you Heal by yourselves?'

He pondered the question for a moment before answering, 'Well, to be honest, I've never thought about it before. We can

Heal minor injuries for each other if we know how. We can't Heal ourselves. I suppose it's because we've always lived in a community with other Fairies and so we rely on others. If we can do it all ourselves, then we wouldn't need each other. We can only do basic magic as we grow up. We go to specialists in a field to become more advanced. If people wanted to become Treaters or any other profession, we would need to get extra training. Most people don't bother, but we do need those professions. Treaters take care of big injuries and illnesses. I could Heal you if you only had one scratch, but if I had to do it one by one, we would be here for ages.'

'What about the salve that you put on me? Does everyone know how to make and use those kinds of things?'

'Uh… no. I learnt that when I was younger. Most people don't know a Treater well enough to be able to learn from them first-hand. Now we must conserve our strength for the flight ahead and not talk.'

With that, the conversation ended. Aria was a bit stunned. There was a tone in his voice that she had not yet heard. *Strange that he did not like to talk about things involving himself,* Aria pondered to herself. After that, she was too absorbed in the scenery to think about the mysteries surrounding Lareo. She felt comfortable and happy in his presence, and that was all that mattered. She hoped that he felt the same about her but couldn't be sure because he kept his expressions carefully guarded.

They continued flying at a steady pace. The trees became more spread out. *Finally,* Aria thought, *we seem to be getting closer.* As if hearing her deliberations, Lareo said, 'We're getting closer to the spot where we can get help. Do you remember the plan?'

'Yes, of course.' *How could I not remember the plan?* She thought. It had been drilled into her for the last few hours. That was all he had spoken about during their journey. Even now she could hear his voice repeating the same thing: 'When we land closer to the village, I will carry you in. You will need to pretend to be unconscious. I will explain that we're survivors from a recently attacked village. I'm hoping they will be sympathetic and not ask too many questions. Then they will call Lady Bia.'

Lareo started descending, and Aria followed close behind him. Suddenly, she felt nervous. She was thinking about the plan she now knew so well, but what if something went wrong? What if they did not believe us? They're going to figure us out, and then they're going to kill us. They'll know I'm not a Fairy and arrest me, or worse. Her breathing got faster, and it had nothing to do with the physical exertion.

# Chapter Four
## HEALING

Lareo ♂

Lareo flew through the forest, happily leading Aria to Brezan's parents' house. The trees were thinning out, so he knew that they were getting close.

He looked forward to reaching shelter and having some good food. Though being outside made him happier than he'd been in a long time, he wasn't very good at surviving alone. He chuckled to himself at his feeble attempts at making meals of berries and nuts; it surprised him that Aria had decided to stick around.

'Aria-' Lareo called over his shoulder, about to tell her that they were nearly there. However, he was interrupted when he felt a strange plummeting sensation.

He couldn't understand this sensation because he was still flying and moving at the same height and speed as he had been a few moments before.

Lareo whirled around to see Aria dropping to the ground.

He dived after her, but he couldn't reach her. He flattened his wings so that he could dive better, but it was no use. She would hit the ground at any moment.

Instinctively Lareo stretched out his hand as if to grab hold of her arm, and the strangest thing happened. Aria slowed down. She slowed down in mid-air.

Instead of hitting the ground with a fatal crash, she landed with a jarring thud. As he neared her, Lareo could see several of her limbs were wrongly angled, but that could be healed in minutes. The important thing was that Aria was alive. He didn't care how it was possible; that was something he would focus on later.

Lareo landed hastily next to Aria and examined her. He didn't want to make her injuries worse, but he had to get her to help and safety. He scooped her up and headed to the village, with an actual reason to explain their story.

#

## Aria ♀

*Not again. I really should stop doing this.* Aria thought. For the second time in only a few days, Aria woke up without any idea of where she was or how she had arrived there.

She tried to move, to get her bearings. Her breath caught in her throat as she clenched her teeth and stifled a scream. Her whole body throbbed with pain. A gasp of breath escaped her, and she whimpered. Even lying completely still was agonising.

'Just breathe into it,' came a familiar voice nearby.

Aria concentrated on what he said and breathed deeply. She focused on dragging air in and forcing it out. The intensity of the pain faded into a distant nagging ache as her eyes fluttered slowly open to a familiar welcome sight.

'Welcome back!' It was Lareo. 'I'm hoping that you remember everything this time?'

'Yes, I do.' She tried to laugh, but that was a bad idea. Every part of her body ached. 'Ouch!'

'How bad were my injuries?' Aria asked the question that frightened her the most.

'They were pretty bad. We were flying quite high, barely starting our descent, and we had reached a clearing. You plummeted straight to the ground. You broke several bones and damaged your wings.'

Aria's jaw dropped, and she made no effort to close it.

Lareo hastened to add, 'However, Lady Bia did manage to Heal your bones and wings, although there's nothing she can do for the bruises. They will have to disappear by themselves.' He continued when she didn't reply, 'The earlier cuts from the rose thorns were completely healed though. She said you would still be sore for a few days because you had quite a fall and all the magic used to Heal you would hurt until it disappears from your body.'

After a brief pause, while he waited for her opinion of this news, he continued talking. Aria tried to find her voice, 'I realised too late that you were falling. I tried to catch you, but I wasn't fast enough, and there was no time for me to use any magic to slow you down. I'm so sorry for not paying more attention.'

That did the trick. His genuine regret and remorse snapped Aria back into focus.

'I don't blame you. You got me here to be Healed. Please don't blame yourself,' Aria said, trying to reassure him. 'I owe you my life, twice now as memory serves.' She grinned at him. He started laughing at that, for which she was relieved.

'That's true, I suppose. Can you remember what happened though?' His mood changed dramatically. 'Lady Bia couldn't figure it out. Only she and her husband know the full story about you, but she didn't understand why you fell. Besides your scratches, you don't have any other problems, and you are in excellent health.'

Aria was caught off guard. What did happen? She thought back to her last lucid moments.

'I remember you telling me the plan and asking if I knew it. Then you started descending, so I knew we were getting closer to our landing spot. Then I'm not sure, but I think I started worrying about whether they would believe us and what they would do if they did not. The next thing I remember is waking up and seeing you.'

The silence returned to the room. Aria looked at Lareo, only to find that his eyes were closed, and he looked as though he was in pain. She started as he suddenly stood up to leave. 'I'll be right back.'

And with that, Aria was left alone to deal with the pain and worry. She couldn't understand what had just happened. *Was it me? Did I say something wrong?* She thought back to what she had said and couldn't find anything that would have upset him. *Is he getting tired of my company already?*

While all these thoughts jumbled around in her mind, Aria noticed that the door had opened, and someone had entered.

An older woman stood looking at Aria. She had light brown hair that was pulled back tightly and tied with something. Her eyes were also light brown and had a kind look about them. She had a big smile and a motherly demeanour. Aria couldn't see her wings as they were retracted.

'I'm glad to see you're awake. How do you feel?'

'Oh, I… uh… I'm fine… um… actually, I don't really know,' Aria answered, suddenly confused.

'I'm sorry; I didn't mean to startle you. I'm Bia. Lareo just told me that you figured out what happened to you before you fell. And I finally understand.'

'And?'

'Well, it sounds to me as though you had some sort of panic attack. You got yourself very worked up and stressed which your body couldn't handle any more, and so you collapsed.'

'So, I'm fine physically, but mentally I'm messed up?'

'No, no, it's not like that at all,' Lady Bia laughed. 'It's perfectly normal. What you have been through in the last few days would make anyone blackout.'

Aria felt slightly better at that. She looked around and suddenly realised something was missing.

'Where's Lareo?' Even to her own ears, she could hear the panic in her voice.

'He… um… well, after you told him what happened, and he told me, he stormed off saying something about how he shouldn't have put you in that situation. I think he was feeling guilty about what happened. He never left your side while you were unconscious. He's such a considerate boy.' And with that, she finished her check-up of Aria and left the room.

*Wow,* Aria mused, *he stayed with me the whole time. It doesn't mean anything, of course. He just feels responsible for me because he found me.* These thoughts carried her off into a deep sleep.

#

Waking up, Aria remembered the room where she had gone to sleep the night before. Just as the last time she had woken up, Aria saw Lareo. However, now he had fallen asleep in the chair near her bed. She felt strangely happy that he had come back and was close by.

Aria decided that she needed to get out of bed and stretch her legs. As she sat up, she felt the pain searing through her body. She let out an audible, involuntary gasp and exclamation.

Lareo awoke with a jump and rushed to her bedside. 'What happened?' he demanded.

'It still hurts everywhere,' Aria cried out as he touched her shoulder.

'Let's get you back down. It's going to hurt again, so just bear with me.' He put his arm behind her back, and as quickly as he could to avoid prolonging the pain, he eased her down.

'There you go, you're lying down. Now, just relax and take deep breaths,' he pleaded with her. Her breathing came out in jagged, shallow gasps. She concentrated on slowing it down.

When Aria was breathing normally, and the pain had subsided, she looked up at him and said weakly, 'You came back.'

'Yes. I'm sorry I left. I got angry at myself that I caused you to panic so much and black out,' he said and hung his head in shame.

'It was my fault. I started panicking that our plan wasn't going to work, and we'd be killed, so I did it to myself. Don't blame yourself. You saved me!' Aria said reassuringly, but it didn't work.

'Something... strange happened. I-I don't even know how

to explain it. It was… so… sudden. I could have imagined it, I suppose,' he trailed off.

'What is it? What happened? Tell me.'

'Well… somehow I sensed that you were falling. I have been over this countless times! I still don't understand it. And then, I reached out to try and catch you, a-and you slowed down. You actually slowed down before you hit the ground! That was how you survived the fall.'

Aria was stunned. 'We'll figure it out. Don't beat yourself up over it. I'm fine, and that's all that matters. You got me here to be Healed.'

He didn't look reassured.

'This picture is wrong. I'm the one in pain, and you're the one that needs comforting.' Aria tried to laugh, but it hurt too much. It did get Lareo smiling, which was the goal. She took advantage of his good mood and asked a few questions.

'Did you sort out your wings?'

Lareo looked confused, so she carried on, 'While we were in the forest you were talking about getting a disguise for your wings…' she trailed off as he understood.

'No, I haven't gotten around to that yet,' he replied.

'Oh. Have you been out in the village yet?'

'Yes. Yes, I've wandered around a bit. Seen the main things…'

'Like what?'

'Er… well, there's the… um… market. Yes, the market is really nice, and it has everything. And, you know, there are houses, and… and trees. Lots of people flying with their wings…'

Aria stared at him incredulously. *Where did the ease of conversation go?* She screamed internally.

'Lady Bia seems lovely,' she said tentatively.

'Yes, she has always treated me as another son.'

'That's nice,' Aria smiled at him.

The rest of the questions vanished as he got up and walked off towards the door.

'You're leaving me again?' Aria asked, trying to sound normal, but she could hear the sadness in her voice.

'Uh… yeah, I need to go and check on some things. I shouldn't be too long.'

Lareo left the room before she could reply. *Now, what do I do?* She thought miserably. She didn't feel tired anymore, having slept most of the past however many days; she made a mental note to ask someone how long it had actually been. While pondering this, Aria looked down at herself in the bed, and saw that she was wearing a plain, loose-fitting outfit. She racked her brain for the word *'dress.'* It had a picture on the pocket: a bottle with a leaf and wings on either side of it. Aria did not have any bandages or wounds or cuts, but she could see many bruises all over herself.

Aria looked around the room properly. It was a medium-sized room with a big window on the right-hand side and two doors opposite. Next to the bed was a small cupboard. Leaning up gingerly onto her elbow, she saw that there was a chest at the bottom of the bed. Next to the main door, there was a big wardrobe. She guessed that the other door must lead to another room. Inadvertently a word sprang to mind, 'bathroom'.

On the first day, after Aria had woken up, Lady Bia had half-carried her to what she learnt was called a 'water-room.' In this room, there was a large grey tub with a tiny drop of lava, in its own little grey container underneath, and another small, grey tub. The large tub was magically filled with water, and then also magically emptied itself. The water was not magically created, but instead was transported from outside. The small tub cleaned itself magically.

Between the wardrobe and another big piece of furniture was a table and chair. Moving over a bit, Aria saw that the big piece of furniture, opposite the wardrobe, was…

A bookshelf!

In her excitement, Aria forgot how much pain she was in, and jumped up. Well, she tried to anyway. She felt the pain searing through her body again and let out an involuntary yell. Two minutes later the door flew open, and Lady Bia ran in.

'What happened?' she asked, breathing hard.

'I tried to get up,' Aria mumbled.

'Why would you do that?!' she exclaimed.

'I wanted to go and look at the bookshelf,' Aria said, feeling a bit embarrassed. 'I was bored just lying here. Lareo left, so now I don't have company. And even when he was here it was a bit awkward,' she added the latter, mumbling again. To cover that up, she hurried on, 'I just wanted something to do.'

'Is that all you wanted?' Lady Bia asked, laughing. 'Well, just between you and me, I don't think you have anything to worry about with Larey,' she said winking. 'Things will get back to how they used to be.'

'Oh,' Aria muttered, feeling heat rushing to her cheeks.

'As for the wanting something to do,' Lady Bia continued, 'you could have simply asked me. If it's a book you want, I'll get you something. If it's company you want, then I can sit with you for a while.'

'Really? You're not too busy for that?' Aria asked, hopefully.

'Well, usually I am, but today one of my assistants is helping me here. I only go out when I'm called for emergencies and big operations. Usually, people come to me for treatment. I had a separate section added onto the house for my patients, called the Treatment Wing. I have one assistant training currently; those that are as qualified as me can train younger Treaters. The problem is that once they are qualified, they go out with the soldiers, which leaves hardly anyone in the village. That is why I'm usually so busy.'

'Can I help you?' asked Aria, with the idea of keeping busy.

'We'll see when you're better.'

Aria sighed with disappointment at this news and carried on examining the room.

'This is my son's room. He hasn't used it in a while,' Lady Bia sounded a bit sad as she said this.

'I'm not in the Treatment Wing?' Aria asked, surprised.

'No, I thought it would be best if you were to stay here in my personal rooms to avoid awkward questions.'

'Thank you.' This consideration touched Aria.

'It's a pleasure. We've known Larey since he was a baby, so he's like family. Any friend of his is more than welcome in our home. And under the circumstances, we can't have you out in the public eye with a lost memory.'

'Why does Lareo keep leaving?' Aria couldn't help

wondering.

'Oh, he just goes-'

She was interrupted by one of her white-robed assistants rushing into the room. The assistant was around the same age as Aria, but she had a hard look in her eyes that could only have come from seeing something terrible, or many somethings as the case might be.

'Lady B, you are needed in the Treatment Wing. A creature attacked them…' She didn't even have to finish her sentence as Lady Bia was up and out of the room.

*Alone again. Great. I can't even get up to examine those appealing-looking books.* Looking out of the window, Aria guessed it was around noon. Of course, she couldn't always judge the time accurately, but she deduced this from the brightness of all the colours outside. Feeling not in the least bit tired, she watched the passers-by through a slit in the window. It was very calming.

#

-

## Lareo ♂

For days, Lareo had wandered around restlessly, torn up with guilt. He blamed himself for what had happened to Aria. Lady Bia had tried to convince him that this notion was wrong. He hadn't caused Aria's collapse – she had been through a lot of stress and her mind and body couldn't cope with more. Lareo understood that, but still, he couldn't shake the guilty feeling.

From the moment he had chosen to trust her, he had made a vow that he would keep her safe at all costs. He felt connected to her in a way he didn't understand.

While wandering around the village, he began to recognise where everything was and who the people were. He had worried that they would recognise him and turn him in. But everyone had welcomed him with open arms and didn't question him. Also, they knew that he was a friend of Bia and Aquila and therefore trusted him unconditionally.

It seemed that the Sentries and servants often came to the village from the castle to shop at the market. He made sure to avoid anyone from the castle, just in case.

He always thought about Aria during his wanderings. When he had put the guilt out of his mind, he shifted to more pleasant things. He looked forward to the time when she would be able to get out of bed and walk around. He wanted to share the village with her, just as he had experienced it for the first time.

There was so much to see, and it was all a new experience to him. The market was now his favourite place. He couldn't believe the collection of stalls selling everything anyone could possibly need. The smells, the sounds, and the colours were so overpowering and breathtaking.

He had taken plenty of money with him when he had left home, and he was eager to spend it. He had never needed to spend money or buy anything before. It was a new experience, getting and doing things for himself. Being independent and able to do anything he wanted, whenever he wanted, was a nice feeling.

The weapons stall particularly engrossed him. It had a wide selection of different weapons on offer: knives and swords, daggers and blades, bows, arrows, and quivers, and shields, all of varying qualities and sizes. He bought a selection of each of the best quality. He soon became good friends with the stall owner.

On his way back one afternoon, he decided to explore the whole market instead of just the weapons stall. He passed various stalls selling food, equipment, and clothes. Stopping by the clothes stall, he realised that he should buy some clothes for Aria. He had a younger sister, so he knew a little about what females wear. He bought what he thought she would need, and the stall owner helped him with the rest. He also got himself some things as he had packed lightly.

For Aria, he had chosen some dresses of varying styles, lengths, and colours. He had gone for dark blues and greens to complement her wings. The owner had suggested a couple of other colours that would also go well with her wings. Her wings had mesmerised Lareo, and he wanted to make sure everyone saw how beautiful they were.

For himself, he got some more shirts and trousers. His few silk clothes were drawing curious glances, so he decided some simpler clothing would be better. He didn't want to stand out as much, so he managed to find some very nice quality items.

Overloaded with his purchases, Lareo walked home. On the way, he noticed an unusual building that was much larger than the typical houses. He realised that it was a library, and he was inspired with an idea. *I can try to find out if there's anything there that could help Aria*, he thought excitedly, and rushed to the house to drop off the clothes and to tell her his plan.

As he neared the house, he suddenly felt shy. That was a

curious feeling. He didn't want to give the clothes to her himself. He was afraid that she wouldn't like them or the gesture. So, he decided to ask Lady Bia to give them to her.

# Chapter Five
## NEWCOMER

<u>Aria</u> ♀

Standing in the middle of nowhere, I look around. What I see all around me is strange. There are tall, square-looking things with windows in them. Looking up, I see the sky, a brilliant blue. I start moving and notice that the ground under my feet is hard. Looking down, I see it's completely black. Beside me, I see large, strange things moving past. Suddenly there is a loud noise behind me. I whirl around and see one of those large, strange objects hurtling toward me. It's going to hit me...

Aria sat up, panting. She could still feel throbbing throughout her body, but not as bad as it had been. She looked around; the room remained exactly as before. It looked darker than she remembered and the bright light shining through the window looked like moonlight, so she must have fallen asleep after all. As she took a few deep breaths, she told herself; it was only a dream... But of what?

All the thoughts that buzzed through her mind were driven out as Aria heard footsteps. She got a bit excited, hoping that it would be Lareo. The door opened, and a tall man stood in the doorway, but it was not Lareo. She grabbed the sheet covering her and pulled it up high and tried to move as far away from the door as possible. This was not very successful, considering how much it hurt, and the limited space of the bed.

He was standing very rigidly in the doorway. His shoulders were squared, and his back was straight. He had dark hair, which was cut short. He had a strong jaw, and his mouth was set in a confused grimace. His wings opened out suddenly, startling her. They were fiery orange with a different colour streaked through them and a slightly lighter colour around the edge. Aria couldn't tell much more about them in the moonlight.

'And who might you be?' he asked, bemused. *He has a lovely voice,* Aria thought, and then realised that she had no idea who he was.

'I'm a patient. Who are you?!' Aria demanded, a little frantically.

'I'm Brezan. This is my room.' He smiled as he said that.

'Oh, you're Lady B's son?' Aria asked, embarrassed.

'Lady B? Yes, she's my mother,' he said, laughing at her familiar way of referring to his mother.

'I picked it up from her assistant,' mumbled Aria.

'Why are you in here anyway?' he inquired, asking the most obvious question.

'Your mother said it would be better. Didn't she explain it to you?'

'She doesn't know I'm here yet. I'm in the area on duty, and I was allowed to come back here for a bit. My mother was very busy doing her early morning preparations, so I thought I'd come up here first. As I was walking here, I heard a scream. Did you have a bad dream?'

His apparent concern for her moved Aria. *He must get it from his mother.*

'Yes, I did. I'm not sure what it was about, though. Nothing made any sense to me.'

'Maybe I can help? What was it about?'

'I think you should go talk to your mother first,' Aria said. She realised that he had no idea about her and her situation, and she couldn't just blurt it all out. 'Wait. Do you have something for me to write down what I dreamt before I forget it all?'

'Yes, of course,' he said. He went over to the table and found a leaf, a pot of ink and a feather which was smaller than the one she had seen Lareo using. As he came back with it, Aria noticed that it wasn't as colourful; it was grey and white and not as elegant. *Strange.*

'Thank you,' said Aria, as she took everything from him. She couldn't even imagine how he would react to the truth. *It will be much better for him if he hears it from his mother*, she decided.

After he had left the room, Aria wrote everything down as best as she could remember. Once finished, she thought about that strange shape coming towards her. Turning over the leaf, after ensuring the ink had dried, she then drew the object as best as she could. It was a very rough example. As she looked at it, it occurred to her that it looked like a snail or giant beetle. That, of course, didn't make any sense considering the size and surroundings. She definitely needed help to figure this one out.

So absorbed in her puzzle, Aria didn't even notice that Brezan had come back. When Aria finally looked up, she saw him standing against the door in a beam of first-morning sun, and she jumped, which sent pain through her body.

Screaming for the hundredth time in only a few days, everyone rushed to her bedside. *This is getting ridiculous*, she thought, *I can't keep enduring this pain every time I move.* Brezan looked at her with guilt in his eyes. Lady Bia was worried.

'I understand that you can't sit still, but you have to try. Your recovery will take longer otherwise,' she said gently. 'I have to get to work, but I explained everything to Breezy, and he said he would sit with you.'

Aria nodded and mumbled a thank you.

'While you're up, I have something to give you.'

She left the room to get it. Aria felt self-conscious as Brezan sat down next to her.

'You've had a rough few days. I'm so sorry for scaring you. I just found it interesting watching you deep in thought.'

'Well, I'm flattered,' Aria said, not really meaning it. 'Help me lie down again, please?' she added resentfully.

He walked over and put his hands behind her shoulders and held her weight until she was lying down.

'Can I?' he asked, as he picked up the leaf that she had dropped.

'Sure, if you can make sense of it,' she said doubtfully.

He read through it and then shook his head. As Aria had assumed, he could make no more sense of it than she could.

Lady Bia entered the room, followed by Lareo. *Lareo was back!* Aria rejoiced. *I wonder why he is here now after so many days away. Why does he look so upset?* She pondered, *that is very odd!*

Lady Bia bustled around the room. She carried some clothes that she said she had organised for Aria, who felt pleased at the thought. Lady Bia put them into the wardrobe and told Aria to sort through them when she felt better. Then Lady Bia left.

Brezan stood up and went over to greet Lareo.

'Hello, Larey. How have you been? I haven't seen you in ages!' he said cheerfully, happy to see his old friend again.

Lareo, on the other hand, did not seem to reciprocate his enthusiasm, 'Hi Brezan. I've been good... you know. So, uh, what are you doing here? Shouldn't you be back at the castle on duty?'

'I-.'

But Aria interrupted him before he could explain further, 'You're a Castle Sentry?' she cried in astonishment.

'I... uh... Yes, I am. I thought you would have known that. That's how I know...' he trailed off.

*How odd*, Aria wondered as she glanced from one to the other. Lareo looked a combination of angry and scared, which she had never considered possible before that moment. Brezan, on the other hand, looked guilty. Both reactions did not make any sense at all. Aria had clearly missed something important.

'What's going on here?' she demanded, looking at Lareo. It was Brezan who answered, 'His father was an advisor to the King. He mediated the needs of the common villagers to the King. My father also worked at the castle as a Sentry. And we met each other while our fathers were busy with their respective jobs.'

That made sense, but it did not explain the tension and looks on their faces. Aria chose to drop the subject for now.

#

The next morning, Aria woke up in the dim early morning light. Gingerly, she turned over and spotted Brezan fast asleep in the chair, which looked extremely uncomfortable. Aria smiled at the sight. They had spent most of the day yesterday talking and had become friends very quickly. Now she felt bad because she had taken his nice comfortable bed. Aria sat up slowly. The pain was significantly less, but still present. She decided to try walking a bit.

She slowly eased her legs over the edge and reached the floor. She sat there for a few minutes as she got used to the movement. Slowly, holding on to the wall, she pushed herself to her feet. *That wasn't too bad*, she thought.

Still holding the wall, Aria moved one foot forward and put her weight on it. That was fine. She walked carefully around the edge of the room to the other side. It was slow going as she did not want to injure herself again.

Aria headed toward the desk, but as she reached the wardrobe, she decided to stop and look at the clothes, which pleased her very much. There were some pretty dresses, but also some trousers and shirts. She held a couple of the dresses up against herself and saw that they came to a reasonable length just above her knee. The material was thin but durable. The dresses were flowing but not frilly and would not get in her way or get tangled in anything. The trousers were flexible, and the shirts, like the dresses, were practical. And the colours were lovely. Dark blues, purples, and greens, and a few light pinks for variety. She set one aside for later.

She finally made it to the desk and sat down to have a closer look. It all looked normal: leaves, inkpots, and feathers. She turned to look at the books; they all had wooden covers. Picking one up, Aria saw the pages were not thick parchment, but neither were they as thin as the commonly used leaves; these were made of something in-between. Most of the books were about wars or weapons, which made sense considering the owner of the room. There were some books on herbs – Lady B's attempts at encouraging her son as a Treater, no doubt. Then there were some books on the history of the area and other villages. Aria took one of those first, since weapons and fighting did not appeal to her.

She sat at the desk and read about the fascinating history. There was one Royal Family and one village originally. Slowly, over the years, the population grew bigger until there were four villages. There were four royal families – one for each element – that ruled over specific areas. Each had a village.

There was no clear explanation in the history book that would account for the transition from the one village and Royal Family to the four; despite the population growth, it didn't make sense. It was as if there was a chunk of history missing.

What interested Aria the most was what it said about how each person had a higher affinity with a particular element which determined the village they lived in. What she couldn't understand was, what if a person was stronger in an element which was different to their family and village? Did that mean that if they were different, they were banished? Were the wars Lareo spoke about between the elements or others? Wouldn't they be stronger if all the elements were joined and used together?

So engrossed in her studies, she did not realise that the room had grown lighter with the sun streaming in. Aria was still thinking hard when she looked up and around the room. She saw Brezan still in the same chair, watching her with amusement.

'What?' Aria asked defiantly.

'Nothing. You're just cute when you're thinking so hard. What have you got there, anyway?'

She showed him and asked him the questions that puzzled her.

'How long have you been up?' he asked, surprised. 'That's a lot of thinking you've done. I don't have the answers you're looking for, however.'

Before Aria could voice her disappointment, the door opened, and Lady Bia came in.

'I thought I heard talking up here,' she said, smiling. Then her smile slipped from her face as she realised where Aria was sitting.

'You're sitting up!' she exclaimed. 'How are you feeling?'

'Still a little sore and, while I was walking, I felt a bit stiff, but mostly fine.'

'Come back to the bed, and I'll examine you again.'

Aria slowly walked over to the bed and gingerly laid down again, facing Brezan in his chair; he gave her a reassuring smile.

Lady Bia examined Aria thoroughly. It did not hurt as much as before, but she still felt some dull throbbing.

'Everything is on the mend, but I think it would be best if

you let the last few cuts and bruises heal completely without more magic. Also, your wings still need a bit more rest. Just take it easy,' she insisted, and gave Aria a look that said, 'or else'.

Aria smiled sheepishly but agreed.

As Lady Bia left the room, Brezan said, 'I need to finish the business that I came here to do, but once I'm done, I could keep you company.'

Aria was happy about that; it gave her something to look forward to.

#

A couple of days later, Aria wondered why she was still alone. This house was constantly bustling with activity, but other than mealtimes and check-up visits from Lady Bia, she didn't see anyone. She understood that Brezan was busy working, but where was Lareo? The loneliness hung heavy like a weight on her shoulders, and it was an effort to do anything. She tried to occupy herself, but nothing distracted her from the darkness that enveloped from her being alone.

Aria thought about Lareo. Lately, she hadn't seen him at all... *Where is he? Why isn't he here keeping me company? Is the novelty over? Am I no longer entertaining?* There was a Lareo-shaped void when he wasn't around. She had grown very close to him during their time in the forest; she couldn't stop thinking about him, and the good times they'd had together. Every time she heard footsteps outside, Aria would get her hopes up and then be slightly disappointed that it wasn't Lareo.

Now, however, she would be happy for anyone to show up. She was so bored that she couldn't occupy herself in any way.

Not even the thrill of having so many beautiful new clothes could cheer her up. The first couple of days with them had been so much fun. There were only one or two outfits that she didn't really like, but otherwise she had loved them all.

Now, however, they were all a reminder of not having anywhere to go to. They were mocking her. This morning, she hadn't even glanced at them when she chose one at random.

Aria sighed heavily. She got up to get a book. Walking was a lot easier now. Having been getting up and moving around, she no longer felt stiff. The cuts had almost completely healed, and the dull throbbing of the bruises had gone. She had been waiting to tell someone since breakfast, but she still hadn't seen anyone.

Aria chose a book. It was about a soldier in some war, or another. She sighed. This was a boy's room. What else did she expect? Putting the book away, she walked over to the window. It had been a bad few days. Water had been pouring down between the trees; Aria wracked her brain for the word: rain. She smiled at her achievement and then remembered that she had no one to tell.

Today was different; the sun was shining. Everything outside was no longer a dull imitation of what it usually was. It was bright and full of colour. There was a fresh, renewed quality to everything, which made things seem worse for Aria.

From the window, she could mostly see other houses. Aria saw people walking up and down, looking happy. Small children were bounding backwards and forwards. Some people were carrying parcels. She figured that they must have been coming back from a market of some kind. How Aria wished she could be bounding along with them.

Stepping back, she sat down on the bed without even bothering to look at it. She picked up the leaves she'd been writing on. Aria had had several more dreams like that first one. They still did not make sense. However, there were more of the big grey things with windows. She shoved the leaves away and sighed heavily.

'What did those leaves ever do to you?' Aria heard a voice laughing from the door. She turned around and smiled as she saw Brezan.

*Finally!* Aria thought.

'What they did was not give me the right answers,' Aria replied, a lot happier with them than she had been a moment ago.

'I must apologise. I promised I would keep you company, and I was gone for the whole day yesterday. You must have been very bored cooped up here this whole time,' he said kindly.

'Yes!' Aria almost screamed. 'I couldn't settle on anything.' She explained how she'd been up and down, trying to take her mind off things.

'How about I get my mother to give you a check-up now? You look all healed,' he suggested.

'Yes, please!'

He came back shortly, followed by Lady Bia. She checked everything thoroughly and came up with a verdict.

'Well, everything seems to be fine.' Aria could hear the 'but' in her voice, 'But I don't know what to do about your lack of memory.' She sounded concerned.

'What does that mean?' Aria tried to make her voice sound even.

'It means I may need to get someone to help you. But the problem is that it will need to be kept very quiet because the memory loss is strange on its own, but coupled with the fact that your wings don't look like you've been using them for your age is a concern.'

'How can you tell that?' Aria asked, surprised by that news.

'Your muscles aren't as developed as someone else your age. But let's wait another few days while I try to figure out something.'

She left, looking thoughtful. Aria sat up and looked at Brezan, who's expression changed a few seconds too late...

'Don't worry. My mother is one of the best Treaters in this territory. She also has the best connections. She'll figure something out for you.'

Aria considered what he had just said. While his words were reassuring, there was a slight edge in his voice that worried her.

He must have seen the worry on her face because he said, 'Why don't we take a book and go sit outside, at the back of the house? My mother chose this house for the enclosed back garden so that her patients could get some fresh air and still have privacy.'

Aria agreed to that plan. She picked up the history book she had been reading while he went to choose one. Naturally, he avoided all the books except the war books. As neither of them wanted to read what the other had chosen, they compromised on a storybook. This would be the first time she had left this room except for short trips with help from Lady Bia out of necessity. Aria almost skipped out of there, happy to be getting out finally.

Brezan walked next to her, holding her elbow, for which she was grateful. While walking across the room was manageable, Aria feared that walking down the stairs would be an effort. She was right. Walking through the passage, she noticed there were several other rooms. The walls were the same oak colour – and the floors were the same mahogany colour as her room. Aria limped down the stairs and entered a hallway. There was a statue standing in one corner that Aria felt a magnetic pull towards.

When she got nearer, Aria saw that it was a woman. She looked regal: the robe she wore had an elegant cut, and it looked as though she stood in a breeze; she had waist-length hair that looked windswept, and she seemed to be quite young but had wisdom in her eyes. Aria was drawn to her; she had to know who the woman was.

'Who is she?' Aria asked Brezan, still staring.

'She was part of the Aurious. They were the unified rulers of the Fay world. They used all the elements equally and, because they had balancers among them, there were never wars or trouble. Then they were attacked by the Spectres – the evil Fairies. They caused so much strife that the Aurious split. They broke apart and sided with their element and kept themselves separate. That's the basic story, anyway.'

At these words, Aria felt a shiver down her spine and an

inexplicable feeling of anticipation. She could only stare transfixed at the former Aurious.

'What element was she?'

'Air,' he said solemnly. 'She was the Air Aurious who then became the Queen and founded Aer. They named their separate Faydoms after their element, but not exactly the same; for example, we are the Aer Faydom from the element of air.'

'There must be more to the story than that?' Aria had a sudden urge to know more.

'There probably is, but it's not widely known. Only the Royals and the Wise Leaders know more about it now. So, shall we carry on to the garden? Are you hungry? Shall I bring us a picnic?'

Aria allowed herself to be ushered into the garden. She was too distracted to notice how beautiful the garden was.

She couldn't help dwelling on the story she had just heard and its many gaps. *And why did Brezan look so uncomfortable?* She wondered.

When Brezan returned, he brought some food with him. They ate in silence, but it wasn't awkward anymore. Aria had resolved to find out more, but she wouldn't push Brezan for it. They sat comfortably in the silence until he suggested reading the book they had brought with them out loud.

The story was about humans. None of it sounded familiar, though. It was about a girl named Belladonna who, though she was a servant, was a close friend of the Princess, and they shared many secrets. One secret was how unhappy the Princess was, and they switched lives...

# Chapter Six
## HUMAN TALE

There was once a human girl who lived in a castle. Her name was Belladonna. She wasn't a Princess, but she was the Princess's maid. She hadn't always lived in the castle. She had grown up with her parents. She was their only child and was very much loved.

Belladonna had gone to the castle to work for the Royal Family at their personal request. Her parents had had little money and felt that the opportunity couldn't be passed up. She was still allowed to see her parents, so it was not too bad.

As a young child, she did not have to do anything for the Princess other than be her friend. As she grew up and became more able, she became the Princess's maidservant.

Belladonna did everything for the Princess. She enjoyed what she did and took great pride in being the Princess's personal servant. But she had a secret: she envied the Princess's glamorous life.

She had not known when she was younger why she had been specially chosen out of all the girls in the kingdom. When she grew up, they told her the truth.

Belladonna was a particularly good friend to the Princess, who had very few friends in the castle because of a curse that had been placed upon her by an evil sorceress.

The Princess had been born with a gift; she had the power to manifest things in nature. This was such an unheard-of ability that all the sorcerers in the area had flocked to the castle when she was born. One particular sorceress was evil and coveted the power and had, therefore, placed a curse on the Princess. The curse prevented everyone from talking to her.

The only way people could communicate with her was through song. Of course, the only problem was that everyone else could not sing. Not for lack of trying, but because the curse stopped it. This was the sorceress's way of driving the Princess into her reach.

That plan would have worked if it were not for one special person.

Belladonna was the exception to the curse. She was born on the same day and at precisely the same time as the Princess. This coincidence of fate made her invulnerable to the curse. She was the only person in the entire kingdom that could sing and, therefore, was the only one who could talk to the Princess.

She told the Princess stories. She passed messages to the Princess from the outside world, especially from her parents, the King and Queen. And she sang. She sang the most beautiful songs for her.

Among their many topics, the Princess's unhappiness came up frequently. The Princess had her own secret: she desired nothing more than to run away and break the curse. Belladonna felt so helpless. She wanted to help her friend so much, but she did not know how to.

Then one day, Belladonna was sent on an errand for the Princess: to go to an apothecary to get special herbs for the Princess's perfume. She had an idea while there, and with the apothecary's help, she came up with a plan.

She went back to the castle and tentatively told the Princess what she had in mind – terrified about losing not only her job but also her best friend.

Instead, the Princess was overjoyed.

So, under the cover of night, they went out into the forest and met the apothecary and another man. This man was a wizard.

The wizard cast a spell that was so powerful it affected the whole kingdom. With this spell, he convinced the entire kingdom that the Princess was Belladonna, and that Belladonna was the Princess.

The Princess ran off into the forest to find her new future, which was to be a guardian of the forest and to help people in distress.

With the Princess gone and Belladonna in her place, the magic power coveted by the sorceress disappeared. The swap had broken the curse on the Princess and the entire kingdom. The people's voices were raised in song every day as a celebration.

They both missed the other, but they found a way to communicate. Not long after they had parted ways, they found out they could talk to each other in dreams. At first, they had not known whether it was real, but over time and with increased occurrences, they realised that it was real. It was part of the leftover magic from the switch.

Belladonna was pleased to hear that her friend was out in the forest. She knew the forest needed protection from damage, and she could not think of anyone better than the former Princess who loved and longed to be out in the open.

As for Belladonna, she lived out her days at the castle and found a handsome Prince. She had children, which made her overjoyed. She eventually became the Queen and helped the people live in health and happiness.

'The end,' said Brezan.

# Chapter Seven
## THE VILLAGE

When Brezan finished the story, Aria had an odd feeling that, as with the history of the Auriouses, something was missing. It also did not ring any bells, nor bring back any memories. Something about what the Princess was doing in the forest after the swap kept nagging at her mind, but she couldn't place what it was. Aria shrugged it off.

They sat for a while longer, enjoying the garden. As Aria looked around, she muttered 'Wow!' There weren't many trees, but the few that were there provided plenty of shade. The flowers filled the space around the paths and the outside of the garden. In the middle, the grass was so lush and soft that it made the perfect bed. And there were a few benches for patients to sit on.

Opposite them, Aria noticed a small pool, that on closer inspection, she found filled with red liquid. *Lava*, the word popped into her mind.

Brezan confirmed her thoughts, 'My mother chose this location because of the pool. To clean and heat medical things…'

Aria nodded.

'Are there many around?'

'Not too many. There are two main ones by the castle and in the centre of the village. And a few small ones – like this one – scattered around the rest of the Faydom. Of course, fire isn't our element, so you can hardly expect too many.'

*Hmm*, Aria pondered.

They heard footsteps and turned to see Lady Bia coming across the garden. She carried a book, and her eyebrows furrowed as she noticed them. Her eyes widened as she looked Aria over from head to toe, then her face split into a big grin.

'You are up and walking around!' she exclaimed. 'Does it hurt anywhere?' she asked as she hurried over.

'No, I'm feeling perfect,' Aria replied, equally happy.

Aria got a clear view of Lady Bia's wings, which were out; the details of the colours and patterns glimmered brilliantly in the sunlight. From afar, Aria had thought they were a beautiful soothing blue, but on closer inspection, she noticed that there was more to them; they were light blue but had streaks of pale orange through them and a yellow border around the edge. The orange made her think of Bia's fighting spirit underneath her motherly nurturing.

Lady Bia examined Aria again and said that it was only her memory that still needed to heal. Aria was relieved that she was now able to do anything she wanted. They left Lady Bia to her book and walked back inside with a carefree energy.

Brezan suggested that they go out into the village that afternoon. This excited Aria. *Something different after the same monotony*, she thought.

Stepping out through the front door was exhilarating. Aria could see the village from her room, but the experience of being out there was completely different. She followed Brezan, looking around and trying to take everything in. They were in the centre of the village, which provided easy access for any injured people.

They walked through the village. Aria loved it. Although the houses all shared the same colour of yellow, each was unique. They were all various sizes; the windows had a range of shadings, and the yellows were also multiple shades, with patterns in different colours.

The other buildings were decorated in many colours too. They walked past the library and the community centre, which had a big grassy area where children were playing.

Fairies bustled along around them; all of them had their wings out because they were out in the open. Brezan and Aria joined them and unfurled their own wings. She understood immediately why they would open their wings if they could; while it did not hurt in the least to have the wings retracted, the freedom and relief when they were loose was unmatched.

Aria marvelled at the glorious colours, in every shade imaginable, and every possible combination. *How amazing*, she thought, *that the colours all worked so beautifully together; there is no such thing as an ugly combination.* Also, some combinations were similar but never identical. Not one set of wings looked the same, even if they had similar colours, except in one way.

'Everyone has yellow along the edge of their wings?'

'Yes,' Brezan replied. 'We're all from Aer, and our element is air, which is reflected in the yellow of our wings. You have the same yellow. Look.'

Aria spun in a circle as she grabbed hold of a wing and moved it around herself to see that he was right. The outer edge was yellow like everyone else's; although the colour seemed to have grown darker than the previous time she had looked at it.

She looked at Brezan's wings properly for the first time. They were a bright orange as she had glimpsed when she had first met him. They had Lady Bia's blue streaked through them and the yellow edge. Lareo was right; all wings are beautiful, no matter their colouring. She swallowed hard and pushed the thought of Lareo out of her mind.

They followed the streams of people that Aria had seen through the window. They were all heading towards the market, so that's where Aria and Brezan decided to head. They wandered through the crowded market and looked at the stalls, which were filled with everything imaginable; food and drink, herbs, crystals, clothes, books, and much more. Everything was overwhelming to her senses after being kept in a sterile enclosed house for the past few days.

Aria didn't know which of her senses to follow first; the sight of the jostling crowds, the smell of food, or the sound of buzzing chatter. They wove their way through the people and eventually reached the stalls.

Aria examined each stall, and then she spotted a bookstall; making a beeline for it, she spent ages studying the volumes. She found a fascinating book on herbs, listing every herb and its uses. There probably was a similar book in the Treatment Wing, but she wanted one of her own. Aria hesitated when she realised that she did not have anything to pay with. However, Brezan jumped in and bought it for her.

He held out his hand to show her some coins. There were two sizes: one was the size of her thumb tip, and the other was about the size of a walnut. They were light grey with small, multi-coloured flecks throughout, and had Fairy wings on one side, and the number on the other.

'The big one is ten and the little one is one,' he explained. It seemed easy enough.

Brezan spent a lot of time at the weapons stall. They all looked so beautifully crafted; the blades, whether thin or wide, conveyed the wicked deadliness of their nature; the jewelled stones glinted on the hilts and shields; the bows twanged as people tested them. If it weren't for their purpose, Aria would have found them exquisite; however, she found them distasteful.

Brezan bought a few items before they made their way out of the market. They had spent so much time in there that they hadn't noticed the sun moving lower in the sky. As they started on the path home, they met Lareo, who greeted them with a scowl.

'Hello,' said Aria excitedly.

'My mother cleared her physically,' Brezan explained. 'So, I thought a walk through the village would be nice. Would you like to join us?'

Aria looked at Lareo, eagerly awaiting his agreement.

Lareo stared at Brezan for a moment, then grunted 'no' and walked off.

As Aria watched Lareo walk away, she felt sad. But amid her sadness, there was a hint of something else, a feeling unusual and yet familiar, although very faint; it was the same impression she had had every night in the forest. She had forgotten about it until this moment. It was an intrusive presence that was also watchful. As Lareo left them, the sensation diminished. *Weird*, she thought.

They walked through to the other side of the village, heading towards the forest and the perimeter. As they got nearer, Brezan told her that the houses at the edge of the village were mostly for the Sentry.

In an empty area, a fair distance from the forest, Brezan took out his weapons to demonstrate to Aria.

'I have a specialised power also, you know.'

'Really? Like a Treater?' Aria asked, interested.

'Well, it's not Healing. It's the opposite,' he said, slightly hesitantly. 'I was trained as a Sentry, as you know. I have a special talent for it, I guess.'

'Oh. What can you do?'

'I am more than capable with weapons. Anyone can, of course, pick up a weapon and strike, but you need skill to be able to do significant damage. Training can only take a person so far. I've seen plenty of Sentries who weren't cut out for the tasks. The extra skill or power heightens all the qualities that are important to a Sentry: discipline, endurance, speed, accuracy. And we all have a proficiency with a specific weapon that makes the strike more... um... effective. Mine is with swords.'

They made their way back towards the village and spent a bit more time out in the open. Sitting alongside the path, they watched the sunset over the forest. Then, despite the deepening darkness, they wandered around for a while longer, before walking back along the river. There were some houses along there, but not as many as further in. It was lovely to be in the open space after being cooped up in the house all day. Aria felt so energetic that she spread her wings wide and then started flying. Brezan soon caught up with her, and they flew back to the house.

#

## Lareo ♂

Lareo watched them walk away. Jealousy jolted through him. He resented Brezan for showing up. He made his way slowly back to the house in the setting sun, thinking. He had tried to talk to Aria today, but when he showed up, he had found them sitting in the garden laughing and telling stories, so he had stormed off to the village. *But they had had the same idea*, he thought, clenching his teeth.

He felt ashamed that he felt this way towards his oldest and best friend, but he couldn't help himself. Brezan had always had the life he had envied. Most people envied Lareo for his life, but the truth was that he hated it.

He contemplated the story he had overheard Brezan telling Aria. He felt as though he was the cursed Princess. He could talk to everyone, of course, but they did not want to talk to him. That's what it had felt like to him. Everyone was always polite and formal towards him, never doing or saying anything that might upset him in any way. Even his parents had treated him as another pawn in their schemes and not as their son.

Lareo was no longer a carefree child listening to that story and running around with the Head Castle Sentry's son. No, he was now a grown man, and he had many responsibilities. His parents had chosen a future wife for him, and he had many duties to perform.

It was more than he could handle. Being considered a pawn in his parents' scheming was not the life he wanted to live. The pressure was more than he could take. If only he had had more siblings, then his parents would have more children on which to spread their expectations; however, he only had one younger sister. Despite her young age, their parents had also planned her future. However, those plans were minor and did nothing to remove any of the family duties necessary, which meant that he would have to shoulder most of the burdens of the family legacy.

Lareo had had an argument with his parents about his future. When they wouldn't listen to his point of view, he had decided that he was tired of trying to convince them, so he had chosen to leave, and thus began his journey. He had thought that he would like to join the Sentries in a more permanent and involved way. But as soon as he had left and was on his way to the Sentries, he realised that that did not feel right either. He had then decided he would have to take some time to figure out what it was that he really wanted. He knew this much, he would be in control of his own destiny.

He didn't have much knowledge of the forest or the village, which could have proved problematic. All he had known was that the forest stood between his home and the village, and that he was heading towards the village where he hoped that he would find sanctuary. Laying low for a while and getting familiar with it had been the plan. Despite wanting to travel around the kingdom, he had never seen much of anything.

He had come here in the hopes of making up for what he

had missed. He sought out the attention that his affectionless parents had deprived him of.

Brezan had been the only one to treat him normally. They were honest with each other and had never treated each other formally. They were able to be themselves. And following their son's lead, whenever Brezan's parents were with Lareo, they had treated him as they treated their own child. That was why he had chosen to run to them. He had wanted to slip right into Brezan's place in the family, but that hadn't worked.

Brezan had shown up and not only had he taken the attention of his family, he had also stolen the admiration and interest of the girl Lareo was falling for.

Lareo had wanted to spend all his time with Aria, but he was prevented from doing so. Every morning when he had gone to Aria's room, he had found Brezan sitting at her bedside, sleeping. The notion tore him up.

Lareo didn't know what to do any more. Jealousy consumed him, and he didn't know how to stop it. He considered leaving, but he couldn't go without Aria. She had a magnetic pull over him. He had to be near her at all times.

He spent most of his time thinking about her. He had been going to the library every day to look for something that would help with her problem, but he hadn't found anything useful. A part of him was glad about that. He was scared that helping her recover her memories would mean losing her. He couldn't bear that. But more than that, he wanted her happy and safe. If getting her memories back meant she would return to the place where she belonged, and would be happy and safe, then he would help get her there.

He trudged back to the house, feeling more confused and hopeless than ever before.

# Chapter Eight
## CALLING

<u>Aria ♀</u>

'It's strange, though,' Lady Bia said to Aria the next day. 'I can't find anything that can help to retrieve your memories.'

This was not good news at all. The helplessness flooded in, and Aria tried to stifle it, but all she could think about were the implications. She wouldn't be able to go out into the village and live with the rest of the Fairies without raising suspicion about why she didn't know a lot of things. Spending the rest of her life – in this case, it would be a very long time –if she couldn't change back, was not an appealing thought.

Lady Bia must have seen the look on Aria's face because she said, 'I think I could teach you to help out around the Treatment Wing. I don't expect my students to know much about anything.' She gave Aria a wink and a small comforting smile.


#


Over the next week, Aria learnt about the herbs and their uses. This was complicated work because there were many herbs and they could be combined with many others to make new concoctions. The book that Brezan had bought for her helped. She wrote down all the extra information that the book didn't explain, in an empty book Brezan had given her. But it was not only the herbs that were used. Different crystals were also used in Healing, and she had to learn about those as well. She needed to be able to identify them and know their uses.

Aria's days were suddenly very full because of all the work Lady Bia had her doing. Bia kept her busy with cleaning and organising the Treatment Wing. She helped Bia's assistant, Coloma, with making the herbal concoctions. The pair became friends, but Coloma didn't know the truth about Aria, which made things difficult at times.

Everyone was told the story that Lareo and Aria had come from an outside village which had been attacked. This had been the most plausible story, and Bia had made sure it spread quickly around the village. They hoped that no one would look too closely at them. Lareo had mentioned to her in passing that no one here was able to help conceal his wings, and also that no one looked closely enough to notice.

Brezan also helped around the Treatment Wing, so Aria got to spend a lot of time with him. She didn't think about it too much, but she vaguely wondered how strange it was for him to still be there.

Brezan and Aria took over Coloma's duty of gathering herbs. She had shown them what to get the first day and then left it to them to do this every second day. Aria always carried her book of plants with her on these trips. While they were out there, she always felt at ease. Maybe it was a result of being cooped up in the house recovering for so long, but Aria relished being outside in the open air.

When Coloma had explained what they needed and what

it looked like (and given Aria a chance to draw and write down everything in her book), she left them to get familiar with all the plants. She had given Aria a special pouch to carry on her hip for the essential plants; Coloma herself also wore one attached to a belt.

Brezan explained how they treated nature. They had to make sure they were very diligent when they were gathering. When they could, they took the leaves that had fallen off of their own accord. But sometimes they needed them fresh, and they were cautious; never taking an excess of leaves, harvesting the oldest-looking leaves and cutting precisely to remove only the leaf needed. This caused no damage to the rest of the plant.

On the first day they had gone out collecting, Aria had seen a couple of big animals pulling a cart piled with plants. Brezan whispered 'food' in her ear. Of course, the Fairies ate plants, but they did so in the same manner as the gathering of the herbs. They were precise with what and how much they took, and the same was true of any materials that they needed from the environment – everything was in moderation with no damage.

'What about the animals?' Aria pointed in the vague direction where they had seen the animals pulling the cart of food.

'What about them?'

'Do you eat them?'

Brezan looked horrified. 'Why would we eat them?!'

Aria shrugged. She honestly had no idea why she would even ask such a thing.

Brezan regained his composure. 'No, we do not eat animals.' He looked faintly green in the face at the thought. 'We find everything we need to stay alive in the plants. Animals are used only for transporting things for those with less power, who are unable to move their carts.'

This stirred in Aria a strangely vague sensation, as if she was grasping for a memory that eluded her. This was getting more and more common over the weeks, but she could never quite place the feeling or the memory. This time, it was something to do with the plants and the method they were using. It felt unusual, and yet it was comforting at the same time. Eventually, she placed the feeling: it felt right.

#

One day while Brezan and Aria were both scrubbing herb pots, Brezan said that he felt as though he was Belladonna, which made them laugh until they were crying. Through the tears and howls of laughter, Aria thought she had seen a shadow pass the door and heard a door slamming far away. But carried away with the joke, she didn't dwell on it.

Lady Bia came in at that moment, saying, 'So this is how my assistant's work?'

The laughter died away, and they glanced at each other guiltily.

'Sorry,' they both mumbled.

'I was wondering if you would like to assist me with a patient today?' Bia said to Aria. 'Coloma has gone out to collect more supplies.'

'Can I really? That would be great!' Aria exclaimed.

Bia told Aria the basics before they entered the room

and made sure she was prepared so that she wouldn't be too nervous. The patient was a boy who had fallen out of a tree and cut his arm. Aria wouldn't need to do any of the significant Healing as Lady Bia would do that. She would only get the herbs ready and clean the wound so that Lady Bia could seal it.

Aria followed Bia into the Operation Room. Sitting on the bed was a young boy, with his parents behind him. He had a deep gash along his arm.

'This is my new assistant, Aria,' she told the parents.

They went to the boy's side, and Lady Bia examined his arm. 'The bones are not broken, which is good. We'll just clean the wound with some herbs, and then I'll seal it. Aria, get some of the tea-tree please.'

Having made and packed all the cures, Aria knew where to find the disinfectant. She got it quickly and held it out to Lady Bia.

'You do this part,' Bia encouraged her.

Aria opened the bottle and poured some onto the gash. Lady Bia handed her a cloth to wipe it evenly.

The bottle slid through Aria's numb fingers and smashed to the floor as everything went black.

*I am standing next to a bed with silver edges. I'm wearing a white coat. The person in front of me has a deep cut on his hand. I'm cleaning the wound with something that smells very strong.*

*'Very good. Now the doctor will stitch it up,' I explain gently. I turn to the older woman next to me, and she smiles encouragingly. I hand her the forceps with the needle on it. She starts working on the gash, closing the wound with tiny stitches.*

Aria came to and found herself lying on a bed. *How long was I out for?* She wondered.

'Are you alright?' It was Lady Bia's voice. Aria focused and saw her standing next to the bed, with Brezan, his father, and Lareo standing behind her, all looking concerned.

'I had a flashback,' Aria explained as she sat up slowly. 'I've done this before,' she waved around the room. 'I was cleaning a wound similar to that little boy's, and then I turned to a woman that I called a 'doctor'.' She was careful with that word. 'I think that's what the humans call Treaters. She then took some long pointy metal thing that had thread attached and started closing the wound,' Aria told them exactly what she remembered. They stared at me in shocked silence.

'So,' Lady Bia began, 'this is where you belong? Healing people?' she asked tentatively. Aria felt the rightness of her words and smiled.

#

After the big revelation, Aria spent her time not only making the cures but also working with Lady Bia and Coloma on patients. They both showed her the basics of Healing, which happened without magic. It mostly involved cleaning and treating wounds with herbs and using the crystals to promote natural healing. Lady Bia insisted on doing it this way because she wanted the body to Heal by itself if it could. Using too much magic would diminish the body's natural strength and vitality.

They saved magical Healing for severe injuries such as

broken bones, internal damage or severe sicknesses. There were a surprising number of these kinds of cases, mostly Sentries with training injuries. But life in the forest was also rough and led to many people with injuries. Because of their healthy diet and magic, Fairies didn't get sick often. A Treater would only treat sicknesses sporadically.

In these cases, Lady Bia would show both of them the Healing with magic and then encouraged Coloma, as the more experienced of them, to try after the demonstrations. Aria only watched when this type of Healing took place as she had no magic. Coloma believed that Aria did not attempt any magical Healing because she was too inexperienced. Aria still took notes on all the injuries and how they were healed magically. It was fascinating to watch.

The Treater had to use a crystal that had no exceptional power other than its natural properties, which lean towards Healing. What a Treater does is send their power through the crystal to the person, and that power then forms an aura around the body, allowing the Treater to seek the location of the problem. The crystal acts as a magnifier and conveys the magic to the patient. The Healing magic surrounds the person like an aura, then enters the body and gathers in the centre.

The Healing magic then spreads through the body to the affected part, where, with careful control, the Treater is able to Heal the injury. The Treater has to know how each part functions in order to send the right kind of magic to fix the problem.

However, before any of the big magical Healing can be done, the patient needs to be in a deep sleep. This is also the case with non-magical Healing that might cause discomfort. Usually, Lady Bia takes a herbal concoction – which is a combination of herbs that creates a profound sleep – and amplifies the fumes in a controlled bubble around the patient. These are the herbs that Aria and Brezan collected, so it was useful to now see how they are used to help with the healing of patients.

Aria learned about a few of the main crystals and their properties. They were not as important as the herbs, however. A Treater only ever needs one crystal, but it is up to each individual to choose their own, so they need to know the different properties. Of course, the crystal needs cleansing, and this cleansing fell to Coloma, who did it with magic. Lady Bia covered for Aria, saying that she wanted someone more experienced in charge of this.

#

One Healing session with a patient raised questions about Aria. It was a case of a male Fairy who had escaped an attack. He had come from one of the other Faydoms, but he was too afraid to say which one. He had sustained brutal injuries but somehow managed to find his way to Aer's main gates, where the guards found him and brought him to Lady Bia.

He had a vast amount of injuries: broken bones, deep cuts across his body, and many bruises. He was so close to death that Lady Bia didn't hesitate and used magic straight away.

When he woke up, his discomfort was a mystery. He said that he felt dizzy and nauseous and couldn't seem to breathe properly. Lady Bia was baffled. She had to send out messages on the fastest birds to get answers.

Eventually she got a response saying it was the altitude. It was so rare because not many outsiders came into Aer. But the fact that Aer was situated on a mountain made other people sick because they weren't used to it.

After she had made the patient as comfortable as possible, she took Aria aside.

'Did you ever feel out of breath or nauseous?'

Aria shook her head.

'You came from a high altitude then,' she stated.

This was another piece of information that Aria could store for future reference. It didn't mean anything to her, however.

Aria was allowed to try some of the procedures that didn't need magic, such as setting bones before they could be healed, so that they would Heal correctly. Slowly she got the hang of the non-magical techniques.

# Chapter Nine
## DISCORD

Even though Aria was fully occupied, she missed Lareo, whom she hardly saw any more. He always had supper with everyone, but left as soon as the meal was finished. Aria had no idea where he spent his time or what he did.

During these meals, Aria got to know Brezan's father, Aquila. He was a very nice person and was like an older version of his son. He knew a lot about the history of the Fairies; every night, he would tell a new story. He was kind enough to keep the gory war stories to a minimum for Aria.

However, the one thing Aria wanted to know, he couldn't tell her; how the Auriouses came to be. Their beginnings were unknown. Only the years after they grew to full power and began governing the Fairies were known. Even their end was uncertain, though it had happened more recently. Aria felt compelled to learn more about it. She decided to ask Brezan for help one afternoon.

'I can try to look in the library here in the village, but I don't think there's anything interesting to find. Why are you so fascinated by this?'

'I just want to learn more about the Fairy people,' Aria sighed. 'I want to be able to fit in if I can't return to my own world,' she said in a small voice.

Brezan came over to her and wrapped his arms around her. It was very comforting, and it felt safe.

A sudden cough broke the silence, and they sprang apart.

'Sorry to disturb you. Lady Bia sent me up to call you two down for dinner,' Lareo said, sounding very formal, and turned to walk back down.

The meal was awkward that night. Aquila told a story about the early Air Royals, and how the ruling Princes and Princesses of the four Faydoms got together to try and recreate the Auriouses. They were, however, discovered by their angry parents and were punished for running away.

This story seemed to make Lareo even angrier. He kept shooting looks at Brezan and bolted down his food. He excused himself before everyone had finished. That night, when Aria went up to bed, she saw Brezan setting up blankets out in the passage. It seemed that he had been locked out of the room he and Lareo had been sharing.

Aria felt horrible. 'Please take your bed back,' she pleaded with him. 'You have become a refugee in your own house.'

But he refused, insisting that the room was hers now.

#

The next morning, down in the kitchen, Aria gathered herself some breakfast before she began her work. Brezan came down and grabbed a bit of her food. He seemed to have taken last night's ill-treatment in his stride. Aria's respect for him grew.

'Best get your Belladonna shoes on for my mother,' he joked over the fruit he had stolen from Aria. They were laughing so hard that they didn't notice that they had company. They stopped when Lareo grabbed some of the fruit laid out and abruptly stormed out of the kitchen. Silence followed the slamming of the front door.

'I'll go check the library for you today. And I'll try and talk to Lareo and explain about last night.' He sighed and left before she could reply.

Aria went to the Treatment Wing and asked Lady Bia about it.

'I think Larey was always a bit jealous of Brezan. He grew up very differently to how we raised Breezy. I think his parents weren't as hands-on as Aquila and me. Perhaps he's upset that he's busy working hard to find information for you now and Brezan is relaxing at home,' she said with a concerned look.

'How come Brezan isn't back at the castle?' Aria asked, acknowledging for the first time that it had been weeks since he came home.

'He didn't want me to tell you, but he asked for extra time off to take care of you. He said you were family and were very ill,' she said softly.

Aria was speechless. Lost in her thoughts, she couldn't think about anything else while doing her work. Late in the afternoon, a new patient came in. She was a young woman, hardly much older than Aria. She had a few cuts and bruises on her arms and a gash on her head. She said that she had been gathering water when she lost her balance and fell into the river.

She wore a shirt and some trousers in a coarse material Aria had never seen. It was black, which was strange; the Fairies loved bright colours. Her hair looked stringy, and her eyes were watery and shifty.

'Please, can you open your wings so that I can examine them?' asked Lady Bia.

They looked odd to Aria. They were not the shimmery brilliance of every other set of wings she had seen. She had only noticed that quality in them now, when faced with the stark absence of it. The colours looked dull. They were red, just plain red. There was no other colour streaking through them. And there was no yellow or any colour along the edge. Aria shrugged it off. What did she know about wing colours?

Setting to work, Aria cleaned the wound on the patient's head while Coloma healed the cuts. Lady Bia said that she would like the girl to stay overnight just to make sure everything healed properly.

By the time they had finished, it was growing darker. As Aria tidied up, and Coloma helped the patient to the sleeping quarters, her stomach clenched, and her heart pounded. She had had this feeling a few times now; the watchful presence. Aria turned to look around the room, but it looked normal. Coloma ushered the girl away.

*Weird*, she thought.

#

## Lareo ♂

Lareo sat in the back garden as it grew darker. He liked it out there. The fresh air, the flowers and plants soothed him. He had gone quite far out today, nearly to the forest. He had tried to shake the bad mood he had been carrying for days, with no success. He had never been this angry before. But then again, he had never been in love like this before either.

He also felt incredibly useless. He kept trying to figure out what to do with his life, but nothing came to him. He had left home, running away from a forced existence. He had turned his back on what his parents wanted for him. And now he was trying to keep busy in the place he really wanted to be in. And the thing that made him feel completely helpless was that he wasn't the one helping Aria. He couldn't fix her, nor had he been around to keep her company. Anger simmered inside him for leaving her alone and allowing Brezan the opening.

Not that he could hate his best friend, despite appearances. He regretted his treatment of his oldest and only companion, but he just couldn't help it. He felt drawn to her and yet blocked off at every turn.

He couldn't fix any of it. He sighed heavily.

'Oh dear. That doesn't sound good,' a voice said.

Looking up, Lareo saw that it was Lady Bia. She had a kind, understanding look on her face. As Lareo looked at her, he realised he had never seen that look before; it was the look of a worried mother. She sat down next to him and took his hand.

'There is no need to be angry with Brezan. Despite him being here, we still have plenty of room in our home, and our hearts, for you. I know your parents didn't make it easy for you, but they just wanted what was best for you.'

Lareo nodded. Under the anger, he knew this was true. He knew his parents loved him in the only way they knew how.

Lady Bia continued, 'You don't need to compete for our attention. You are a second son to us. And we love you,' she hugged him tightly.

They stayed like that for a few minutes as Lareo savoured this affection. His parents had never shown emotion; they had their strict ways and kept to them rigidly. It may have been a terrible idea, but he was glad to have left that environment. The only thing that bothered him was leaving his sister behind.

Being ten years younger than him, they had never been playmates. But Lareo loved and protected her, nonetheless. He hoped she could manage in his absence. But as he remembered her stubborn little face, always demanding attention, he knew that she would be fine. She could force emotions out of their parents, as he never could. He also remembered teaching her to stand up for herself and was satisfied at how strong she was. She was strong and brave enough to fill the gap he had left behind.

She was still a few years from being married off. That was both good news and bad news. The problem was how Lareo's parents would treat her now that he had left home. She would need to learn how to take his place. He hoped she would be able to change things for the better and not stick to their parents' strict rules.

He pulled his thoughts back into the present. He enjoyed the last moments of a mother's embrace. As they broke apart, Lady Bia said, 'I also don't think you need to be fighting over a girl. Just tell her how you feel.' She smiled encouragingly with a twinkle in her eyes.

#

## Aria ♀

Aria tried to talk to Brezan when he got home, but he was distracted. He handed her a few pages, saying that that was all they had. Then he disappeared into his father's den.

Aria went into his room – it still didn't feel right claiming it as her own – and read the pages. It wasn't much. It just described the castle that the Auriouses had built. It had four towers dedicated to each couple for their elements. Then the rest was dedicated to their unity. It also described how they formed couples, which happened before they had found each other by chance and come together as the Aurious.

*That's strange*, she thought, but did not have time to dwell on it. Brezan came into the room.

'Tha-' Aria was cut off.

'I'm leaving in the morning,' he said, looking pained. 'I need to return to the castle. I've been away for too long.'

'Is this about Lareo?' Aria asked.

'Just leave it alone. I belong at the castle, doing what I was trained to do. I'm leaving early so I'll say goodbye now.'

'Goodbye?' Aria refused to show any hurt. *What am I going to do without Brezan?*

'Yes. I don't imagine I'll see you again before you find a way to return to your world.' She caught sight of a glint in his eyes that betrayed the hurt he also felt.

Aria couldn't find any words to say.

'It has been a pleasure to know you. I hope you have all the happiness you deserve back in your world. Goodbye.' He turned to leave.

As he reached the door, Aria managed to whisper, 'I'll miss

you,' but she was not sure if he had heard. Then he was gone.

She sat crying on the bed – the bed she had commandeered from its now far-away owner – for what felt like hours. The room was a fresh reminder of its previous owner and the time they had spent there during her recovery. Aria could no longer bear to sit and stare at the painful memories. She fled the room to the only other place in which she felt comfortable – the Treatment Wing.

There were patients there today, so she did not go to the sleeping quarters. She stayed in the surgery side, where all the medicines were stored.

Lareo eventually walked in. The tears had stopped flowing, but Aria still breathed shallowly. She couldn't bring herself to look at him just yet.

'You sent him away,' Aria said with a bitter edge to her voice.

'It was time he returned home. He doesn't belong here.'

Aria gasped. She crossed slowly to where he stood. With all the strength of will in her, she controlled her temper. 'We. Do. Not. Belong. Here,' she growled at him. 'You have driven him away from his home. I don't even belong in this world, but I am here. You were a guest in your friend's house, and now you have driven him from his kind and hospitable parents because you couldn't stand him being my friend. How dare you?' Aria glared at him.

He looked ashamed. *Good*, she thought, *he needs to be brought down from his pedestal.*

'No one has ever spoken to me like that before,' he said, genuinely awed.

'Well, I'm glad to be of service,' Aria snapped.

He stepped closer, beseeching her.

'I thought you loved him. I couldn't bear that I was doing all the hard work for you, and he got your admiration and friendship,' he said quietly, looking at the ground. For the first time, Aria saw how vulnerable he really was. Her anger began melting away.

'I love him as a friend and brother, that's all. He was there to keep me company when no one else was.' Aria glared pointedly at him. 'But even if I did, why does it matter?'

'Because... because I...,' he was struggling to find the words. His face crumpled in resignation. With his eyes closed, he said, 'Because I love you.'

Aria's heart was racing, her breath caught in her throat. Her stomach was in knots and fluttering... as if there were butterflies in her stomach (*what a strange expression*, she thought for a split second).

While Lareo's eyes were still closed, Aria took a step forward and placed her hand on his cheek. It felt like an eternity had passed between them. He looked at her as if uncertain of her response. Aria smiled at him and whispered, 'I'm in love with you too.'

Lareo beamed at her.

He was so close to her now that she could feel his body heat radiating out. All her anger had vanished. Aria stared at his face, taking in every detail. All she could think about was how beautiful his bright green eyes were, reminding her of spring. He was like spring, full of life and bursting with emotion that was previously hidden away.

Consequently, he made her feel full of life and emotion too. It was as though her life was finally starting. This was a new beginning for her, and she was overjoyed.

Slowly, Lareo put his hands on Aria's shoulders. Taking her stillness as willingness, he leaned in and gently brushed her lips with his. His hands dropped to her waist and pulled her in. The kiss deepened as their bodies pressed together. Aria's hands found their way up to his hair, which was as soft as feathers.

When he pulled away, he looked down at her, smiling. She returned his smile, feeling happier than ever.

'I want you to have this.' Lareo pulled out a necklace with a stone on the end that Aria knew from her studies with Lady Bia.

'Fluorite,' she whispered.

'Yes. It's for clarity,' he said, as he put it around her neck.

The stone was dark purple with light green streaks running through it. It entranced Aria. It was an oval-shaped stone, with a hole near the top, where it hung on an elf-made silver chain. Aria tucked it into her top. 'Thank you. It's beautiful.'

'Now I think I should walk you to your room and bid you goodnight before anything else happens,' he said with a twinkle in his eyes.

As Aria snuggled down in bed that night, she realised how happy she was. *I don't need to be changed back*, she thought to herself, *I'm perfectly happy just being here.* And she fell asleep thinking of how perfect her future could be if it just carried on like this.

#

## Lareo ♂

Across the house, Lareo lay in his bed, thinking similar thoughts. He fell asleep feeling the happiest he'd felt since he was a child.

When he woke up the next morning, he was excited to start the day and see Aria. He had finally told her how he felt, and to his surprise, she felt the same way. He couldn't believe he had wasted all that time thinking she had feelings for Brezan. He got up, eager to get to breakfast. She was always up reasonably early and always before him, so he knew she would be waiting for him. He dressed quickly and went downstairs.

When he got to the kitchen, only Brezan's father was there.

'Good morning,' he greeted the old Fairy cheerfully. He had always felt closer to him than his own parents. Aquila had personally trained Lareo when he was old enough to join the army. He had come to think of him as a father.

'Bia is in the Treatment wing, but Aria hasn't come down yet,' he informed Lareo.

*That's strange*, Lareo thought. But he didn't dwell on it.

He went to the wing to see Lady Bia. He didn't feel like going to the library as he had done every other day. He hadn't found anything so far that could help Aria with getting home or retrieving her memory. He suspected that the Wise Leaders safely guarded that information.

'Good morning, Lady Bia,' he greeted the Treater.

'Oh, hello, Larey. What can I do for you?' she asked distractedly.

'Nothing. Actually, I was wondering if I could help you.

It seems Aria hasn't come down yet. Is something wrong?' he asked with concern at her worried expression.

'Yes, one of my patients left during the night. She was healed, but I wanted to check her one last time before she left. And she left something behind. But I have no way of Tracking her because she didn't live in the village,' she explained.

'May I see what she left behind?' His military training kicked in.

Lady Bia went to the Recovery Room and came back, holding a small metal object.

'It's just a pendant, but I thought it might be important to her. It looks like it's a family crest,' Lady Bia said as she handed it over.

Dread washed over him. This was no family crest. It was the mark of the Spectres; Fairies who were corrupted by the Shadow and turned evil.

'Aria!' he exclaimed as he sprinted out of the Treatment Wing. He flew up the stairs, in too much of a hurry to bother with manners. He reached Aria's room and threw the door open. It was empty!

# Chapter Ten
## KIDNAPPING

<u>Aria ♀</u>

*Not again! Why does this keep happening?* Aria thought angrily. Once again, without opening her eyes, she had no idea where she was. She was not in her comfortable bed, surrounded by the soothing smell of Brezan's room. She couldn't hear Lady Bia downstairs humming, as she lovingly cooked a delicious breakfast for them.

Instead, Aria was on a hard surface covered in the thinnest blanket. She could smell the outdoors which was a bad sign for her. She heard voices arguing but couldn't make out the words over the sound of creaking wood.

Sighing, Aria decided that she had better open her eyes to find out what was going on.

Peeking through half-opened eyelids, Aria could tell she was inside as it was quite dim. She detected a rocking, jarring movement and heard a creaking of wood. They were moving. *Great! That's just what I needed*, she complained to herself.

Aria gave in and opened her eyes fully. It was a small space, and the walls were slatted wood, which let some light in. It looked empty except for a heap at the back. Sitting up, she found she wasn't hurt in any way, although she did feel a bit drowsy. She put her hand to her chest, happy to discover that her necklace was still there. Quietly, she slid herself closer to the heap at the back of the space, to try and see what it was.

As Aria got closer, she realised that the heap was a blanket that moved gently up and down. Gingerly, she pulled at the blanket and it fell away, revealing someone hidden. Except that she wasn't like anyone Aria had met so far. Her face was longer and narrower, she looked slightly taller than the average Fairy, and her ears were pointy. And, most shockingly, she had no wing bumps on her back. Aria gasped.

The other creature stirred awake at Aria's exclamation. She opened her eyes and sat up slowly, turning to look at Aria, who saw that she had short brown hair. Her eyes were also a vibrant brown colour. She looked surprised to see someone there.

'Sorry, I didn't realise there was anyone else here with me,' Aria explained. 'Do you know where 'here' is?' she asked her.

'Yes, you are in a caravan. You must have been kidnapped by a Spectre and some Goblins, as have I.' She added the last bit, looking downcast.

'But why? And what are they?' Aria asked, confused.

She did not reply; instead, she turned her back to Aria. As she turned, Aria heard a sharp intake of breath. *She must be in great pain,* Aria thought.

'I could help with your injuries if you want.'

She glanced at Aria over her shoulder, and even in the darkness, Aria could tell it was a contemptuous look. *She does not think me capable of helping her,* Aria mused to herself.

Aria slid over to investigate. *Why am I uninjured?* Aria puzzled. *I suppose a sleeping Fairy is less able to put up a fight than a fully awake one.*

'I am an apprentice Treater. I can help you,' Aria explained, using a tone that Lady Bia had taught her.

'No, thank you,' she said harshly. 'I don't need the assistance of a Fairy, never mind a novice.' She practically spat the words at Aria.

Even though Aria knew she wasn't a Fairy, she took offence at that. 'I have been trained by one of the best and most talented Treaters around. She taught me everything she knows, and I have spent weeks at her side,' Aria explained angrily. *Not to mention that this all came quite naturally to me as a result of whatever I was in the human world*, she added to herself. 'I also happen to be the only one here to help you. So, you can sit in pain if you like, or you can let me help you.'

'Fine,' came the grudging reply.

Aria moved over to her and gently reached for the arm she was clutching. After a thorough examination of every part of her arm, Aria discovered that her patient's shoulder was dislocated. Aria had only done this once before, so she was panicking inside. But true to Lady Bia's training, Aria showed a brave and calm face.

Aria spoke in a soothing voice, 'Your shoulder is dislocated. I will have to set it, but it will probably be excruciating,' she explained.

Aria felt around and found a piece of wood that must have broken off the caravan's wall. Aria handed it to her, and she took it and put it in her mouth. When she had done that, Aria got into position and grabbed her patient's arm, closed her eyes and pulled as hard as she could. Aria could feel her stiffen and arch her back and a moan issued from her throat, although the piece of wood helped prevent any screaming. The arm slid into place and Aria quietly sighed in relief.

'There you go,' Aria said as she folded her patient's arm. Aria tore a piece off her shirt and tied it around her patient's arm and neck as a sling. 'It will hurt for a few days, but it's fine now. I'm sorry it hurt so much.' It bothered Aria that she had no magic to ease the pain.

'Thank you,' she whispered with sincerity.

It felt good to help someone. Aria smiled to herself. *This is where I belong.*

'To answer your question, the Spectra and Goblins are evil mutations. I don't know why you are here, but I am an Elf. My people are powerful, but our numbers are dying out. They have kidnapped me in order to gain my people's magic,' she explained weakly, still whispering.

'Can't you use your magic to get us out of here?' Aria asked, confused.

'No,' she said simply. As Aria looked at her expecting more, she sighed and continued, 'They have put a seal on the caravan preventing any use of magic. You wouldn't be able to use any of your magic either.'

That startled Aria. *Me? Having magic?* Aria never considered that she could have magic, and no one had mentioned it to her before.

'As far as I know, I don't have any magic; I'm not a true Fairy,' Aria said quietly.

'I know that you are a human who has been transformed. My powers may be blocked, but I can still tell. Besides all the knowledge you possess, I can see that there is a lot of magic in you just waiting to be used. That is why you are here, and I don't just mean here in this caravan.' As she said this, she became less sad and more determined. 'You have done me a great service, even with my contempt. I will help you in any way I can, when I regain my strength.'

'They call me Aria, by the way.' She smiled at her new friend.

She nodded. 'I am Elvya.' With that, she closed her eyes and fell into – what Aria hoped would be – a restful sleep.

#

When Aria woke up again, there was something different about the caravan; it wasn't moving. She couldn't hear any voices either. But she felt that strange sensation. It was the bad presence that she kept sensing. So, they had been watched and followed from the forest. If only she had realised sooner and raised an alarm.

As Aria glanced around, she noticed a flicker coming from a spot on the caravan wall. She crept across to investigate and felt the place with her hands, discovering splintered edges and a hole. Looking through it, she couldn't see much because it was dark, but as she shifted, she caught sight of the glow of a fire nearby. The light showed two figures lying down and one sitting, apparently on guard.

The figure sitting up was different to the other two lying down; there was a distinctly female shape about that one as she moved forward and stoked the fire. Aria felt a jolt of panic as she recognised the woman; it was the patient who had come into the Treatment Wing the day before. She looked slightly different, though. Aria stared for a few minutes as the firelight got brighter before realising what it was; her wings. Despite it being night-time, Aria could tell that there was absolutely no colour to them. They were a dull shade of grey, with no trace of any colour. She must have disguised her wings so that she wouldn't be noticed in the village.

The other two figures looked more prominent than the female. They seemed bulky and misshapen, but Aria couldn't tell more about them in the dark.

Aria did not know if this was good news or bad. She sat down again. Slowly, Elvya woke up.

'How is your arm feeling?' Aria asked quietly.

'It's still stiff and sore but much better,' Elvya sounded grateful.

'Good. I managed to get a look outside, and I saw that two of our captors are sleeping and there is a guard. It looks as though there are three of them.'

'I think you may be able to get us out of here with your magic.'

'What?' Now Aria was confused. *How can I, not even being a Fairy, get us out of here, when she, who is a powerful Elf, can't?* she thought.

'You have magic that is unknown to most,' Elvya explained. 'The Spectre will have guessed somehow what you are. But they will have no idea of the magic you possess and therefore won't have known to put a block on your powers as they have put on mine. I will teach you how to access your powers to get us out of here.'

Aria stared in bewilderment.

She hadn't even considered having powers before, never

mind using them. This was a lot to deal with. *Was it possible for me to have powers?* There must be a possibility, or she wouldn't have been captured. And who better to learn from than a powerful Elf? If the numbers of her kind were as low as she had said, then it was a huge honour to even be in her presence, never mind learning from her. But Aria hesitated, *she could be wrong about me.* 'Well, I suppose I could try. I don't know if I'll get very far, though.'

And so the training began.

#

They didn't have much space in which to practise, given their confinement. Their captors opened the caravan twice a day to give them food, and the Spectre stopped the caravan every night to sleep. They were forced to conduct the lessons in whispers, even though Elvya had regained full strength.

'You can fly, right?' Elvya asked when they started.

'Yes,' Aria stated hesitantly.

'Flying is only possible if you have power. Tell me how you learnt to fly?'

*How had I learnt to fly?* Aria smiled, remembering the day in the forest when Lareo had taught her. She felt a pang of longing as she thought of what a great day it had been. But that was not what Elvya wanted to hear.

'I was taught to get a sense of my wings, where they join at my back. Then I had to concentrate on getting control of them to start moving. And slowly I got used to using them,' Aria explained, remembering every detail of those moments.

'Good. A similar process is involved when accessing your magic. I have spent time with a few Fairies who have explained how they use their magic. They have said that they feel, in the environment, for their element and draw power from that. I, and my kind, access our magic within ourselves. You would probably be able to access the elements, but I am not sure. But I do know that you can access the magic within yourself,' Elvya explained.

That was quite a lot to grasp.

'Do humans have magic?' Aria asked.

'Not as far as I know. I suspect your magic has something to do with your transformation. Now concentrate.'


#


After a day, Aria began to identify a power source within herself. She started trying to use this power. It took a few attempts, but slowly she could access it more easily. She could do small things like create tiny sparks between her outstretched hands that gave them a little light. Soon she was able to maintain those sparks to provide them with some warmth, although she couldn't light anything to make a fire. Aria could also create a bubble of unformed energy that she could shape slightly.

'We might be able to use that bubble to get us out of here,' Elvya said one evening. Their captors were a small distance away from the caravan, preparing their camp. 'We shouldn't do it at night because they will hear us. The best time would be while we are moving. It will disguise the sound a bit, but it will make it more difficult for us to get down,' Elvya said, as she sighed and glanced at her arm, which was still in its sling.

'Is there no way to ease your pain with magic?' Aria had been wondering this for some time now.

'I would rather you use your magic to free us than to make me more comfortable,' Elvya replied.

Thus, the plan was set. Tomorrow, while they were moving, Aria would force her bubble through the door to open it. Elvya wasn't sure what effect that would have, but it was their only option.

'So, once we open-,' Aria was interrupted.

'How much longer until we get to the South Perimeter?' the male's voice asked. Aria and Elvya had never heard them speak more than a few complaints before now. Aria looked at Elvya and saw her horror reflected.

Those words took Aria back to a morning in the Treatment Wing. While she was cleaning instruments, Brezan had explained about the Faydom to her. He told Aria about the village and the castle and the Wise Leaders. She had learnt all of that from Lareo during their days in the forest, but she hadn't known about the perimeter. It was at the edge of the Faydom, guarded by soldiers and magic. The weakest part of the boundary was the west side, which was closest to Spectre Land, and had suffered the most damage from attacks. It had been reinforced with an extra wall and increased security from the Sentries.

'- tomorrow night,' replied the woman's voice. The rest of the conversation was drowned out by the night sounds.

Speechless, Aria just stared at Elvya. Slowly, she recovered enough to understand the meaning.

'Why are they going to the South Perimeter?' Aria asked, confused.

'The female is a Spectre Fairy,' Elvya explained in a forlorn voice. 'She is corrupted. She would know that the Western Perimeter is the most heavily guarded and would avoid it. She let the Goblins through, in the first place.'

When Aria stared at Elvya without understanding, she carried on, 'There is a powerful magic placed on the forest around the perimeter which repels Goblins. Only Fairies and Elves have the nature and magic for subtlety. The perimeter protects against obvious threats, but it doesn't protect against concealment. That means that anyone who makes an obvious attack or who has conspicuous power is repelled. It's essentially designed to prevent Goblins from coming in. Their magic, like their very nature, is violent and conspicuous; they can't hide in any way. I think that is the reason we are here.'

Aria was impressed and shocked at the same time; impressed by the complex nature of the magic she found herself a part of and appalled as the last realisation raised two thoughts. Firstly, if the Goblins could get in, then they were on their way out. Once they were out of the perimeter, there would be no need for hiding so they would head straight to Spectre Land. Secondly, as only Fairies and Elves had the power for subtlety, the Goblins would most likely use them in some way to give them that power.

'Why are they called Spectres?' Aria voiced the random idea that was bouncing around her head. 'Are they actual ghosts?'

'No. They are as solid and corporeal as you and I. From what I know, they got the name because they become a shell of their former selves. Anything good that was there was taken over by the evil Shadow.'

They were silent for a few moments, and then Elvya said, 'We must get out of here as soon as we can, which means that you shouldn't waste your strength tonight. Get some sleep and focus on our escape.' Elvya was suddenly fiercer than Aria had seen her so far. But she was right; Aria could still get them out, which was the most important thing.

Aria lay down and took a deep breath. She went through the calming exercises that Lady Bia taught her and fell asleep quickly.

#

The next morning, Aria awoke to the movement of the caravan. She became aware of a different feeling from the past few mornings. Today she felt determined. Aria sat up and saw that Elvya was already awake. *Good, now we can get started,* she thought.

Aria did not waste any time but got straight to work. She remembered her lessons. Aria took a deep breath and concentrated. She didn't need to work very hard to use her power now; it was ready. She quickly made a bubble and directed it towards the door. She felt the resistance as it reached the door.

Aria could feel the wood and moved the bubble to the edge. Once she got there, she could detect the magic that sealed it. She also realised that it was weak, much weaker than her magic, which surprised her. Changing the bubble into a blade shape, she pushed it into the seal. It slid through as easily as if there wasn't anything there.

Sliding the blade around the edge, Aria met no resistance. Once she had gone all the way around, she let the blade vanish. Aria went slowly towards the door, checking the surroundings for any other trace of magic. There weren't any.

'They didn't give the caravan much protection,' Aria commented as she reached the door.

'Yes, you're right. They believed that suppressing my magic was all they would need,' replied Elvya.

Aria nodded in reply. She pushed at the door, and it opened easily. She decided to try hooking the door to the outside of the caravan so as not to give them away. It took a small amount of magic, but she thought it necessary. Aria turned back to Elvya and saw that she was standing up. Elvya walked over carefully, and Aria could see that there were two blankets in her hands. She handed one to Aria. It was a good idea, but it magnified the gravity of what they were about to do.

'Now for the tricky part,' Elvya said reluctantly.

Aria had avoided thinking about this part. It wasn't too far to the ground, but at the fast pace they were travelling at, they wouldn't land easily. Elvya couldn't afford any more injuries. Aria thought quickly, *Maybe I have enough magic to help?* Then an idea occurred to her, and she hoped that she had enough power to bring it about.

'Elvya, do you trust me? I have an idea to ease the jump,' Aria told her.

'Yes fine, let's just get this done,' Elvya replied stiffly.

Aria took a deep breath and concentrated. She took hold of Elvya, holding her arms securely.

'When I say jump, we jump,' Aria said.

Concentrating again, Aria made them feather-light. As she reached out with her magic, Aria noticed first that she almost picked them both up and made them lighter. Aria also realised that despite Elvya being taller, she actually seemed to weigh less. Aria could only hold this briefly as the weight she was lifting was adding to the pressure on her. 'One, two, three, jump,' she whispered.

The feather-lightness helped them land gently. As soon as their feet touched the ground, Aria dropped the magic. It had drained her completely. Elvya grabbed Aria's arm now and was pulling her along. They ran towards cover, and when they got there, they hid themselves, not daring to move.

# Chapter Eleven
## SAFETY

They remained hidden until the light came directly down through the trees, and Aria started to recover some of her strength. They slowly got out of their hiding spot and checked their surroundings. There was no one around.

Aria took them further undercover and set up camp. They didn't have anything other than the two blankets they'd had in the caravan. Aria laid those out.

Before they did anything else, Aria turned to Elvya and said, 'Please can I try to use magic to Heal you?'

Elvya nodded. 'Do you know how?'

'Yes, I've seen Lady Bia doing it, and she explained it. I need to find a crystal, though.'

'What for?'

'I need to magnify my magic. The magic is not powerful enough to manage on its own.'

'Your magic is different. Try!'

Aria was sure that it wouldn't work, but she agreed. Lady Bia had said that if they tried without a crystal, nothing would happen. It wouldn't affect her in any way.

Elvya lay down, and Aria knelt next to her. Aria placed her hands over the middle of Elvya's chest and closed her eyes to concentrate. Aria focused on calling on her magic as she had before, and she felt it channelling out.

Opening her eyes, Aria saw a magical aura around Elvya.

It was astonishing; that shouldn't have worked, but somehow it had. Aria worked on getting the aura to penetrate the body. Once inside, the magic moved to the centre, and then Aria moved it to Elvya's shoulder. In a matter of minutes, Aria sent out soothing magic to chase off the pain. There was nothing else wrong with Elvya's shoulder, as Aria had fixed the dislocation correctly. She then let the magic withdraw from Elvya and disperse.

'It worked!' Aria beamed.

Elvya stood up, flexed her shoulder and stretched her arm, which was back to proper working order. She grinned at Aria, in a much better mood now. She was almost a different person. Having been imprisoned for so much longer than Aria, she had lost so much. It was not surprising that it had all taken a toll on her.

Now that Elvya was free, there was a fierce fire about her. It was as if she had gained a purpose in life again. While they bustled about gathering the things they needed, they chatted about nothing specific, idle banter. It was a comfortable feeling, as though they had always been friends. Aria thought about that and smiled; they were friends. They had bonded when they had both needed someone more than anything else in the world.

Elvya collected extra material for bedding. While she did that, Aria went off in search of food. Her days with Lareo had taught her about survival. She was glad that he had found her and showed her the important things.

Thinking about him sent a pang of regret through Aria. She had put him out of her mind since checking for his necklace, to avoid feeling even more hopeless.

#

## Lareo ♂

Lareo thought about Aria; he had been Tracking her for a few days now. He was thankful that he had given her the fluorite necklace. It wasn't only for clarity, as he had told her. It contained powerful tracing magic. He had the other half of the original stone that was used to make the necklace. It was drawing him in her direction.

He had grabbed his and Aria's belongings and left Brezan's house as soon as he had explained to Lady Bia and Aquila what must have happened. He had also asked them to send word to Brezan. He needed someone with more practical fighting skills than he had.

He had followed all day. He went on foot because he couldn't use his Tracking power and fly at the same time. He had picked up their path easily as he spotted some wheel treads; he examined the size and spacing between the wheels, and he realised that they belonged to a caravan which wasn't used in these parts; they were strictly Goblin creations, for this exact purpose.

Although he had spent so much time alone throughout his life, he now felt lonelier than he had ever felt before. Emptiness of this kind was entirely new to him; Aria's absence was painfully evident. While he had wandered about the village, he had spent a lot of time alone. But that was different. He had always known that Aria would be there when he returned. Now, however, he had no idea if he'd ever see her again.

He had stopped to make a camp the first night. While he was sitting there, he had come up with a plan. He decided that the caravan wouldn't stop during the day as that would be too risky. They would also stick to the thickest part of the forest, and it looked as though they were travelling south. Lareo had decided he would sleep for half the night, then start moving before they were likely to. He hoped that by doing this, he would catch up to them.

Two days later, as he walked along the path he was Tracking, he heard something. It was around midday, judging by the light. There was movement up ahead. Creeping through the bushes and peering through, what he saw made him almost jump for joy – he had found her! But she was with someone – female, he thought, guessing from her hair. Then she turned around, and he gasped in surprise. She had no wings: she was an Elf. He didn't recognise her, so she wasn't part of the clan that lived near their Faydom.

He made his way around the bushes. As he did so, both of them froze and stared at him. Dropping the bags of their belongings, he held his arms open wide. Aria was first to recover and shot across the space into his embrace. He held her tightly.

#

<u>Aria</u> ♀

After the first excitement of seeing Lareo again, they sat down and filled him in on what had happened.

'They were heading to the South Perimeter?' Lareo exclaimed. 'That's not far from here. I had better get Brezan to round up the Sentry and head them off.' He went off to send a letter.

Aria turned to find Elvya looking at her curiously.

'Who is he?' she asked.

'He's Lareo, the one who found and rescued me,' Aria told her.

'Yes, I can see that he found us and will rescue us. But who is he?'

'Oh, I didn't mean now. He was the one who found me after I was transformed and had no memory. He took me to the Treater whom I learnt from.'

'I guess we didn't have a chance to talk about our stories,' Elvya started saying but was interrupted by Lareo's return.

'Brezan should be on his way. He will find us soon,' he told them as he sat down.

They ate the food that Aria had collected, while she explained to Lareo what had happened and how they had escaped.

'You told her about yourself?' Lareo asked, raising his eyebrows.

'It was crucial to our escape. And she guessed,' Aria said, shrugging.

'So, you have magic now?' Lareo asked with surprised interest.

'Yes. Elvya helped me discover it and encouraged me to use it. But it was your flying lessons that helped me to access my magic,' Aria elaborated.

'I should have thought to try. I didn't think it was possible,' Lareo replied apologetically. 'How did you know?' he asked Elvya.

'I could sense the power within her. She just needed to focus on finding it within herself,' Elvya said.

Lareo grew quiet and pensive. Aria carried on eating and pondered, *I wonder if I would have discovered my power if Elvya hadn't told me to look for it?*

While they were all deep in thought, they heard a rustling as something moved through the bushes. When Lareo had arrived, he and Elvya had combined their magic to form a shield around them. Elvya said that it was potent, but would it be enough to protect them against Goblins? They all froze.

Lareo recovered first. 'I sent a message to Brezan. It's probably just him,' he tried to assure them, but his worried expression didn't change.

They listened as footsteps came closer. They were well hidden among the bushes and couldn't be seen from afar, unless someone was right next to them. The footsteps stopped.

'Larey?' a whisper called out.

Lareo and Aria sighed with relief. That was Brezan.

Lareo stepped out of the bushes to greet him. Elvya looked at Aria questioningly, who nodded her assurance. There would be time later to explain the complicated connections. Lareo and Brezan returned together moments later. Aria hugged Brezan; Lareo would just have to deal with it, especially after what she had been through.

'Breezy, this is Elvya, an Elf,' Aria told Brezan, whose

eyebrows shot up. She continued, 'The Goblins captured her before me. She helped me use magic for our escape.' Aria threw the last part in, anticipating even more shock. *I guess no one ever imagined I could have magic*, she deliberated. *Well, no one except for whoever turned me into a Fairy*, she added bitterly.

'You have magic?' Brezan asked, looking around as if it were a joke.

'Yes. Elvya detected it and taught me how to use it,' Aria said as they all sat down. She started again at the beginning of the story.


#


## Lareo ♂

While Aria explained everything to Brezan, Lareo contemplated Elvya. He had met the Elf clan living near the Wise Leaders. He knew their history and never had reason to worry about them. Now, however, for the first time, he realised how powerful they really were. She had been able to sense in Aria what none of them had – not even Lady Bia, who had examined her thoroughly.

As he had so often lately, he glanced down at his stone. *Is it still working fine? Or have I just been hoodwinked into a perilous situation?* He wondered about his companions. No, he reasoned, this was his childhood friend, who had done him a favour at a potentially significant cost to himself. Aria was who she claimed to be, as she genuinely didn't know what was going on, and he was in love with her.

The Elf, however, he wasn't sure about. All he had to go on

was their nature in general, and the fact that his stone wasn't alight. About the former, it could be argued that she might not be like the clan he knew and could, in fact, be dangerous. About the latter, it could be due to the fact that the stone was Elf-made and only infused with magic by the Wise Leaders, so she may be able to deactivate it.

Even if all that were true, he had the bigger problem of getting them all safely away from this part of the forest and from the Southern Perimeter. Lareo reached this conclusion just as Aria had reached her conclusion. *Now we need a plan*, he thought. He voiced as much, and the others agreed.

'I think we need to advise the Sentry of their presence. Hopefully, they can catch them before they catch us,' Brezan said. *Ever the Sentry*, Lareo mused.

'I think we need to have an exact location before we call the Sentry. They don't have the numbers to go scouring the forest for renegades,' said Lareo, as the leader that he was.

'What?' exclaimed Aria. 'You want us to go after the evil Goblins and Spectre Fairies who abducted Elvya and me? Not to mention injured her?' *She seems very attached to the Elf*, Lareo noted.

This pulled them up short. *We couldn't in good conscience ask them to do that after being so traumatised*, Lareo thought. Then it would just have to be Lareo and Brezan on this mission. Brezan exchanged a knowing look with Lareo.

'You two stay here. We'll track them and then come back,' Brezan told the girls.

Aria instantly looked worried. She looked pleadingly at Lareo.

Lareo hesitated, 'It's our duty to ensure they are caught. We have to go.'

Usually he and Brezan would have spent some time strategizing. This was especially important for Lareo, as a leader. He never did any of the actual fighting – his parents wouldn't have allowed him to be put in harm's way. But he was an excellent planner, which helped his army. There hadn't been many threats to Aer-Faydom. He had to ensure the Perimeter stayed strong, especially the Spectre Land barrier. Now all that effort seemed wasted, as they had found a way in any way. He would need to get word back to the army commanders.

But in the meantime, they needed to track the Goblins and the Spectre. He had to think about how they could find them.

It would be possible to follow their magical trace, if the Spectre wasn't blocking it. *Curse the renegade Fairies*, Lareo thought, infuriated.

He was one of the few who had learnt the rare and complex magic of Tracking; it had been taught to him at a young age when magic is more malleable. It required deep concentration to pick up a Magical Trail left behind after being used. This was made infinitely more difficult due to all the magic in the air. Usually, he would need something of the person to narrow the search, but, luckily, Goblin magic was so obvious and different. Finding them would be like finding a rock among leaves.

He took a leaf and placed it on the ground in front of him. He held his hands over it and channelled his Tracking power into the leaf. It spun around, becoming a green circle until slowly, it came to a stop. The leaf pointed in the direction that they needed to go in. He then fished in his bag and took out a small transparent box. He broke off part of the leaf that he had magicked and placed it into the box. It mimicked the big leaf, settling into the same position as the big one, and the box began to glow.

Lareo looked around smugly, only to be greeted with puzzled expressions.

'I'm a Tracker. And this is an Elf-made, Wise-Leader-infused box to enable me to track without having to keep stopping,' Lareo explained expectantly to the others. Only Brezan's expression changed to one of understanding.

*This is going to take some explaining*, Lareo sighed to himself.

#

## Aria ♀

Aria had been watching Lareo arranging the strange objects. She was relieved to see that at least she wasn't the only one who didn't understand. And then he started going on about Tracking and Trails, which only Brezan seemed to understand. This strange behaviour was triggered by his announcement that he and Brezan were going to go off in search of the Goblins. The idea terrified Aria. *I have a bad feeling about this.*

Lareo explained in greater detail, 'Tracking is an advanced magic taught to certain children. It involves picking up a person's Magical Trail, which is what lingers behind for a short time after magic is used.'

'Did you use it to find me?' Aria asked, finally understanding how he had appeared to rescue her.

'No, actually. I Tracked the clarifying necklace I gave you. I had a fragment of it that I placed in the box to lead me to you. I honestly had no idea you had magic,' Lareo said ruefully.

*Mystery solved*, Aria thought. 'It's good to know how you did it and that it's rare. I was worried the Goblins might find us the same way,' she added aloud.

'Yes. Well, moving on. What I was doing actually had a purpose. I have Tracked the Goblins. If we hurry, we could catch up with them,' Lareo said the last part to Brezan, who nodded his understanding.

Aria's stomach dropped; Lareo really was going through with this. She started to protest, but they had already started planning. Aria turned to see Elvya looking pale.

'Are we supposed to just sit and wait here?' Aria demanded.

'Well, yes. I don't see what else we can do. We'll put up the protection shield. Once we've found the Goblins and sent word to the Sentry, we'll come back,' Lareo stated with the authority of a leader.

Aria was speechless, but she sighed and shrugged. They had no choice, as Aria had no idea where in the Forest they were.

Elvya looked at Aria with a resigned expression, which Aria was sure she was also wearing.

#

Lareo and Brezan had started strategizing as soon as they had finished discussing things, and then they left.

Now the girls were all alone again. They weren't sure what to do with themselves. They had plenty of debris to use for the fire. They had eaten earlier while explaining their story. And they had nothing else that needed doing.

Aria had checked Elvya's shoulder when they had arrived, and it was perfectly fine, though a little stiff from lack of use.

So now they just sat and contemplated things.

'How do you all know each other?' Elvya asked timidly.

'It's a long story which is good seeing that we have nothing else to do with our time,' Aria said. 'I think I should start at the beginning,' she added.

And so Aria did. She told Elvya about waking up with no memory of anything, how Lareo had found her and taught her the essential things to blend into Aer and learning to fly – which Aria had briefly mentioned before. Then she explained how she had recovered after the second fall and how she had joined Lady Bia in the Treatment Wing and the flashbacks that followed. Aria told Elvya how in all that time she had befriended Brezan but fallen in love with Lareo. This brought them full circle to where they were now.

Throughout Aria's story, Elvya's expression was one of surprise and awe. Now, however, it was one of deep sadness.

'What's wrong, Elvya?' Aria asked, concerned.

Elvya did not answer straight away. Aria gave her a chance to recover.

'I was in love once,' Elvya said quietly.

'What happened?'

Elvya paused to gather courage. 'He was killed with the rest of my tribe. We put up a fight against the attack. We wouldn't go down quietly, but the Goblins were too strong for us. I was taken hostage rather than killed. I was spared because I am a

Light-Keeper,' she said bitterly.

'A Light-Keeper is what the Auriouses called their advisors. We helped them retain their balance so they could rule efficiently. Goblins never used to exist. They were Elves who were changed by the Shadows. The Shadows came from the first ever Spectre-Fairy. But it's not known who this was or how they came to be,' Elvya explained.

Aria sat transfixed. She had been trying to find out exactly this; having realised that there was a lot more to the history than what she had been told.

'How do you know all this? I've been searching for this ever since I first heard about the Auriouses,' Aria asked eagerly.

'That is my purpose. I am the Light-Keeper. I preserve the truth of the past so that one day, I – or whoever comes after me – may help the Auriouses to reunite and rule again,' Elvya answered. 'The true Aurious heirs, I mean. Not Princes and Princesses trying to fill their roles,' she added wryly.

'You mean the Auriouses will be recreated?' Aria asked her, puzzled.

'Yes. There is a prophecy among the Light-Keepers of the new Auriouses who will have powers that the rest of the Fairies don't. That is why the Goblins captured me; to gain those secrets. I'm not the only one, but I fear there may not be many of us left. We pass our knowledge on down the generations, but now there is no one left to pass it on to.'

They sat in silence for ages. Aria pondered the significance of all that she had heard. Aria looked at Elvya and saw the pain on her face, which was streaked with tears. Aria vowed to help her find her people and with her quest. Aria wished Lareo and Brezan would hurry up so that they could get her to safety.

#

## Lareo ♂

They had been following the compass box through the forest. Lareo could feel the trail getting more substantial and reliable.

Night-time had fallen, so they were forced to stop and find shelter. They found a hollow tree and settled in. They took out some food which they had packed and began eating.

'We must be getting closer. The box is glowing brighter,' Lareo said when they had finished.

'We'll set out at first light. Hopefully they won't do the same.'

Lareo slept poorly. He kept worrying about Aria. All he could see when he closed his eyes was her helpless expression when they had set off. He was wretched with guilt for leaving her out in the forest, after all she had been through.

He also did not know where he stood with Brezan now. He felt peeved that he was back, even though he had sent for him. He didn't want to remind Aria of their friendship, just as he had got her back. But she had chosen him, which had to count for something. He felt more at ease remembering the night before her kidnapping. It had been the best moment of his life. He held onto that memory in the face of the unknown ahead of him.

It came as a relief when the sky lightened. They set off, leaving no trace behind.

They had been walking for half the morning when–

'What's that?' Brezan whispered.

They stopped to listen. It sounded like the forest was being torn apart.

'They must be packing up their camp. This will be good news for the Sentry. Let's send word,' Lareo replied.

'I'll go find an air current to send the message,' Brezan said as he sneaked off.

Lareo peered through the bushes and saw two Goblins nearby, clearing up their surrounding camp. They looked very disgruntled. He listened closely.

'How were we supposed to know the human-Fairy had magic? She didn't know either. The caravan had all the confinement magic we had. If she wasn't in such a hurry to get out of here, she could have done something about it...'

*They also hadn't known Aria had magic, but unfortunately, they do now*, he thought.

'They really are a tiresome, annoying lot. Aren't they, Princey?' a cold, female voice said behind Lareo.

That was the last thing he knew before everything went black.

# Chapter Twelve
## WORST MISFORTUNE

<u>Aria</u> ♀

After the intensity of the day before, and because of Elvya's story, they were now doing something cheerful. Elvya carried on with the lessons on magic - they were levitating objects. Elvya said that this would be more difficult than what Aria had done in the caravan. What she had done then was feel the magic around her and force her way through. Aria hadn't been able to repeat what she had done to make them weightless, which meant that Elvya had to cover the basics with her again.

Aria concentrated on the berries they had collected earlier in the morning for breakfast. She started to get the idea of it eventually. She had had to go through it step by step, but finally she had achieved the weightlessness of the objects as she had done before. Aria sent the berries flying over to Elvya, who smiled as she plucked them out of the air and ate them.

Curiosity stirred in Aria, and she broached the subject while they enjoyed the berries.

'How does your magic work?'

Elvya didn't reply straight away. She looked slightly puzzled.

'I assume you mean creating objects?'

Aria nodded.

Elvya thought about it, and then she explained, 'There are

two ways that we can make things. The first is by combining existing materials, and the second is by making a new material with our magic.' Then she started to make something.

Aria watched in awe. It was such a spectacular sight that it took her breath away.

Elvya held out her hands, a hand-span width apart. Aria watched that gap closely. Between her hands, a material was forming. It was dark grey and shiny like the net – which Lareo and Aria had used to carry all the apples back to camp – and the necklace chain. The blob of material slowly began to take shape. It slowly flattened out and rounded itself until it was slightly bigger than a ten coin.

While it was still spinning, Elvya looked up at Aria and said, 'This will be different to the coins you may have used in the village. Those coins are made with rare metals and crystals that only a few Elves have access to. It's to stop any unauthorised coins.'

The spinning stopped, but Elvya looked intently at it. Then it flipped over, and the same concentration was applied.

Elvya's concentration eased off, but the round object continued floating in mid-air. Slowly it drifted over to Aria, and she looked at Elvya, who nodded encouragingly. Aria reached out and pulled the round flat thing out of the air.

She placed it in the palm of her hand; it was about the size of the berries they had been eating. Aria looked at it carefully and saw that it had writing on it: ARIA, LAREO, ELVYA in a spiral. On the flip side was the same spiral, but with just a line, no letters.

Aria looked up and smiled, 'I love it.'

Aria was really touched that Elvya tied herself to them in this way. Even though they had only known each other a few days, they had formed a tight bond. Aria slipped the coin into her Treater's pouch which, much to her surprised delight, Lareo had brought with him.

#

They spent the next couple of hours in idle chit-chat. It was relaxing after the stress of the last few days, and the concentration that was needed while learning. But the peacefulness did not last long.

Suddenly there was a crash through the trees, and Brezan landed in the clearing. He was breathing hard, and the absence was too conspicuous.

'Where's Lareo?' Aria asked, starting to panic.

Brezan looked up, and Aria saw his face: despair.

'No!'

'He's not dead as far as I know,' Brezan tried to assure her. 'He was captured.'

'Where were you?' Aria spat at him.

'I was sending word to the Sentry. And then I was knocked out.'

Aria glared at him. Him and his stupid Sentry! What use were they?

'Why don't you send it now?' suggested Elvya.

'I can't. Lareo wouldn't want the Sentry to rescue him.'

Aria's anger momentarily abated. 'Why? They can go rescue him. Isn't that their – your – job?'

'Lareo isn't all that he appears.' Brezan paused; he took a deep breath and continued, 'he is the Crown Prince of Aer.'

Aria was shell-shocked. She certainly wasn't expecting that.

'Why is that a problem for rescue?'

'They would drag him back to the palace and charge him for desertion despite the fact that he's the prince,' said Brezan.

'What do we do?'

'We'll have to go after him ourselves.'

'And they'll be in the same place?' Aria asked, confused.

'I don't know. We'll start there and see what we can find.'

Aria looked at Elvya. This would be hardest on her. Aria knew she would do whatever it took to find Lareo again, but Elvya didn't need to be part of any of this.

'You don't have to come with us. We would all understand if you wanted to stay as far as you could from any more danger.'

Elvya nodded. 'I will go with you and save your love. I owe you my life. And it's my job as Light-Keeper.'

*She must feel a tie to the regular royalty now that the Aurious no longer exists*, Aria mused vaguely. But she didn't have time to dwell on it. They needed to get going to find Lareo.

*Hang in there, Lareo!* Aria thought fiercely. *We're coming!*

#

## Lareo ♂

The irony of his situation wasn't lost on Lareo. He had switched places with Aria, but he didn't have the advantages she had had. He had only survived until now because the Spectre had recognised him as the Prince. They were contemplating using him to extract secrets and then for blackmail.

He had to figure a way out, and fast. Unfortunately, the Goblins had learnt from their previous mistake. They had put extra magic around the caravan and had also tied him up to be safe.

He considered his options and mused at how fortunate Aria had been that her powers weren't blocked, when he heard it.

**Hang in there, Lareo!**

It was Aria! But how was it possible? He must have imagined it; after all, he had just been thinking about her.

**We're coming!**

What did it mean?

Was he really hearing her or was he hallucinating?

Was she here?

No, he would have heard if they had found her. It was a major source of resentment that they had lost her and Elvya.

Should he try to call her?

'Aria,' he whispered.

Nothing.

This was a hallucination, after all.

Regret filled him. Not for running away. That was the best thing he had ever done because it had brought him to Aria. *I should have listened to her about whether or not to follow the Goblins.*

*Aria, I'm so sorry,* he thought despairingly.

#

## Aria ♀

They hurried towards the area where Brezan and Lareo had seen the Goblins camping. They travelled faster than the boys had done because they knew where to go. Brezan had reasoned that the Goblins wouldn't travel backwards so they would be safe.

Now they approached the campsite cautiously, in case they hadn't moved on; they needn't have worried; the camp was empty.

Feeling an intense despair that wasn't hers, Aria froze. The others looked at her with alarm.

***Aria, I'm so sorry,*** Aria heard. Looking at the other two, it was clear that they had neither said it nor heard it.

'I've just heard Lareo saying how sorry he is,' Aria told them.

'That's not possible!' Elvya exclaimed.

'Well, I'm aware of that, but I definitely heard him in my head.'

'No, I didn't mean it wasn't possible to do. It's extremely rare. It has only happened to a small group of people,' Elvya paused and smiled. Her eyes were twinkling. 'Talk to him,' she encouraged.

Confused, Aria tentatively thought his name. Nothing. She shook her head.

'You need to be thinking only of him and nothing else.'

Aria took a deep breath and closed her eyes. She pictured Lareo and how he made her feel.

***Lareo!*** Aria mind-called

***Aria?*** Lareo responded. Aria could feel his confusion. ***Is***

*that really you?*

*It is!* Aria exclaimed. *Are you alright?*

*I'm fine. They have me tied up in the caravan, though.*

*How long have you been travelling?* She asked.

Lareo paused. While Aria waited, she reassured the others that he was alright. They smiled with relief.

*I don't know how long I've been out.* Aria could feel the hopelessness behind Lareo's words.

*Don't worry, we'll find you!*

Aria looked up at the others. 'He doesn't know how long they've been travelling, so let's just say he's been moving since he was taken.'

'Let's keep moving,' Brezan said. 'Use your new-found talent, or whatever it is, to tell Lareo to let you know if anything changes.'

Once Aria had passed on the message, they set off.

They searched the campsite for any clues. After a short while, they had some luck. Brezan called out, 'Over here! I found something.'

The others rushed over. He was standing over wheel marks.

'It doesn't lead very far, but it gives us their direction. We'll go in that direction, which is heading towards the Southern Perimeter.'

So that was exactly what they did. Now and then they came across more partial marks along the way, where the ground was damp. They made good progress but slowed down after some time. They didn't know how far to go, so they proceeded cautiously.

#

Lareo ♂

After hearing Aria's voice earlier, he felt slightly better. He did not want her putting herself in danger, but he still needed to get out of this situation.

Judging by the light, which was dimming somewhat, Lareo guessed that they had been travelling for half a day. He hoped this meant that they were stopping. He listened carefully for any indication.

'Are we stopping tonight?' a gruff voice asked.

There was a pause. 'Very well!' snapped a female voice as the caravan stopped. Lareo heard footsteps coming around the side, and then the door opened.

'Well, well, Princey, you're in luck. I'm travelling with the slowest creatures ever, so you will be spared another day,' the Spectre said in a bitter tone. 'Here,' she dumped a plate of food by the door and shoved it towards Lareo with magic. Half of it spilt over. She threw a blanket into the caravan, which landed next to Lareo's feet, and then she slammed the door shut.

The ropes securing him to the caravan did not give much leeway. He edged towards the plate and stretched for it. He slowly brought it to him and began eating. He was ravenous. After he had cleaned his plate, he pulled the blanket closer with his foot.

He put it around himself and settled in. There was nothing else to do but sleep. He was starting to drift off, when the realisation that they had stopped hit him.

*Aria!* He called out in his head.

*Yes?!* She replied frantically.

**We've stopped!**

\#

## Aria ♀

'We must move,' Aria exclaimed to the others. 'They've stopped for the night,' she explained.

'We are nearing the Perimeter,' Brezan whispered.

They stopped to search, and as they scoured the area, they heard the crackle of a fire and whispering voices.

They crept closer, when Brezan and Elvya suddenly stopped. Aria turned to see them looking alarmed.

'What?' Aria hissed.

'We can't go forward,' Brezan said.

'We must be repelled because of our magic,' Elvya explained.

'What do we do?' Aria asked, starting to panic.

'You'll have to go in by yourself,' Elvya said. 'You can do it!' she encouraged.

Aria took a deep breath. She thought for a moment and then crept closer to their camp. It was easy to locate all three of them. The Spectre was standing guard, throwing disgruntled looks at the two Goblins who were leaning against a tree, fast asleep.

Aria sent her magical sense out until she could feel their presence. She didn't have much time to think, so she did the only thing that came to mind. Aria put them into the deep sleep that was used when curing severe injuries. She had only seen it done a few times, but she knew what to do. She remembered the technique she had learned from Lady Bia. The process was to take the herbal mixtures and cause the fumes to be released and inhaled by the patient. Aria didn't have any herbs with her, but she imagined them in the forest around them.

Aria created an invisible bubble around the three evil guards in front of her. She pictured the plants that she hoped were inside the area she had sealed off. She visualised fumes coming off those plants and filling the bubble. While Aria couldn't see the fumes to tell if it worked, she saw the Spectre, then the other two, slump over.

Aria didn't like using Lady Bia's techniques on anything other than Healing, but she had no choice. Once they were asleep, Aria had more time. They would be like this for a few hours.

She went to the caravan and peered in. Lareo was there, asleep but tied up. Concentrating on the lock, she blew it open. She went to the back, knelt by Lareo and shook him awake.

'No! You got captured!' He looked distraught.

'No, Larey, I'm here to rescue you,' Aria said, smiling.

He looked past her and saw the open door. Relief washed over his face as Aria started untying him. The knots were tight, but she got them undone, eventually.

They jumped out of the caravan and ran to find Brezan and Elvya. They looked as though they had been talking the whole time Aria was away. Brezan looked relatively at ease, but Elvya looked a little annoyed at being stuck with him. Aria smiled at how they were such opposite characters. Such an unlikely pair, sitting there together, trying to pass the time. They were happy, however, to see Lareo.

Aria went back into the camp and took the food, which the Goblins had collected. She returned to the others with her arms full of goods. With their bounty, they walked further into the forest, putting some distance between the Goblins and the Southern Perimeter and themselves. They set up their own camp and sat down to eat. Meanwhile, they told Lareo what had happened on their way to rescue him and about Elvya's story. Aria glanced at Elvya and saw she was a little uncomfortable, but she didn't object.

After the explanation, Brezan looked up and said to all of them, 'I must send word to the Sentry to come and get the Goblins before they wake up.'

'I can't be here when they come,' Lareo said, then looked at Aria guiltily.

'And why is that? Could it be because you are a runaway Prince?' she asked sarcastically.

Lareo looked at Aria, nonplussed.

'Your secret is out,' she smiled at him.

Lareo shot a dirty look at Brezan, then turned back to Aria and tried to apologise.

'It's fine. It's understandable. But we have more important things to deal with. Like, for example, what are we going to do?'

'I think we should go to the Wise Leaders,' Elvya announced.

They all looked at her, confused.

'Well, it's where I wanted to go when I escaped,' Elvya

explained. 'Also, didn't you want to find out about yourself?' she asked Aria.

'Yes, I suppose so. Lareo, can you take us?'

He nodded.

Aria turned to Brezan with a questioning look.

'I'm going to stay here for the Sentry. It will also give all of you a chance to get away,' said Brezan.

Aria noticed a pained look in Brezan's eyes that she had been too preoccupied before to notice. *I guess he figured out about Lareo and me*, Aria thought. She smiled apologetically at him.

'Thank you,' Lareo said.

With a plan to follow, they tidied up the area. Brezan suddenly stopped and stood with his eyes closed and his mouth moving, but he made no sound. Aria looked at Lareo, puzzled.

'He's sending word to the Sentry over the air,' he explained. 'The wind carries the message which constantly repeats until it reaches its destination. We can all do it, but we don't because everyone can hear the message. The Sentry uses it to get messages to each other quickly, but they use a secret code so as not to alarm everyone.'

Once the message had been sent, they said goodbye to Brezan and set off.

# Chapter Thirteen
## FLIGHT OR FIGHT

<u>Aria ♀</u>

While they walked, Lareo told the girls that the Wise Leaders lived in a tower at the base of the mountain. They would follow the river, and it would take a few days to get there on foot.

They decided that they should find somewhere to sleep for the night and could then set off again in the morning. Lareo refused to stay anywhere near where the Sentries might show up, so they began moving through the forest, away from the Southern Perimeter towards the mountain. They moved at quite a fast pace; Lareo wanted to put as much distance between them and the Sentries as possible.

They had reached the river when Lareo decided that it was far enough for that day and, in silence, they set about making a camp. After so many days out in the forest, they all knew what to do without discussing it. Aria laid out the beds, Elvya gathered debris for a fire, and Lareo went off in search of food.

Once the fire was going, and the food was prepared, they sat down to eat.

'Are we going to be able to see them when we get there?' Aria asked between mouthfuls.

Lareo paused for a moment. 'They can't deny me entry,' he said reluctantly. 'I… uh… I learnt my Tracking there… from an expert in the field. Usually, children don't learn directly from the Wise Leaders… but in my case…' he trailed off.

*Oh,* Aria thought awkwardly, *he's the Prince. So of course nothing was off-limits to him.* She just nodded, not trusting herself to speak.

They continued their meal in silence. Once they had finished, they laid down to sleep. Lareo put a perimeter shield around the camp for protection and to alert them to anyone's approach. Aria couldn't keep her eyes open for a moment more, and she fell asleep straight away.

#

When Aria woke up, every muscle hurt. Despite being drained from all the magic she had used, she felt exhilarated. She was with Lareo again, and they were safe and on the move. Her happiness diminished slightly as she pondered what she had learnt about him. Lareo had kept a secret, a big secret at that, but he'd had his reasons, and she understood them.

Sighing, Aria sat up. In the bed next to her, Elvya was still sleeping. Glancing around, she saw Lareo sitting by the fire, and went to sit next to him.

'Good morning,' she greeted him.

'Morning,' he said quietly. He handed her a cup of water.

'No more secrets,' Aria told Lareo firmly.

He looked at her beseechingly. 'I'm sorry.'

Aria nodded. She couldn't stay angry with him, and he smiled in relief.

'What happened yesterday? With the mind thing? Have you ever heard of that happening?'

'No. It was as if you were right next to me. But I felt what you were feeling; the intense desire to find me?'

'Yes. And I felt despair?' Aria questioned.

'Yes,' Lareo said, looking away. 'I knew you would come looking for me, just as I had done. But I felt guilty about that because I didn't want to endanger you. I suppose that was pointless?' he added, smiling.

Aria smiled bashfully.

She heard Elvya getting up and watched as she came over and sat down next to them. They prepared breakfast with leftovers from last night. As they ate, they planned their journey; they would follow the river, which would lead them to the mountain.

Packing up as soon as they had finished, they set off alongside the river, but still under cover of the trees. The conversation died out as they left the camp and headed into the forest.

After a while, Aria was glad they weren't talking. The forest was difficult to navigate on foot, but flying wasn't an option, because of Elvya. The ground was slowly getting steeper. Thankfully, they weren't travelling as fast as yesterday.

As they collected the fruit and roots, Aria decided to ask Lareo about his past.

'Why did you run away?' she asked tentatively. Elvya looked up curiously.

#

Lareo ♂

Lareo had expected this question ever since he found out that Brezan told Aria the truth. Once he had heard what Elvya really was, he was in awe. All of his doubts about her disappeared.

He took a deep breath before saying, 'My parents were controlling me, and I couldn't follow their plan. I wanted something different,' he said, without looking at either of them. 'They want me to rule Aer the way they do, by making deals with the other Faydoms, and enforcing their ways. They are also more interested in that than listening to what their people are saying. I want to earn our Faydom's loyalty and respect, as well as the other Faydoms. I could not live up to their expectations, so I thought that I should get out while I still could.'

He paused and took a deep breath. *I've never told anyone any of this before – not even Breezy.* Considering his oldest friend and now these new friends, he realised this: *I've been hiding these feelings for so long that they had become a constant companion. No one else, besides Brezan, had cared enough to know my deepest feelings. I owe these three the full truth – and, more importantly, I* want *them to know.*

'It was more than that, though. I really did try it their way. I tried my best to do things the way they wanted me to, but I just couldn't. They constantly found ways of finding fault with every little thing I did. No matter what I did, or how much effort I put into pleasing them, I always seemed to fall short. The disappointment was a daily experience for me. But no matter how hopeless it felt, I kept trying to win their approval. The only time I ever heard anyone say how proud they were of me was when I was studying under Spiro. It was the only time I felt accepted. And with him, it felt real. I doubted it in most people because of who I was, but with him I could tell he really meant it. But of course, my parents ordered me back home, and I never saw him again.'

'I had thought that maybe I wanted to take a more permanent role with the Sentry. But that didn't feel right at the time. And then everything happened.'

He looked up now. He expected to see them shaking their heads reproachfully for how petty he had been when they had suffered more significant troubles. But instead he saw them nodding, showing understanding and sympathy.

*They accept that, and therefore me?* Lareo mused, somewhat amazed. He had been so used to people being kind to him out of obligation that he had never had any real friends, except for Brezan and his family. Now he realised that he had found some more. It was also such a relief to have all that off his shoulders. He had been suffering for so long in silence. Talking with his friends was the best thing that could have ever happened.

With the truth out in the open, things were a lot more comfortable. He had no more secrets, and he could finally let loose and be himself.

After eating, they set off again. They would have to spend another night in the forest before they made it to the tower. He told the others this.

While they walked, they did not say much. They had touched on a sore spot for each of them, talking about family. Lareo did not know which of the two girls to feel more sorry for; Elvya who had lost not only her family but all her people;

or Aria, who couldn't remember them at all.

When darkness began to fall, they found an enclosed area for their camp. Lareo watched as the girls set to work. Aria kindled the fire, while Elvya collected food in the area.

'Aria, catch,' Elvya called.

Aria looked up and smiled as some leaves spiralled towards her. Catching the leaves out of the air, she used some of them in the fire and sent the rest back to Elvya.

*They have come a long way*, Lareo thought as he got some water from the river.

Once they had satisfied their hunger, they all fell into a deep sleep, exhausted by the long journey.

#

## Aria ♀

*I'm sitting at a table that is set for three people. The smell of delicious food is wafting from the kitchen, so I assume it's nearly ready. I help dish up, and then we sit down to eat. I'm talking with the other two people – my parents. I am telling them about my day at university, talking about the procedures that I'm learning. I know they don't understand what I'm talking about, but they act interested. It's just a typical family dinner, and I smile happily.*

Aria woke up abruptly; the dream had startled her. She remembered her parents, probably from hearing Lareo talk about his parents.

She looked around; it was still dark, but it was getting lighter as it was close to dawn. It was peaceful, even with the birds chirping. Aria had calmed down and was processing what the dream was about. She took out her collection of leaves that Lareo had brought for her, adding the newest recollection to the growing story. As she was pondering the story that she'd been gathering, her story, she stared off into the forest. Suddenly she sensed that the forest was staring back. She felt a familiar evil presence out there. Quickly she rushed over to Lareo and woke him up. He sat up, startled.

'What?' he asked urgently.

'I felt as though there's someone out there in the forest watching us,' Aria told him, trying to stay calm.

He jumped up and went off in the direction she pointed to. Aria sat near Elvya while she waited. After a little while, Elvya awoke and sat up, just as Lareo returned.

'I searched the immediate area, but I didn't see anyone or any evidence that anyone has been here but us.'

Aria nodded.

'Did you have another dream?' He pointed at her stack of leaves.

'Yes.' She handed it to him.

As he read it, Aria asked, 'How do you know about the human world?'

Lareo frowned slightly, 'I must have learned about them when I was a child, I suppose. It's not something everyone knows. I guess, because I was the prince, I was told about the important threats.'

It was a subdued morning. They had some food and then packed up the camp. They had woken up so early that they set out before the forest had warmed up. The light was very pale.

Lareo said that they were close; they should make it there

before nightfall. This made Aria feel a little better, although she was still uneasy with the thought of someone evil nearby. She shook off that feeling and concentrated on the path.

#

When the sun was shining brightly overhead, they discussed whether to stop or keep going. They decided to stay for a short time and have something to eat to sustain them for the rest of the journey.

They had been walking for a couple of hours when Aria started to say, 'I think we -...' but she stopped suddenly.

There it was again: the presence, but this time it wasn't a faint feeling. It was powerful. Aria had felt that kind of power twice before. She spun around, looking wildly for the source, and to her dismay, she discovered she was right.

'No!' Aria exclaimed out loud. The other two turned to see what she was looking at and were horrified.

The Spectre who had captured them stood there, with a wicked grin on her face. Aria was utterly shocked. *How is this possible?*

As if hearing her thought, the Spectre answered, 'You really think you can outwit me? I have more power than you can possibly imagine. Although I must compliment you on your performance, knocking us out,' she sneered. 'I have never been defeated before. But it didn't last long. I woke up only to discover my Goblins still down and one pathetic Sentry standing guard.'

Aria stared at her blankly. As the meaning of her words

sank in, Aria gasped.

'You killed him?!' Aria practically screamed.

'No,' the Spectre chuckled. 'I didn't bother wasting my energy. He wasn't even looking at us; he was looking out into the forest, waiting for something. I just sneaked away. It was the easiest thing. I found your trail, and I've been following you ever since. It took me less time than I thought. You make so many stops; you're almost as bad as those idiots I've been lugging around,' she mocked. 'I managed to catch up with you during the night.'

'It was you that I felt in the forest.'

That caught her off guard. 'You actually sensed me there?'

'I... Uh... Yes.'

'That's not possible!' she shrieked furiously. 'Night is my domain, and it shields me!'

In the blink of an eye, the Spectre had gathered up power and hurled it towards them. With an instinct Aria didn't know she had. She pulled the wind around them as a shield.

The Spectre grew even more furious and began sending power surge after surge at them. Aria held up her shield easily. This was a deadlock; they were too evenly matched. Aria knew the Spectre would keep throwing surges at them unless she did something. She ruminated over what the Spectre had just said: *night is her shield. If that's true, then she can't shield unless it is night-time!*

Cautiously, Aria felt around the wind barrier. She concentrated and pulled the air towards her. Before the wind reached the barrier, she directed it at the Spectre with great force. This created a gale that was so powerful, it lifted the

Spectre and flung her against a tree, causing the tree to break in half and topple over onto the ground. The Spectre lay at its base in a crumpled heap.

Aria let down the shield and stared at what she had done. She was partly relieved the Spectre was finally dead, yet horrified at what she was capable of doing. She was also afraid of what her friends would think.

Her knees gave out, and she collapsed to the ground. As Aria crouched there, Lareo and Elvya rushed over and sat down next to her. Aria braced herself and turned to look at each in turn. They were looking at the fallen tree with astonishment.

'How...?' was all Lareo could manage to get out.

Aria shook her head. She was trying to process what had just happened. 'I don't know. I saw that she was about to attack, and I just threw up a shield of wind,' she paused, thinking of the deadlock. 'Then I could see we were at a stalemate because my shield was so strong. I thought of how she had said that the night was her shield, and I threw a gale-force at her. And then that...' she trailed off.

Elvya and Lareo gasped at the same time.

'What?' Aria asked, confused.

But it wasn't either of them that answered.

'What, my dear, is that no one can control the air to do their bidding.'

As one, they jumped and whirled around. They were facing a Fairy older than any she had seen until now. He was wearing light yellow robes with a silver belt around his waist. He was tall and full of authority; his eyes were a light grey colour but gleamed with wisdom, and he had dark grey hair and a matching beard. His wings were dark green with blue streaks running through them. There was the usual yellow around the edge, but there was a silver glitter sparkling in the light.

Startled, Aria realised he must be a Wise Leader. That was the last thing she remembered before blacking out.

# Chapter Fourteen
## WISE LEADERS

Lareo ♂

Lareo didn't need to look at the speaker to know who he was. He had spent many years under his tutelage. He knew this man better than he did his own parents. Spiro had been the first to detect the ability of Tracking in Lareo. Although he was young enough to be moulded towards whichever branch of magic was necessary at the time, the Wise Leaders preferred to teach the specialty that the child had the most significant natural inclination towards. Spiro had detected the ability before the King and Queen had even thought of training him in anything.

Lareo had gone to live in the Wise Leaders Tower from then on. He had been afraid at first. But Spiro had been so kind and patient with him, which had eased Lareo's fears. He had known little of that type of treatment; genuine interest and kindness and Lareo flourished under Spiro's care and training. He had left the tower an exceptionally skilled Tracker and became a great asset to the Sentry. Soon he had risen to be a general, because of his abilities rather than his royal position.

In his years at the tower, he had learnt secrets from different Wise Leaders as well. He hadn't learnt anything in great detail as with the Tracking, but he knew the basics. He had also learnt the secrets to their defences and was sworn to secrecy.

*They must have had a forewarning of our approach*, thought Lareo. Naturally, they would be on high alert for intruders.

What had shocked Lareo was Aria and what she had done. Seeing her not just draw power from the air, but actually control the wind, was unbelievable. When he was studying with Spiro, he had learnt about the one who would recreate the Auriouses. He remembered asking what the difference between what that person would be able to do and what they already do.

'Well, what we do is draw our magical power from the surrounding element, in our case, air. What this person, and the rest of the Auriouses, will be able to do, is control that element and direct it to their will,' Spiro had said many years before.

Lareo could remember that day clearly and how he had felt incredible awe that there could be someone who would be able to do that.

Now he felt that awe again. Aria was the one who would recreate the Auriouses, and they would defeat the Spectres. What would this mean for them? Lareo didn't know much about the Aurious, but he did know some of the histories. He didn't think there could be much of a future for them if she genuinely was an Aurious. He decided not to think of it at the moment.

Aria had collapsed. Lareo suspected that she had used too much energy, or she wasn't accustomed yet to the amount of power she had unleashed. Picking Aria up and carrying her in his arms, he followed Spiro and Elvya back to the tower. They had finally reached their destination. They were exhausted.

Spiro guided them up the tower, to a floor with lots of doors spaced along the walls. Spiro instructed Lareo to lay

Aria down in a room where she could recover. Lareo kissed her forehead, appreciating the last moment they would share alone together, and silently said goodbye. Then Spiro pointed out two other rooms for Elvya and Lareo himself. Lareo was so tired he barely managed to mumble a thank you before disappearing into the room that had previously been his.

~

## Elvya

Elvya went into the other room and collapsed on the bed. She was physically exhausted, but her mind was racing. The scene in the forest had rattled her. In all her years, she had never dreamed that this would be possible.

*Could Aria truly be an Aurious?*

The Elves had the prophecy that the Aurious powers would return, and Elvya had been taught from a young age that this was her sole purpose.

Elvya's original plan of finding another Elf tribe to join had become obsolete. Her entire life had changed the moment that Aria had woken her up in that wagon.

#

## Aria ♀

Aria struggled to wake up the next morning; the bed was so warm and cosy. She hadn't felt this comfortable in days.

She was about to drift off to sleep again, when her odd surroundings registered.

Aria sat up quickly and looked around. She was in a beautiful stone-walled room. Looking out of the window, she saw a breathtaking view of Aer. The bed was big and soft, and there was a bookshelf, a desk, a chest of drawers and a cupboard. There were two doors at opposite ends of the room.

Aria got out of bed and pulled on some clothes from her bag. which was sitting at the foot of her bed. She wanted to go and find someone to ask what the heck was going on and where she was. But before she could cross the room, the main door opened and Elvya came in.

'Morning,' she said happily.

Aria smiled and returned her greeting.

'We finally made it,' Elvya said excitedly.

'Yes! With several complications and worrying discoveries,' Aria replied less enthusiastically.

'We'll figure that out while we're here. That's why we came, after all.'

She was right.

When they left Aria's room, Elvya pointed out her own room, which was right next door. They were discussing where they should go to find Lareo when he walked down the passage.

'Morning. We can go and see Spiro now and discuss things. This way,' he said abruptly, as he walked off. Aria glanced at Elvya, bewildered. He had not even looked at her.

They followed Lareo at a distance. *Clearly, he knows his way around*, Aria thought, feeling utterly disorientated. Aria glanced again at Elvya, who seemed to feel the same, judging by the bemused way she had attempted to walk in the opposite direction. Thankfully, it was not too far away.

They caught up to Lareo as he stood in front of a heavy, dark wooden door, knocking. As the girls reached the door, it opened. Spiro welcomed them in and directed them to seats.

'It is an honour to have met you. I, of course, expected visitors,' Spiro paused at Aria's confused look. 'We have ways of seeing things.'

Aria nodded.

'I had no idea it would be a trio of some of the most powerful people to exist in hundreds of years,' he continued.

Aria drew breath to speak, but nothing came out. *A trio of the most powerful people? Surely, he doesn't mean me? I didn't do anything that out of the ordinary, did I?*

'I don't understand,' Aria said quietly.

'That is perfectly alright. Together we'll find the truth about everything. This is the place where lost truths come to rest,' Spiro said, smiling gently.

'I don't remember my life,' Aria said, looking down.

Spiro remained quiet. Aria looked up. He nodded with a pondering look. 'We'll solve that mystery as well.'

Warmth spread through her body, washing the dread away. *I will finally know who I am.*

'The first thing we need to do is to research the history. We need to know all about the Auriouses and find out how you gained their powers. This is fairly straightforward, but it will take some digging through books.'

'I don't understand,' Aria said again, frowning. She recollected what she had heard about the Wise Leaders before. She remembered learning that the Wise Leaders knew all the history and kept track of it all. She said as much to Spiro.

'Yes, that's true,' he agreed. 'But we don't all know everything. What I mean is, we all have our areas of expertise. I, for example, specialise in magic, specifically Tracking...' he let the sentence trail off, making them draw their own conclusions.

'So, we just have to find the expert on the history?' Aria asked tentatively.

'Yes. But there is no 'just' about it. We don't know where this history expert is. He's a recluse, and no one knows exactly where he hides himself. He's probably on one of the library levels.'

*Great*, Aria thought, *more secrets to uncover.*

'I will go and speak to some other Wise Leaders and see if anyone knows where we must go. You can stay here if you want. I'll make sure lunch gets sent to you.' And with that, he walked out.

They sat in silence for a moment.

'This makes a change, no searching for food,' Aria said pleasantly to break the mood. They laughed happily together, although she didn't hear Lareo join in.

'I feel relieved that we're here,' Aria said.

'Yes. Safe,' whispered Elvya.

Aria nodded in agreement. She hadn't felt safe since she was in Lareo's arms in the Treatment Wing. She thought back and realised that she had always had a lingering feeling of unease. Even when they had escaped and Lareo found them. She didn't realise it at the time, because she was so happy to see him, but now, knowing that she was truly safe, she felt so much better.

Lareo still looked preoccupied. He did not join in with their relief. After a while, he wandered out of the room. Elvya drifted off to sit by the window and meditate. That left Aria with nothing to do.

She got up and wandered over to the bookshelf and saw that it wasn't a full library. Instead, it was mostly a collection of information on different aspects of Tracking. There wasn't much that she found interesting. This confirmed her earlier idea that Lareo had been taught Tracking here by Spiro. She took a book at random and sat down. It was about technical things that a Tracker had to do when Tracking. It didn't mean much to her, but she had nothing better to do or read.

Around midday, a couple of servants came in, bringing food. Aria put the book down and saw Lareo coming in behind the servants. They thanked the servants profusely and gathered around the spread. *This is delicious! Such a relief to have proper food after having lived for those few days, on scraps and whatever we could find along the way. Eating a well-prepared meal is the best thing ever.*

Lareo did not say anything during the meal and then left as soon as they were finished. Elvya went back to meditating. Shortly after Lareo left, one of the servants from earlier came to collect the empty trays.

While the servant gathered the plates, she seemed most fascinated by them. She wanted to hear everything about them. She told Aria some of her story, but she couldn't stay for all of it as she had to get back to work. Aria hadn't realised how others would see them; it was a surprise.

Aria tried again to read the book, but it was far too involved for her to understand. She got up and walked over to replace it on the bookshelf. She was just about to search for another book when the door opened.

Spiro came in, followed by Lareo. Spiro looked happy about something.

'I have some good news,' he said, coming to sit opposite Elvya and Aria.

'You found someone who knows the history?' Aria asked excitedly.

'Well no, not that good. I'm still looking. I actually found someone to help you retrieve your memories,' he said happily.

Aria gaped in astonishment. She looked across the room at Lareo. He was looking away from them, and from what Aria could see, his face wore a cold expression. She turned to Elvya, who was looking at her eagerly. Aria was confused when she turned back to Spiro, who looked expectant. She thought about the implications, which scared her. I have come to know and love this world. If I remember where I came from, would that still be the case? But it was essential to know everything.

She just smiled and nodded at Spiro. 'Thank you. That will be really helpful.'

He beamed at her. 'Good! So tomorrow you can go to Sya. She's our expert on the mind. And in the meantime, we'll continue with our other quest,' he paused as if trying to convince himself to do something difficult. He took a deep breath and turned to Elvya, 'I made contact with the Elf tribe that we work with, and they would be more than happy to welcome you into their tribe.'

It was Elvya's turn to look around, bewildered.

'Is that not what you were coming here for?' Spiro asked, confused.

'Uh, yes, it was my original plan. But I couldn't leave my friends. We are in this together, and it's my duty to stay with them,' she said without hesitation. Aria hadn't considered what this would mean for Elvya, but she was extremely relieved to hear that she didn't want to leave them. She couldn't bear to lose her friend.

'Very well. Tomorrow you will join Lareo and me in our search while Aria goes through her own personal search. Now let's get some food. We'll be eating in the main dining hall tonight.'

Aria was excited to see the rest of the tower. She hadn't seen anything except the two rooms and the passage. On the way to Spiro's room earlier, Elvya had explained that Aria had had some sort of power overload and collapsed. *I need to get past this weakness*, she thought furiously.

They followed Spiro out into the same passage that they had used before, but instead of going towards the rooms they were using, they went the opposite way.

There were windows along the passage, and Aria paused to look at the view. From this side of the tower, she could see part of the castle. The top of the mountain, with a cascading waterfall, blocked the rest of it. She focused on the passage and caught up to the others.

They walked a bit further, and then Spiro and Lareo, who were ahead of Elvya and Aria, came to a stop. Spiro opened a door and led them through. On the other side of the door was another passage, but this one was around a huge hole in the ground. There was a banister around the edge. Aria looked at the others, puzzled.

# Chapter Fifteen
## SEARCHING FOR ANSWERS

Lareo ♂

Lareo had kept very quiet for the whole afternoon. After breakfast, he went to his old hideout. When he'd studied here years ago, he had needed a place to get away from everyone. He would sneak into one of the less popular libraries and hide there for some time alone. Today he went back there to think. Yesterday had brought so many new revelations that he didn't know where he stood any more. He was going along with everyone, but he was too preoccupied to participate.

He noticed Aria's confusion now in the vertical passage and knew what was on her mind. After keeping quiet for so long, he finally spoke, 'It's the way they get around. There are no stairs here because the tower is too big, and it would take too much time. So, they created this passage, so to speak. It goes vertically to allow them to fly up and down.'

Aria turned, startled, toward him, but she just nodded.

They walked to the barrier which had a gate to give them access to the vertical passage. Elvya turned expectantly to Lareo, and he just nodded and picked her up. *Of course, as an Elf, she has no wings, so she needs help.* Last night when he was busy carrying Aria, Spiro had taken Elvya easily. But now that he was free, he didn't hesitate.

Spiro had already gone on ahead. Aria watched what Spiro did before she attempted anything. She prepared herself, but Lareo noted that she still hesitated for a fraction. Any other Fairy wouldn't have. *She is much better*, Lareo thought, *but it will be no use anymore as she will soon remember her past and go back.*

He took off and flew down. They were about halfway up the tower, so it didn't take them long to reach the bottom. As he landed, he set Elvya down. They walked through the main entrance to the dining hall. He had seen the dining hall many times when he had taken lessons here. But he had forgotten how big and majestic it was. He looked at the girls, and he saw the complete amazement on their faces.

As they got further into the hall, everyone stopped talking and turned to stare at them. They were all eager to see the new Aurious. They were probably used to Lareo because of all the time he had spent there. She, however, was a new face and vastly powerful. She didn't realise how much power she had.

As he watched her, he saw her falter as she sensed them all staring at her. He had to do something before she bolted.

#

## Aria ♀

All the noise around the hall had stopped. Aria looked around to see what was going on. They were staring at her the same way that she had been staring at the room. She didn't know what to do. She couldn't understand why they were looking at her with such awe.

As she tried to figure out what to do, she heard Lareo's voice in her mind saying, **Stay calm. You have nothing to fear. You are more powerful than you know. Use that confidence you have in your powers.**

Aria nodded. He was right. She wasn't this person; she wasn't shy or scared. Feeling the profound power in herself, she knew that she could handle anything. She took a deep breath, held her head high, and kept walking. Aria smiled at everyone, and everyone smiled back, and then continued with their conversations.

They sat down at an empty table which seemed to be reserved for Spiro. Soon after, the servant from earlier brought them a selection of food and a jug of water. They ate and talked cheerily, and even Lareo joined in.

After they had eaten as much as they wanted – which was such a pleasant feeling – they went back up the vertical passage. As they were walking down the hallway on Spiro's floor, Aria glanced outside and saw that it was night-time. They bade each other goodnight and went to their rooms. Aria was preoccupied with pondering the happenings of the last few days while she was getting ready for bed.

Lying down, she drifted off to sleep while thinking about what she would need to do tomorrow. She was so nervous about what she would discover that she slept fitfully.

#

Waking up the next morning, Aria felt weary from her restless night. She wasn't sure if they were eating in Spiro's room or if they were going down to the dining hall. She was about to decide when a knock came at her door. Expecting Elvya, Aria was surprised to see Lareo.

'Morning,' she said tentatively.

He just nodded in reply. He walked to the window and looked out. Then he turned around and faced her. It looked like he was struggling to say something.

'What is it?' Aria asked.

#

## Lareo ♂

Lareo looked at Aria, not knowing what to say. He had spent the whole night tossing and turning, feeling guilty. He had had a glimpse into Aria's mind when he had encouraged her. He had seen the bewilderment and hurt that she had been feeling at the time. *Despite her excellent Treater facade, I know that my actions are affecting her. I... just... I don't know what to do. Is it too late to fix it?*

*Everything changed with the discovery of her powers. She – can she be – an Aurious? If she is... then what about me?* Lareo shuddered. *If I had known, it would have been different. I would have kept my distance, not let myself develop feelings. But now... it's too late. She is a part of me, and I can't lose her!*

He couldn't stay silent, however. He had to apologise to her. And find a way to make her understand. He took a deep breath and started, 'I wanted to apologise for my behaviour yesterday,' Lareo cringed inwardly. He sounded so formal, as though he was trying to impress his father's council.

Watching her closely, he could see the pain in her eyes, despite her impassive face. He continued, 'I think we need to focus on figuring out what's going on, before we can consider us.'

She paused, as if trying to compose herself before speaking, 'Yes, you are right. I need to know where I belong before making any kind of decisions about… us,' she said wryly. Her expression had changed from impassive to scornful. 'Shall we?' she asked bitterly, pointing to the door.

Lareo followed her to Spiro's room. Elvya was waiting, already eating breakfast. When she saw Aria, she looked concerned. Aria sat next to her but didn't say anything. She just grabbed some food.

Lareo went to another tray of food and made his selection when Spiro walked in.

'Good morning,' he said, beaming. 'I see you're all eating, that's good. We need our strength for today. We have lots to do. Aria, I will take you to Sya once you've finished your meal. Lareo and Elvya, we'll start in one of the least popular libraries. There are only a few which are unused and therefore are unknown to the rest of us.'

They finished their breakfast in silence. Lareo noticed that Aria was wolfing down her food, obviously in a hurry to get started on her discoveries. She finished quickly and got up. Lareo tried to wish her luck, mind-to-mind, but found he was locked out. It was as if he had hit a wall. He felt the sting of rejection. *Well, what did I expect?* He ruminated, resentfully. *That things would carry on as if we were best friends*, he admitted.

He shook his head, getting a grip on himself. *This is not the time for petty problems. She is the key to resolving the wars. We need to focus on that.*

He looked around and saw that Elvya was staring at him contemplatively. There was something that he couldn't quite place with her. He didn't think she was evil – his stone hadn't reacted to her. He could sense that she wasn't telling them everything; however, he had more important things to worry about.

Spiro returned a short while later. They followed him out of the room and up the vertical passage. They went farther up this time until they were near the top. They were one floor away from Lareo's secret hideout.

Lareo landed and put Elvya down. 'I thought this would be a good place to start as it holds some documents on our history. You two can start looking around here, and I will carry on asking about the historical records that we need,' Spiro said.

He took off as Lareo and Elvya walked into the library. It was a single room, about double the size of Spiro's office. In comparison to the other libraries in the tower, it was a small one, although it was filled with rows and rows of tall bookshelves. It was daunting to look at, and they had no idea where to start. He walked at random and started skimming the book titles. These were about structures such as the tower, no use to them.

'You don't trust me, do you?'

Lareo turned to Elvya. She did not look angry, just dismayed.

'No, not entirely,' Lareo replied tentatively.

'Why?' she asked nonplussed.

'You're hiding something from us,' he said bluntly.

She was taken aback. 'Yes, I am.'

Lareo was impressed that she hadn't denied it. He expected her to get defensive and claim ignorance. He respected her for her honesty.

'I can't tell you now. It may interfere with destiny. But eventually I will tell you the truth. Please trust me on that,' she said beseechingly.

Lareo thought about it for a moment. She admitted to hiding something, but only so that it wouldn't interfere with anything. He really didn't have any reason to doubt that or her. He would just have to trust her.

'Fine. I'll let you tell us when you think it's the right time. My turn to ask a question?'

She sighed with relief. 'Of course.'

'How did you know Aria had magic?' he asked. It had been bothering him since he had first learnt about it.

'It's my gift. I can sense people's magic. For example, I could tell that you're an exceptionally accomplished Tracker.'

Now it was Lareo's turn to be shocked. Exceptionally accomplished? How could that be? Spiro had never said anything like that. He had learnt the same as any other Tracker. He can't be more advanced than them.

He couldn't stop thinking about it for the rest of the afternoon. They didn't find anything useful amongst the books through which they looked. They chatted pleasantly throughout the search, despite Lareo's preoccupation.

Once he had put aside his feelings of distrust, Lareo discovered, to his great surprise, how easily he got along with

Elvya. He felt that he could trust her because she had been honest with him about having hidden something. At least if she could not tell the complete truth, she was open about it. Also, Aria trusted her completely, so he thought he should give her the benefit of the doubt.

'I never lived in the mountains,' Elvya said quietly, looking out of the windows.

Lareo stayed quiet, not interrupting her.

'I lived in the flatter area, just north of the Faydom.'

She closed her eyes and took a deep breath. She turned to look at Lareo.

'I'm a little afraid of the height,' she laughed.

'Don't look down. That's what I always taught my sister.'

'You have a sister?' she sounded surprised.

'Yes. She is the cutest thing ever. I was quite a bit older when she was born. I took her under my wing and taught her to be brave and strong. She will be a fierce ruler one day…' he trailed off.

'I also had a sister,' said Elvya. 'And a brother. They were older than me. We were close in age, so we grew up and played together,' she paused as if to steel herself. 'They were killed first. The Goblins rampaged through the village and killed everyone in their path as they looked for me. They didn't know who I was exactly, only that I existed, and that I was part of my family. A traitor either sold me out or turned into a Goblin.'

'They came to my house and tortured my parents. They were trying to force them to say which one of us was the Light-Keeper. When they would not say, they began torturing all of us to see the power that was released. They killed my brother first because he was the oldest. Then my sister next. When they turned to me, they realised that it was me they were looking for. They killed my parents and then took me. I tried to fight them off, but they put a block on my powers. They knocked me out to get me into the caravan. When I woke up again, the Spectre was already in the village. I tried to escape when I thought the Goblins were distracted. They dislocated my arm in the struggle.'

'They somehow channelled or used my powers to find you. I don't know how they did it. They assumed it was you because you were the Prince. But instead they took Aria.'

'It's not your fault,' he reached out and took her hand. 'We are all together now, and that's what we must focus on.'

That made him trust her even more. He could see the pain in her eyes, but he could also see her strength and resolve to move on. In his view, she was incredibly brave.

When Spiro joined them, he had no news to tell them other than that which they already knew; the history records would be in one of the libraries on the higher levels. Lareo and Elvya also had nothing to report.

They made their way back to Spiro's room, waiting for Aria to return from Sya. While there, Elvya seemed as preoccupied as Lareo. Finally, she voiced her concern, 'With this memory recovery process, can Sya see what Aria discovers?'

As the significance of this question dawned on him, Lareo gasped. He hadn't even considered it. The information from the human world would be disastrous in anyone's hands. The Spectres had already tried to capture her for her knowledge.

'No. Relax, both of you. I would not have sent her there

if I had not first made sure that no one will ever know the memories and information she carries.'

That was a relief. Lareo couldn't take any more problems. They were already trying to solve too many as it was. They sat in silence for the rest of the wait.

After a while, the door opened, and Aria came in. In all the time they had known her, none of them had ever seen her looking as tranquil as she looked now. She sat down next to Elvya.

'How was it?' Spiro asked pleasantly.

'It was amazing!' Aria beamed.

'So, you remember everything?' Elvya asked excitedly.

'Most of it. We didn't get to the last few weeks before I was brought here, so I still don't know how that happened. But I remember my parents and friends. And I was studying to be what is called a 'doctor'. It's the human equivalent to a Treater. That's why I was so good with Lady Bia,' she enthused. 'And my name is Arianna.'

Lareo's stomach dropped. He was happy for her, of course. But her excitement meant that she would want to go back. He would lose her!

# Chapter Sixteen
## MEMORIES

<u>Aria</u> ♀

Not even Lareo's lousy mood could dampen Aria's happiness. She had spent the day going through her memories; it was what she had been waiting for since she'd woken up that first morning in the forest. She ignored him while she explained to them what she had done.

Sya had first taken Aria through meditation to help her relax and release her negative energy. Sya had assured Aria that she wouldn't see anything. She was only there to walk Aria through everything, and to help Heal her memory with magic.

'It took most of the morning, but she helped me access the memories slowly, so that they wouldn't overpower me. I saw the most amazing things. The human world is completely different from this world – both good and terrifying. But my parents…,' Aria paused. She couldn't explain how she missed them. She had felt their love in all the memories with them. *I am an only child, so I am all they have. And I have left them. I can't even imagine what they must be going through right now,* she contemplated.

Elvya put her arms around Aria and whispered, 'It's all right. Don't be sad. We'll figure something out.' Aria thought that Elvya meant that they would find a way to get her back home, so she nodded and pulled herself together.

After her revelations, everyone felt more subdued. Spiro got his servant to bring their food to the room.

'How much about the human world is known to the fairies and elves?'

'The Elves don't know much,' Elvya said. 'In fact, as far as I'm aware, we only know that they exist and that they have terrible weapons.'

Aria nodded.

Spiro said, 'There are old texts that certain Wise Leaders have studied. Old, as in, predating even the Auriouses. The rest of us are told basic information, little more than what Elvya has said. We know that they have evil weapons. It is believed that is the evil that created the Spectres and the Goblins. It entered through some kind of tunnel or tear in the worlds.'

Once Aria had finished eating, she excused herself and went back to her room. The day had exhausted her, and tomorrow would be the same, but she couldn't sleep. After the excitement of rediscovering her parents, Aria recalled the rest of what she had learnt. But the more she considered it, the more she realised how much was wrong with that world.

The human world was a scary place. After the quiet tranquillity of the Faydom, the human world was too loud and busy and crowded. But more than that, there was so much death and destruction. The humans were destroying everything around them. It was heartbreaking to see that the nature around them was almost gone.

Aria thought back to one of her earlier flashbacks. The tall, square-shaped, grey structures were called buildings. These were often homes for humans. They could only be compared to trees, but they went much higher than any tree she had ever seen. The hard ground she had been walking on was a road covered in tar, which was for the strange moving objects, which were called cars.

There were so many gadgets and things to make life easier. But they all contributed to the dwindling of nature. It may have made things more comfortable, but it certainly didn't make it better or healthier.

As Aria saw and remembered what miracles doctors achieved, with their fantastic medicine and advanced surgical equipment, she realised that there was a great need for those doctors and cures in the human world. Yet the Fairy world had absolutely no need of these. The hurts and injuries were minor, and illness rarely happened. This could be due to the magic, but in her opinion, it was because of the way they lived.

She tossed and turned most of the night, thinking of the bad things she had seen. Finally, she fell into a fitful sleep of terrifying dreams about the slow ruin of all that she had held dear.

#

Aria did not open her eyes as she woke up. Instead, she lay in bed for a while, thinking. After the night of bad dreams, she forced herself to remember the good things she had seen. She thought of the day ahead and everything she had been through yesterday. Even though Sya had eased the process of revealing Aria's memories, it was still a lot to deal with. She had a life there, with friends and family who cared about her. And she had been on a career path that would save many lives.

*What am I doing here? Why did I end up here?* she couldn't help wondering.

These two questions were on her mind as she got ready and made her way over to Spiro's room. She barely heard them as they discussed their plans for the day. She also barely registered that Lareo looked as preoccupied as she did. Aria was still deep in thought as she made her way to Sya's study.

She greeted Aria cheerily, however when she saw Aria's face, she asked,

'What's troubling you, child?'

'Just relearning all these things about myself and my world. And I'm wondering what comes next.'

'Ah yes. That's what everyone seeks to know, what comes next, what their destiny is, and why things happen as they do. I believe things happen as they are meant to and in their own time. You have come here for a reason. You'll figure it out soon enough,' she said, smiling. Sya had no idea that Aria was not a Fairy; no idea that she didn't belong anywhere in this world.

'Shall we finish up your journey?'

Aria nodded. This was the part she was most eager to see, and yet, at the same time, she was afraid of what she would discover.

Sya took Aria through the same meditation as the day before, which helped to calm her down. Sya gently placed her fingers on Aria's temples. Aria felt a soothing heat where she touched; this was the Healing magic at work. Aria took a deep breath and watched the scenes unfold.

*I see days and days of university lectures and studying, with the occasional lunches, dinners, and parties with my friends.*

*Medical school is all-consuming. Though I have many friends, it is superficial. I haven't much time for any meaningful connections. I also have no time for love. I am so focused on achieving my end goals that I have lost all enjoyment in life. It all flies past me in a monotonous string.*

Then one day stands out differently from the rest:

I'm sitting in class. The book in front of me says 'Neuropsychology'. We are learning about the brain this semester. I turn to look around the lecture hall. It is one of the smaller ones on campus. Medicine is such a specialised and challenging course that the number of students is not large. I focus back on the professor and take notes.

After class, my friends want to go for lunch, but I say that I have too much studying to do. They smile and wave goodbye.

I get into my car and drive home. I make myself a sandwich and take it back to my room. Sitting at my desk, I look around my room. I still live at home with my parents. All of my friends had lived in dorms and then moved into apartments together. I had decided to stay at home a little while longer. My room, like the rest of the house, is old. Everything had been renovated except the structure. I am just about to swing back to my desk and start working, when something catches my eye.

In the corner of the room, along the skirting board, there is a drawing of some kind that had not been there before. I crouch down and take a closer look. It is a Fairy etched into a panel of the wood. I feel around the edges to see if I can remove the panel to look at it better. It comes out quite easily, but instead of the wall behind it, there is a hole. I look inside and see a leather-bound notebook about the size of my hand.

I pull it out. The pages are thick and look very old. I get up, sit at my desk, and open it carefully. There is a loose page at the beginning; it's a letter, written in elegant, old-fashioned writing:

> *My dearest child,*
>
> *If you have found this book, then you are destined for great things.*
>
> *I came to this world from another – a world of Fairies. I was the Aurious Princess and then the Aer-Faydom Princess. I chose to run away out of fear and grief. The Aurious Castle had been attacked, and the Spectres haunted me. I made an agreement with my servant and only confidant, Ria. We contacted an expert Wise Leader, who gave us two spells: one to make everyone believe that Ria was me, and another one to take me to the Human world. She took my place, but I do not know what became of her other than that she kept our story preserved and hidden.*
>
> *I was contacted many years after the swap via a dream. In it, another Wise Leader told me of a prophecy that a descendant of mine would return to the Faydom to save everyone. I drew a miniature of myself as the Princess on a panel of skirting board. With a spell, I hid it until the right time for the true saviour to find it. Because you have found the picture and this letter and book, you are the one that must go back.*

*This book contains the spell that brought me here and another one that can take you there.*

*I would not ask you to do what I did and abandon your parents, but there is no other way. I have tried to make up for my past with the family I created here.*

*There is another spell to contact people via dreams. You cannot bring them into the Faydom. They were not meant to be in the Faydom as they did not find this book. It is a lot to give up, but it is your destiny, and it will save many innocent people as well as having a positive effect on the Human world.*

*I wish you all the best, my child.*

*Yours truly,*
*Arabella*
*Formerly,*
*Princess Abelia*

I deliberate over that letter and book for days. I keep going backwards and forwards with my decisions. I can't bear leaving my parents; I'm the only child they have, and I know what it would do to them for me to just disappear. The other thing holding me back is my career. I worked hard to get this far into a medical degree. Abandoning it now would be like forsaking all the people I could help.

But on the other hand, it seems that if I went to the other world, I could save so many more people — not only human people but magical beings that I had only thought of as make-believe folk.

*Finally, I realise that destiny is not something you can run from. I write a letter of my own, to my parents, saying that I have to go away to do something vital. And I will try to contact them as soon as I can and explain everything. And I tell them how much I love them. Then, following the instructions in the book, I write my name on a small piece of paper. Then I place the book in a plastic bag so that I can bury it for safekeeping.*

*In the book there is a map of the forest near the house. It is bigger than the actual forest, but that's not surprising considering how old the map is. I search for a few hours. Eventually, I find the spot where Arabella had arrived. I guess it is some sort of portal. I see a single rose bush near the portal and bury the book in the hopes of finding it again. I take the piece of paper with my name on it and hold it carefully in my hand. This is apparently to channel the magic in the right way. I do not know what will happen once I say the spell. I recite the spell which I memorised, that will take me there. Everything goes black.*

Aria sat bolt upright.

'Are you alright?' Sya asked, slightly panicked.

'Yes, now I remember everything.'

After thanking Sya profusely for her help, Aria ran along the passage and without hesitation, threw herself out into the vertical passage with her wings spread wide and flew back to Spiro's room.

# Chapter Seventeen
## REVELATIONS

<u>Lareo ♂</u>

Lareo, Elvya, and Spiro had spent the morning looking in three libraries. They had decided to split up to see if they could cover more ground. This plan did not work, however. They still came up empty-handed.

They had just had lunch and were waiting for Aria to come back from Sya. She said that she would only need the morning to finish retrieving the last of her memories. Lareo was about to ask them what they would be doing next, when the door burst open. Aria rushed in and closed the door behind her, saying excitedly, 'I know what happened; I know how I got here.'

She sat down and explained. She told them that the last few weeks before she came here had been normal, going about her days and her studies, except for one day, which had changed everything. She had found a book that said that she was the descendant of an Aurious child. That is why she had Aurious powers. It was her destiny.

While she explained all of this, Lareo listened intently. An idea was just beginning to form in his mind. He grasped at it but couldn't quite make it take shape. There was something that he was missing; some big piece of the puzzle he'd overlooked.

In fact, two things puzzled him. The first had been Spiro; he had said that he had not expected the most powerful Fairies in centuries. Then the second thing had been something Elvya had said. She had told him that he was an exceptionally powerful Tracker. If Spiro knew he was one of the most powerful Fairies in centuries, then that meant he was more advanced than his teacher.

He wondered how he could possibly be more powerful when every Tracker does the same thing. They take a piece of something the person has come into contact with and then use that with magic to point out the way. This is what had been nagging at him.

But when Aria told them about the letter her ancestor had written, he figured it out. She had said that the story was preserved and hidden. If the Princess had wanted something preserved, she would have become a Wise Leader to keep it safe in the tower. And if she wasn't still alive, then a descendant of hers would have taken her place. And with that thought in his mind, the Tracking magic stirred within him.

He stood up and said to a startled audience, 'I know where to find the record keeper.'

He walked to the door without waiting for a reply or looking to see if they followed him. He just followed the magic. He walked down the passage and out into the vertical passage. He flew up and then he landed on a floor. He was surprised to find himself following his usual path to his secret hiding place.

He walked into the library he knew so well. But instead of making his way to his hidden corner, he went to the back of the library. He went through a door there and found himself in a study.

He heard the others catching up to him. He was about to turn to them when someone stepped into the room from another doorway.

'Who are you? What do you want?' a Wise Leader asked. He had long hair, which he kept tied back; it had turned to silver as he aged. He wore the typical yellow day-robes and a silver belt. He looked older than Spiro. He also had his wings wide open, as if ready to fly away.

They were red with green streaks, and the yellow outline. The silver shimmer to them looked darker than Spiro's. *Maybe they grow more silver the older someone gets*, Lareo thought.

Spiro stepped forward. 'I am Spiro, and I am a Tracker expert. This is Lareo, and he is the Aer-Royal Prince. This is Elvya, an Elf. And this is Aria, the descendant of Abelia.'

Spiro had purposely left Aria until last for more effect. Lareo was watching closely and saw the Wise Leader's expression change from wary to surprise. He peered closely at Aria.

'You have come at last,' he said and smiled.

'I am Caellum,' he introduced himself. 'I am the great-grandchild of the Princess Ria. I met her as a child when she chose me to carry on with her duty.'

He then turned to Lareo and said, 'That would make me your great-great-uncle.' Seeing Lareo's puzzled look, he carried on, 'My sister took the throne. I became the second record keeper for this particular history. And now that the truth can finally come out. I don't need to worry about training your sister to take my place. Please sit while I get the letter.'

They all sat down. They had barely looked around when

Caellum came back.

'This letter was written by Princess Ria. It is a confession of sorts. The books are all about her life. She documented her life thoroughly. I would imagine it was because of her awe at being able to live such a life. Anyway, it's not important. The important part is this letter. Here,' he handed it over.

It was indeed a confession:

> *I am Princess Ria, of the Aer-Royal Family of Aer-Faydom. I was not born the Princess. It took exceptionally potent magic to change my identity. The true Princess was Abelia, and I was her servant. You might have heard of the legend of the Human Story; that story was based on our history. The Wise Leader involved did not wish to lose the record, and so he turned it into a fable and weaved a moral around it so it would always be heard. He wrote the story along with the spell and left it to a trusted friend.*
>
> *After the attack on the Aurious castle, we fled here with the Air Auriouses. Abelia was so distraught at the loss of her beloved that she contacted a Wise Leader. She wished to leave the Faydom forever. She wanted me to take her place as Princess to spare her parents more pain. The Wise Leader, with help from an Elf, concocted a spell that would replace her with me. It was powerful magic, and it took all the strength of the Wise Leader. He died not long after he had completed that spell.*

*She escaped to the human world using the spell. And everyone thought of me as the Princess.*

*I married someone that my 'parents' arranged for me. I had children, and I was happy for many years.*

*During the early years as a Princess, while I was making my preparation for my wedding, a Prophetess Wise Leader came to me. She said that she had had a vision. This prophecy stated that a child of the Air Aurious would have a descendant who would save us all and be a new Aurious.*

*She, of course, thought it meant my children. But I knew better. I found a Wise Leader who specialised in dreams. I told him everything, and he agreed to help me contact Abelia. He got the message across to her, and she decided to make sure that one of her descendants would find their way back.*

*After that, I lived out my life happily and without further mention of the switch.*

*However, as I neared the age of becoming a Wise Leader, the guilt started eating at me. I decided to guard this secret.*

*I moved to the tower and spent the rest of my life guarding this secret until the true saviour would return. I told only one person, the one that would take over from me. This person had to be of my blood.*

*The truth was to be kept hidden under oath until the true Aurious descendant returned.*

When they had all read the letter, they sat in stunned silence. Then Aria said to Caellum, 'I found a letter in my room in the human world. It was a brief version of this letter from Abelia. She had changed her name to Arabella. It was inside a book of spells and other things. There was the spell that took her there, and another that brought me here. I didn't understand the rest of the spells, though.'

Caellum nodded. 'What happened to this book?'

'I buried it before I said the transformation spell. There's no way it would have come with me, is there?'

'It is possible. We would need to go and look at the site where you arrived.'

Everyone paused for a moment, thinking about the new revelations.

'It appears then that I am a descendant of Ria and not the original Auriouses?' said Lareo, which seemed to be the only part of the letter that had stuck with him.

'Yes, Abelia never had children while she was here. All the Royals are descendants of Ria,' Caellum explained.

Lareo jumped up and whooped emphatically. *I have been worrying for nothing!* He spun around wildly, looking for Aria.

'I thought that we were somehow related,' he said, rushing to her side, and grabbing her hands. 'Since I found out that you were an Aurious, I thought you had to have come from the original Aurious line. But now...' he trailed off, grinning.

He pulled Aria up to him and kissed her passionately. They were entwined in each other. Lareo held her tightly and kept kissing her.

Someone cleared their throat. Slowly, Lareo untangled himself from Aria and smiled at her. Keeping hold of her hand, he turned to the others and beamed.

'Sorry! I'm just so happy!'

'Well, that is, of course, wonderful, child. But we do have more pressing matters to attend to,' Spiro said gently.

Lareo nodded, and he and Aria sat down.

'Can I say something?' Elvya asked timidly.

'Yes, of course,' Caellum said.

'I wish to apologise to all of you. I have been hiding something that now needs to be revealed.

'As I said before, I am a Light-Keeper. This means that I would be the advisor and balancer of the Aurious couple. However, since there has not been an Aurious in centuries, the Light-Keepers have developed an extra power, which is the ability to distinguish a true Aurious. Aria and Lareo, from the moment I met both of you, I have known that you are the new Air Auriouses. And I am your Light-Keeper.'

Her words were met with stunned silence.

Lareo was the first to respond, 'What do you mean by both of us?'

'The Auriouses are all about balance. That is their purpose. They balance magic and their elements, but have all four elements working as one. They have Light-Keepers to keep them balanced, but the pair itself maintains it as well.'

'Does the pair need to be a male and a female?' Aria asked.

Elvya tilted her head and frowned slightly. 'No, not necessarily. Often it is the case, because the male and female energies also contribute to the balance. But it depends on the specific Aurious' energy, not bodily appearance. The important thing is that there are always two,' she emphasised this part. 'They can't function apart. The true couple is distinguished by their ability to communicate with each other mentally, along with their exceptional powers.'

'The mind communication...' Aria gasped.

'But I can't control the air like Aria did,' Lareo was not as easy to convince.

'That only comes afterwards,' Elvya smiled. 'Aria couldn't control the air when she started. She was a gifted Treater first; then came her ability to overcome the Goblin and Spectre barrier. After that came the mind communication, and only then was she able to control the air when under attack.' She turned to Spiro. 'Sir, I don't know if you noticed anything about Lareo?'

'Yes, I have. He had surpassed my abilities within a few months of training. I am one of the most skilled Trackers, which is why I train younger Trackers. For Lareo to have surpassed me means he is exceptionally more powerful than any before him,' Spiro said, smiling at Lareo. 'And then, of course, there is today. That should never have been possible. Tracking needs an object containing a trace of the person.'

Lareo was stunned. He had never known that he had surpassed his teacher. He sat down in a daze.

#

## Aria ♀

Aria looked at Lareo as he sat down. There had been many

startling revelations that afternoon. Lareo had displayed some powerful magic to find the record keeper. Ria had said the same thing as Aria's ancestor, Arabella. The way Lareo had taken off, however, was unexpected. And Elvya's confession and what it meant about Lareo was unbelievable. Lareo didn't seem to be able to grasp the fact that he was more powerful than anyone in centuries.

Elvya had known all along that Aria and Lareo were Auriouses, and that they were meant to be together. Aria recalled and smiled. There had always been something between them.

Aria voiced a question that had been nagging her for the past few minutes, 'So Lareo and I fell in love because we are Auriouses?'

Aria felt a bit dismayed, not because it meant that she loved him any less, but because it took all the romance and choice out of it.

'No, not at all. You fell in love before you got your powers. But, in any case, an Aurious couple isn't about romantic love, which is above and beyond the powers. The couple are simply equal in every way and hold the balance of their power. They don't have to be a romantic couple to rule. The Auriouses are free to choose and love whomever they wish,' Elvya explained.

Aria nodded. Lareo squeezed her hand. She felt better that it hadn't been forced on her. She believed in destiny and that they were meant to be together, but she didn't like the idea that it was because of the powers and not themselves.

'What happens now?' Aria asked the room, as no one else had volunteered any more information.

'You will need to find the other Auriouses,' Caellum said.

'What?' Lareo asked, confused.

'That is part of the prophecy,' Caellum explained. 'You need to find the other six Auriouses. Then, once you're all united, you have to conquer the Spectre Queen and reclaim your castle.'

*Oh, is that all?!* Aria thought but did not voice. 'I don't understand. What do you mean 'need to find them'? If it was so obvious with us, why are the other six unknown?'

Elvya answered this time, 'You are the trigger for their powers to manifest. You had to come back here; otherwise, no one else would be an Aurious either. Also, I suspect the other Light-Keepers have kept to themselves for safety.'

'And my parents?' Aria asked quietly.

'Your parents don't belong here. They can't come here.'

Aria nodded resignedly. She remembered how long she had debated the decision to leave. She knew that this was too important and that a sacrifice would have to be made. But all the same, it was difficult. Lareo wrapped her in his arms, and she cried into his shoulder. Elvya came over and hugged her from behind. How long they stayed like that, she didn't know.

Finally, when Aria had cried herself out, Caellum said, 'Let's have some supper. We don't need to figure everything out in one night.'

Aria nodded. She took a deep breath and confirmed the decision she made when she left.

'I chose to come here. I knew I would be leaving my parents, but I chose to do what was right. However, I would like to be able to explain to my parents and then say goodbye to them. I will let go of my past life. Arianna is no more. Only

Aria. This is where I belong.'

They were a very subdued group that night as they ate. Spiro agreed to talk to the Dream Expert to try to find a way that Aria could contact her parents. Lareo took her aside before the food came, to apologise for his behaviour. Aria understood what he had been worrying about. The idea did not even occur to her, but she saw how it had bothered him.

'If we are going to have to fight the Spectres and Goblins, we'll need to find out all we can about them,' Aria said, breaking the silence.

'There is not much known about them,' Caellum said, dismayed. 'We didn't have many who were willing to talk about them after the exile.'

'Elvya?' Aria asked desperately.

'No. We don't know much, either. There might be more information in the other Faydoms.'

'We have been through a lot today,' Spiro declared. 'We need sleep before we can talk about anything else.'

They all agreed and made their way to their rooms. Aria asked Lareo to stay with her that night. They held each other tightly and talked well into the early hours of the morning.

Lareo apologised again for how he had treated Aria the past few days. She told him that she now understood what he was thinking. Also, she explained that it helped her in her journey and decision. She had chosen to stay here not only for him, but because she knew it was the right thing to do.

Aria told Lareo all about the human world. He was both fascinated and horrified – even more than she had been.

'Cutting down trees! Destruction without a second

thought? That's really how they are? They don't care about conserving the earth?'

'They were more interested in creating new futures than saving the current and past world,' Aria explained.

She explained about all the wonders, but he could not overlook the bad in favour of the good. She told him she agreed with him now.

'Obviously, living in the human world,' Aria confided. 'I did everything that is now repulsive to me, but I hadn't developed this appreciation for the world. I knew that the way the world was carrying on was wrong, but I had a greater need to survive. I also decided to save people instead of the world in which they lived,' she told him.

Aria was glad to be given another chance to save both. She needed to help the human world, even though she would never go back to it. She didn't share this with Lareo. She knew that he wouldn't hate her for the way she had lived, but she also knew that he wouldn't understand. It was still her home; it was where she came from, her roots. And although Aria had renounced it, it was still a big part of her. She would be a good Aurious, not despite her past, but because of that knowledge.

One thing that she did share with him, that she thought he had a right to know about, was her romantic past. Aria wanted him to be without a doubt that she was with him and only him. That there was no one that she had left behind that would have a hold on her heart. He was all she would ever need in this world or the other one.

#

They started planning the next day. They wouldn't take any chances by travelling the same way they had to get here. Now the argument was where they should go first.

'We should go to the Faydom. That would be most beneficial to our end game,' Lareo insisted. 'That is Terra. It puts us in the best position to attack.'

'We aren't ready for attacking yet,' Aria countered.

'I agree with Aria,' Elvya said.

They had been going around in circles; they had all explained each point of view and kept coming back to the same conclusions. Aria looked imploringly at the two Wise Leaders.

'I agree that you are not strong enough yet,' Caellum admitted.

Spiro, who had kept quiet during the argument, spoke now. 'Lareo, I understand that your instinct is to attack, that is your Sentry training. I want you to think of this from an Aurious point of view.'

This was a sensitive topic for Lareo. He had confided to Aria the night before that he did not believe he was truly an Aurious. He thought it was only because she had chosen him and not that they were the proper couple. He still had no idea of the extent of his powers.

'Maybe I can help you access your powers?' said Aria.

# Chapter Eighteen
## THE SECOND AURIOUS

This decision broke the deadlock they had reached. The two Wise Leaders and Elvya were delighted by this idea. They were all eager to see Lareo achieve his true potential. Aria wanted to do it so that Lareo had a sense of meaning. He was relying on his old training to strategise, which seemed to give him drive, but it was the wrong purpose for him.

He reluctantly agreed. Grudgingly, he followed as they made their way down the vertical passage and out of the castle.

Aria realised that she hadn't seen the tower from the outside. She looked up and was astounded by how tall it was. It was a round building made with grey stones; windows were scattered up and down.

She couldn't reconcile this with the height that she had been flying daily. It made her happy to know that she was flying as if she had been doing it her whole life. In the village, she hadn't had much opportunity to fly around. But being here a few days had her using her wings all the time. Stretching her wings and gliding down is a liberating feeling. She loves the feeling of energy pumping through her body when she flies upwards.

Aria thought back to when Lareo had taught her to fly. Now she could return the favour, but she was unsure of how to do this. She knew that regular Fairies drew their power from their element around them. *How is my power different?* She accessed the power from within herself and exerted her will on the element around her. *Am I unusual because I'm human? But what if that's not the reason? What if that was how all the Auriouses used their magic?* Aria had asked Spiro and Caellum, but neither of them knew the answer. It would have to be a trial and error method.

Caellum had asked if he could document everything that had happened and would happen which would spare any future generations the trouble they had encountered. Caellum now took to carrying ink and parchment everywhere, and the scratching of the quill became a constant white noise.

They found a private spot away from the tower, near its protective outer wall. Elvya and the two Wise Leaders sat down on the ground beneath a large shady tree. They had all agreed that they should keep a shield up to be on the safe side.

Aria had decided that the only way for Lareo to access his powers would be the same as it had been for her: in defence.

Aria first explained a few things, 'This will be different to what you have been doing up until now. Elvya taught me how to access my magic in a different way to how you access magic,' she said as she threw Elvya a knowing smile. 'She told me to feel the power within myself and draw on that, instead of drawing the power from the element around us.' Caellum wrote furiously.

Aria pondered more about her power and anything different to the typical Fairy way. She remembered the moments when Elvya taught her to access her magic, but something unusual occurred to her. When she knocked the Goblins and Spectre out, she thought it was because of her

Healing power, but what if it had been her air power? She put the thought aside and focused on teaching Lareo.

For the rest of the day, Lareo tried to do as Aria had explained, but it wasn't working. He was too used to using magic in a specific way. He couldn't feel the source within himself. When it began to get dark, they went back inside. They would need to find a way to help Lareo access his powers.

Aria finally voiced an idea that she had been playing around with all day. 'We need a way for his normal powers to be blocked so that he can learn to access the new power. I was forced to use mine when no one else could do anything.'

They nodded. Caellum disappeared to a bookshelf and looked for something. After a while, he came back with a book called Magical Defensive Spells.

'This is old magic that the Aurious used. They weren't strong enough to guard the castle, and so it was discontinued. There is one spell that has mostly managed to protect the Faydoms.'

Aria looked puzzled at the others.

Spiro answered, 'The shield that prevents Goblins entering in large numbers and limits the Spectres' powers. It is not completely effective, but it limits the attacks, allowing the Sentry to do their job.'

Aria wanted to ask more, but Caellum had found what he was looking for.

'There is a spell that can block the element's power. I don't think it will prevent you from controlling the Aurious side of your power. Elvya, can you make me some talismans that I can set the spell into? We'll need to leave them overnight, and then tomorrow we can try again.'

#

## Lareo ♂

As Lareo lay in bed, with Aria deeply asleep in his arms and her head on his chest, he thought back to the day's events. He had been trying all day to get his powers to work, but it just wasn't happening. He felt the same as when he was back at home with his parents' disappointment hanging over him. Only this was worse.

He was not only disappointing the love of his life, but he was also putting the whole Faydom at risk. The more time they spent trying to teach him, the less time they spent out there looking for the real Aurious.

*I'm just not who they think I'm supposed to be.* Lareo had simply been in the right place at the right time, to meet Aria and help her achieve her greatness.

He was born into the wrong family. He had no talent to rule. He had proven that already while trying to learn from his parents.

Aria was trying hard to cheer him up and boost his morale. He felt better that she was there and believed in him, but it made him all the more uncomfortable. The disappointment from her would be worse now that she had such high hopes for him.

But they spent the night just lying together. Her presence was enough to comfort him. While he lay awake, holding Aria tightly, he thought about her.

Her bravery amazed him. She had given up her life and parents, and even her whole world, to follow what she believed was the right thing to do. She was his rock, and he drew his courage from her. *How ironic! I'm supposed to be the tough Sentry, but I need someone else to help with gaining the strength to face this.*

As Lareo held her tightly, he vowed to try his best. If only to prove that he wasn't the Aurious, so that she could move on to find the real one.

His thoughts travelled to Elvya, who had been with them for a while now. They had all faced many hardships, both together and apart. Was it a coincidence that she had crossed paths with Aria and himself? He never used to believe in coincidences; that things were not connected in any way at all. But lately, after the string of events that had taken place in the past few weeks, he realised that things happened exactly the way they were meant to. And now the last remaining piece to make it all count was for him to access his powers. As absurd as it sounds, he had to try, even if he thought it was pointless. He couldn't let Aria and Elvya down.

#

## Elvya

Across the tower from Lareo, someone else was lying awake thinking similar thoughts. The discoveries from the past few days had drained Elvya emotionally.

*I finally found my Aurious couple! I didn't think it would ever happen. However, it feels as though Lareo feels very unsettled and doubtful. I know without a doubt that he is the true Aurious, but I can't convince him if he doesn't believe it. That person has to want to tap into their powers.* She had known something was different about Aria. At first, she had decided that it was because she was human. But then her powers were unlocked.

She smiled at the thought of her strengthening friendship with Aria and subsequently, everyone else she had met. She had been alone for so long, since her tribe had been destroyed. But now that she had found a new family, things were starting to fall into place and feel right. It was a slow process, but she was getting better. Having others for company and problems to focus on was helping to keep her mind off her own problems.

As the night wore on, she kept trying to think of ways to help Lareo. He needed a confidence boost, but that would only come if he saw his powers. Aria had to help him unlock his powers. All their lives depended on it.

#

## Aria ♀

The next day found them back near the outer wall, with Elvya and the two Wise Leaders sitting under the tree. Elvya had made five amulets, and Caellum had magicked them. They set them in a circle, and Lareo and Aria stood in the centre.

By midday, he was looking very dejected. He couldn't access any magic at all, not his old or the new powers. It was frustrating for all of them to see him so helpless and not be able to help him. Elvya and Aria had already explained in detail how Aria had accessed her power in the caravan. He just could not feel the power source they had meant.

Aria was watching him concentrate when an idea occurred to her.

'Larey?' she asked tentatively, and he looked up, forlorn. 'Do you remember when I fell?' He nodded. 'And I slowed down before I hit the ground? How do you think that happened?'

He shrugged.

'You stopped me! You used the air to stop me!'

'Me?' Lareo started looking hopeful.

'You've always had your powers,' Aria smiled eagerly, and then had an idea of how she could help him.

Aria felt the air around her. It was a mild day with no wind at all. She pulled a warm breeze around her and felt it swirling gently. Then she eased it toward Lareo. It swirled around him.

'Use it.'

He looked less crestfallen and a bit more determined. Keeping the whirlpool around him, Aria could feel his attempts to control it, although they were rather feeble. She changed the air from swirling around him to closing in on him and then retracting from him. This had the desired effect.

Aria sent the whirlpool in again, slightly more forcefully this time. As it neared him, she felt the whirlpool snatched from her grasp. Suddenly Aria was the one with the swirling air. Her hair whipped around madly. Lareo dropped the swirl and laughed. She joined in with his laughter and threw her arms around him.

'See!' she exclaimed. 'You are a true Aurious.'

There was clapping coming from under the tree.

'Excellent, Lareo!' said Spiro, who went over to them and patted Lareo on the shoulder. 'Now try it without having your old powers blocked.'

#

They spent the next couple of days practising, trying different approaches to accessing his powers. Slowly, Lareo began to differentiate between the two types of magic. He was soon able to use each one at will without mixing them.

'Now that Larey is getting to grips with his powers, we can decide where we are going to go next,' Aria suggested to the others.

'Yes, quite right, my dear,' answered Spiro.

'I don't think we can go to Terra,' Caellum said, before Lareo could even try to get his argument across.

'I agree with Caellum, earth enhances Elf-power,' Elvya said. 'I think Fiamme would be the best place to start. The fire village would probably be less well guarded,' she paused, surveying the blank looks around her. 'Fire is a natural weapon against the Shadow, although the Fire Auriouses were never strong enough to beat it. So other than the evil fire creatures that attack, the village is mostly unharmed.'

'Do we all agree?' Caellum asked, looking around at all of them. They all nodded. 'Very well, that's settled.'

#

In the late afternoon, on the third day after Lareo had first accessed his powers, a servant come rushing toward them. He was a young boy, which made him a messenger. He ran up to Spiro and handed him a scrap of paper. Spiro thanked the boy who then ran back to the tower. Spiro read the message and looked up gravely at them.

'The King and Queen of Aer request our presence at the Castle this evening.'

Aria gasped and looked at Lareo worriedly.

'No! I won't go!' Lareo refused.

'We have no choice. They know you are here, and they requested all five of us by name,' he said, as he showed Lareo the letter. 'If we don't go, they will send Sentries and have us arrested. Either way, we will have an audience with the King and Queen.'

# Chapter Nineteen
## ROYAL PAINS

<u>Lareo</u> ♂

Lareo stood in his room, glaring at the formal outfit that had been sent to him. It was the stuffy black uniform of his rank as Sentry General. He reluctantly put it on. Once he was dressed, he went to Aria's room. He knocked, and she called to him to come in.

He opened the door and was stunned. Aria appeared in front of him, surrounded by three servants. She was in a floor-length dress. It was dark blue and shimmered as she moved. Her eyes shone brightly, and her hair was piled up in a complicated twist. It contained jewels that shone as brightly as her eyes.

Lareo cleared his throat and regained his composure. 'You look beautiful.'

'Thank you,' she blushed. 'I hope it's appropriate for your parents?'

Lareo nodded. *She is not what his parents would disapprove of; it is me and my choices they have a problem with*, he thought.

'Shall we?' he asked, holding out his hand to her.

They went to Spiro's room and found Elvya standing there. She was wearing a light pink dress, and her hair was also done up formally. She looked beautiful, but Lareo only had eyes for Aria. Spiro came into the room dressed in the Wise Leader's formal robes, which were silver. Caellum, who also wore silver robes, joined them shortly afterwards.

They set off in a procession down the passage. When they got to the vertical passage, they all hesitated. Conscious of their fancy clothes, they did not want to ruin them. They all unfurled their wings gently. The Wise Leaders went out first. Aria followed. Lareo gently lifted Elvya into his arms, taking care not to tangle her dress.

Outside the tower, a carriage waited for them by the main gate. It gleamed in the setting sun; the wood was varnished, and the wheels were spotless. Through the windows, colourful silk was tied back. As they got in, they saw that the seating was comfortable with cushions covered in velvet. Suddenly, the carriage began to move.

'How…?' Aria asked.

'It's pulled by magic,' Spiro answered.

No one else said anything. They were all too nervous to speak and, in Lareo's case, too angry. *I can't believe that after all that I've done to escape, I'm being dragged back.*

**You are an Aurious now**, Aria's voice said in his mind.

He gasped at that idea. *Yes, I am indeed an Aurious, which means that I don't have to take orders from my parents anymore. I outrank everyone; I am part of a group of the most potent Fairies in centuries.*

Lareo watched Aria as she looked out of the carriage window at the castle. Her face wore a look of awe. He looked at it from her point of view and had to admit it was a glorious sight. It was set at the top of a hill. The main part of the building was the Royal Family's quarters, while the tower on the left was for the Castle Sentries. The tower on the right was where the Royals conducted their business. Many windows were reflecting the setting sun, making the castle sparkle like diamonds.

They drove through the gates and up the path. The carriage came to a stop in front of the doors to the right-hand tower.

A few servants were standing waiting for them. They bowed their heads as each Wise leader descended. They were not sure how to respond to Elvya and Aria, so they just lowered their heads again. When Lareo stepped out, however, the men gave full bows bending at the waist, and the women dropped into curtsies.

Aria gave Lareo a startled look. She had forgotten that he was an actual Prince. He had also forgotten how formal people became around him. He had revelled in being anonymous and being treated like an average person.

Lareo, being most familiar with the castle, took the lead behind a servant. He had opened his wings as he walked away from the carriage. After exchanging puzzled glances, they followed his lead and also opened their wings.

The servant led them into the tower. There was a grand staircase leading up in front of them. To the left, through the open doors, they saw a ballroom. They were led to the right and were told to wait at the door while the servant went inside. Soon their names and titles were called out.

'Wise Leader, Caellum. Wise Leader, Spiro. Elf, Elvya. Treater, Aria. And His Royal Highness, Prince Lareo.'

They entered as their names were called. Lareo was seething at the titles they had chosen to use. He stormed in, ready to set things straight. He barely acknowledged the room they were in, as he knew it so well.

They were in the throne room. In the centre was the largest throne occupied by his father, who wore a long cape of red velvet over his own uniform similar to Lareo's. The next smaller throne was set behind the King's throne and was occupied by Lareo's mother, who was wearing a long dress of the same red velvet. Her hair, wrists, and neck were adorned with many bright jewels. There were two other thrones set even further back and were smaller than the Queen's throne. Only one of these was occupied by Lareo's sister, the Princess. She was about five years younger than Lareo. She was wearing a silver dress and looked like a miniature version of her mother.

They all came to a stop in front of the thrones. All of them, except Lareo, sank into deep bows and curtseys. Lareo just stood there, glaring at his parents.

'You should be the ones bowing,' Lareo said, barely containing his anger. 'You were introduced falsely to us. Allow me,' he mocked. They were taken aback but indulged their son.

'Wise Leader Caellum, descendant of Princess Ria and Record Keeper. Wise Leader Spiro, Tracker teacher. Elf Elvya, Light-Keeper to the Air Aurious. Aria, Air Aurious and fulfilment of the prophecy. And I am Lareo, Air Aurious and I complete our couple of the Aurious,' he said smugly, enjoying the look of shock on his parents' face.

'This can't be...' the King breathed.

*Show them*, Aria thought to Lareo. She nodded encouragingly. He smiled and concentrated.

The throne room, which did not have so much as a draught passing through it, was suddenly engulfed in a gust of wind.

Their fancy clothes flapped around them as their wings opened. The King stood up shakily and felt his cape billow out behind him.

Just as suddenly as it had started, the wind died down. The King and Queen stood rooted to the spot. They were astonished.

'So, it is true. The wild rumours circulating about our saviours returning are true. You really are the Aurious?' the Queen said quietly.

'Yes, Mother. We are indeed. Why have you summoned us here?' He felt better, having released his anger in the small gale.

'We had heard you were at the tower and we wanted to demand an explanation and a return to your duties. But now…' the King trailed off.

'But now, you had better start training Alizée to take my place and find a new Sentry General?' Lareo supplied.

'Yes,' his father said, disheartened.

'Can we speak to you for a moment alone, Lareo?' his mother asked.

'Whatever you have to say to me, Mother, you can say in front of my friends,' he paused and looked at her unconvinced expression. 'These people have my full confidence.'

'Fine,' she said reluctantly.

#

## Aria ♀

Aria had been standing uncomfortably while Lareo confronted his parents. It was good that he was sorting out his issues with them. She felt very awkward standing in the beautiful dress that they had sent to her, watching their business unfold. She looked around at the others and saw that they were just as disconcerted.

Aria felt incredibly out of her depth here. She was standing in these fancy clothes, surrounded by other people who were also in their finery, in the presence of the rulers of a Faydom, in a room that was the grandest and most expensive place she had ever set foot into.

The Royals were intimidating in their own right. Even little Alizée, who was younger than them, presented an appearance of power and majesty.

As always, their wings fascinated Aria. They were vastly different from any she had seen up until now. The striking difference was that they were gold. Not entirely gold, but glittering with gold. All three of them had the gold sparkle on their wings.

The King's wings were a solid red, the Queen's were a dark pink, while Alizée's were a light pink. They were all complementary except for Lareo, whose turquoise wings stood out in stark contrast.

That made Aria remember something that she had noticed when she first got here. She glanced at Lareo's wings and stifled a gasp. He had no gold anywhere on his wings anymore, not even the faint glittering he had had when they first met. But the yellow outline had become more pronounced. She glanced at the two Wise Leaders and noticed that their yellow wasn't as bright. Also, another difference was that in Lareo's yellow, there appeared to be a new pattern. Aria couldn't quite make it out from this distance.

She wondered if hers had also changed.

The Queen's voice cut through Aria's thoughts. She sounded very uncomfortable talking about these private matters in front of others.

When Aria heard Lareo saying that they had his confidence, she felt more at ease. She realised that he wanted them to hear everything so that there would be no more secrets.

The Queen was not happy about this turn of events, but she maintained her composure.

'We would like to know why you abandoned your duty and ran away from us,' she asked.

'I don't belong here,' Lareo replied simply.

The King seemed enraged by this. 'Well, of course, we see that now!' he bellowed. 'But how were we to know that at the time? We raised you the only way we knew which was befitting for you as the Royal Heir to the Throne.'

Aria glanced at Lareo. He looked stumped.

*What has confused you?* Aria asked Lareo mentally.

*I have never had such an honest conversation with them. In fact, I have never really spoken to them at all*, he replied.

Aria supposed he had been too caught up in his belief of the injustice of being forced to be someone else, that he hadn't even considered that they were doing things the only way they knew how to. They really needed to work on their communication.

'I tried to talk to you, but you were never around and didn't care enough to hear me out,' Lareo finally told them.

They all spoke for a few minutes, and Lareo had the opportunity to tell them everything he had always wanted to. They were shocked at how they appeared and made a promise to both their children that they would try to be much better parents.

They reached an uneasy truce. Lareo, while not able to completely forgive his parents for his forced life, was able to accept that they had done the best they could. The King and Queen, on the other hand, couldn't let go of their disappointment that their only son was no longer their heir. They did, however, acknowledge that they had no say in the matter and that his destiny was not something that could be changed.

They were begrudgingly ushered into the dining room, which was set off the throne room. It was not as big as the ballroom, but it was just as grand and exquisitely decorated.

The King spoke to Caellum and Spiro. And the Queen tried to talk to Alizée, who was far more engrossed with Elvya. She had obviously never met an Elf before and threw question after question at her.

Lareo and Aria had only themselves for company. The King and Queen seemed to be ignoring them, either for fear of their rank or because they felt that Aria was the reason they had 'lost' their son. Aria tried to mind her own business and eat her food (which was by far the best meal she had ever had in either of her lives), but she couldn't keep it up for long. When the Queen tried yet again to engage her daughter in conversation without success, Aria lost her cool.

'In case you haven't noticed, Your Majesty,' Aria said wryly, 'you have another child to talk to.' The whole table became silent, and cutlery froze halfway to their mouths.

'Excuse me?' said the Queen with a hard edge to her voice and narrowed eyes.

'I don't wish to pull rank over you, but the way you are treating us is appalling. Besides the fact that we are the Aurious, which means we deserve respect from you, this is your son. No matter what he has done to you, he is here. You should acknowledge that before he stops caring.'

The Queen was shocked into silence. The King answered instead, 'You are quite right. We have not been as respectful as we should. It is difficult to accept a higher rank than ours. We have never had to before. It was known that one day it would happen, but never did I dream it would be in my lifetime. It is an honour to know you. I mean that sincerely,' he added, obviously seeing scepticism written all over Aria's face.

'The truth is,' he continued, 'I am humbled by the immense power you possess. I am proud to be the father of an Aurious.' He said the latter directly to Lareo. The Queen looked as though her world had just crumbled around her.

'Aria, thank you for bringing this to my attention. I am glad you are here. For my son, my Faydom and the whole Fayworld,' concluded the King, who was a wise and good leader. These qualities were evident to Aria in the speech he had just delivered.

Aria glanced at the Queen again and saw that she looked as if she was working up the courage to say something. Just as she opened her mouth, a sentry came hastily into the dining room. He marched up to the King, saluted him, and handed him a message. He stood at attention, waiting for a reply message.

As the King read the letter, his expression grew grimmer and grimmer. He looked up in alarm at Lareo. He took a deep breath and addressed everyone. 'The Spectres and Goblins have started rallying. It is believed that they are aware of the rumours about the return of the Aurious and they are planning to attack Aer-Faydom.'

'We must get the Sentry up and armed,' Lareo said, jumping up.

'No, son,' the King answered calmly. 'You are not the Sentry General any longer. You are an Aurious. And as such, have far more important things to do.' He turned his attention to the messenger. 'Wake the Lieutenant General and have him meet me in the tactical room.'

He then turned to the rest of them. 'I am terribly sorry to have to leave. I need to give the Lieutenant his new ranking. Estimates say the Goblin army will arrive here in a week. I suggest you gather everything you need and leave as soon as possible. You will take a Sentry with you as extra protection, I hope?'

'Yes, if that's alright, Father?' Lareo replied.

'Yes, of course. I will send Brezan.'

'Thank you,' he said, and then he turned to his mother. 'Mother, I am sorry for leaving. I hope you'll forgive me. Alizée, you will make a fine Queen! I will miss you.'

They said their hasty goodbyes and then ran back to the carriage, which took them back to the Wise Leader's Tower at a rapid pace. Once they got there, they flew at full speed back to Caellum's room, pausing only long enough for Caellum to tell the Sentry at the main door to send Brezan up to his room.

'When do we leave?' Aria asked.

# Chapter Twenty
## DREAMS

<u>Lareo ♂</u>

Lareo barely heard Aria as his mind raced, thinking about their next move.

'As soon as Brezan arrives and we have everything we need,' answered Caellum.

Lareo snapped out of his trance. 'What do you mean 'we'?' he demanded.

'I thought we had agreed that I am coming with you?' Caellum replied nonplussed.

'Not with war threatening.'

'But I still have so much information to learn. I must come,' he pleaded.

'Very well. Spiro?' he asked his old mentor.

'You do not need my power. You are more of a master than I ever was.'

Lareo nodded, somewhat dismayed. 'I will miss you. You have been an inspiration.' Lareo regretted saying goodbye more now than with his parents. *Spiro felt more like my parent than my parents ever did*, Lareo reluctantly admitted. *Although, tonight the King had made significant strides towards making things better.*

Spiro beamed.

Before they could all turn to make their preparations, Aria spoke up, 'I would like to say goodbye to my parents before we leave.'

'When we were getting ready earlier, the Dream Expert gave me a spell you can use,' Spiro said, handing Aria the spell. 'And she made it abundantly clear that no one else can touch you at all. She said that the consequences were unimaginable.'

She shivered, and then handed the spell to Caellum to make a copy, keeping true to her promise of letting him document everything.

'Very well,' Lareo said, getting into his 'general' mode. 'Everyone go to your rooms and gather everything you need. I'll watch over Aria.'

They all went their separate ways.

Lareo and Aria went to her room. She laid down and said the spell. Immediately, she fell into a deep sleep. Lareo had no idea how long it would last, so he busied himself getting ready.

He went around her room, carefully checking everywhere and packing everything. She hadn't had much on the way here. But since taking up residence in the tower, she, like the rest of them, had gained a lot of things, especially clothes. He put everything in a bag. He needed to go to his room and collect his own belongings, but he would not leave Aria alone in case she woke up. He had moved some of his clothes into her room since they had officially become a couple. He gathered those few things and put them into another bag. He was just debating what to do when the door opened.

Brezan came through, looking battle-weary. They greeted each other like brothers. Lareo was much happier to see him this time than the previous time he had shown up.

'I need to apologise for what happened after you left me in the forest,' Brezan said disheartened.

'What do you mean?' Lareo demanded. What had happened once they left him in the forest?

'I, uh, let the Spectre escape. And then I heard how she attacked you again,' Brezan said, hanging his head.

'That was not your fault! If you had been in her way, she would have killed you.' He paused to collect his wits. 'It was actually better this way because we found out the truth. Having the Spectre attack us is what released Aria's powers,' Lareo explained.

Brezan frowned, 'Huh?'

'Her Aurious powers!'

Brezan went from confused to shocked. 'What?!'

'I guess the castle's rumour-mill isn't working as well as it should,' Lareo said laughing. 'I'll explain the whole story to you. But first, I need you to stand guard over Aria while I go and gather my things.'

Lareo went to his room, still amused by the look of shock on Brezan's face. He had thought once his parents had found out about them, then everyone would know. But then again, he reasoned, the truth surrounding them was not really known, other than that they had appeared. So, it wasn't surprising that no one knew that the Aurious power had returned. If they had, there would be cause for celebration, and it would bring hope after centuries of being under constant fear of attack.

*But if Breezy hadn't heard about what had happened, how did the Spectre army find out?* Lareo paused to wonder, but then decided he had more pressing issues to deal with. They would discuss those things once they were on their way to Fiamme-Faydom.

He collected his remaining clothes and his Tracker's tools. He paused for a moment, looking at them. Did he need them anymore? Lareo decided he would give them back to Spiro. After all, they had been magicked by him. Spiro had been given the tools by Elves and had then infused them with Tracking magic. He should be able to pass them on to his next student. However, Lareo still had a great need for the Truth Stone, especially for what he needed to do next.

#

## Aria ♀

Aria arrived in a room with a couch in the middle, a couple of armchairs, and a coffee table. Opposite the seating stood a television, and a bookshelf which lined one wall. It was her old home. On the couch, frowning slightly, sat her mother.

Aria had been thinking of both her parents when she said the spell, however, only her mother was present in the room.

'Mum,' she said quietly.

Her mother turned, jumped to her feet and hugged Aria tightly.

Once they parted, Aria said, 'I thought dad would be here.'

As Aria looked around the room, her father materialised. 'Dad,' she said, running to her father and throwing her arms around him.

'This is an odd dream,' he said, looking around.

'It's not a dream. It's a spell.'

'A spell? Your family's madness again?' he looked around at his wife.

'It's not madness, dad. It's all real. And what do you mean our family, mum?'

'My father passed along a story down the ages. About how one of the family will be special and destined for something great. Some great magical adventure that would mean that person would leave forever to do something spectacular that would not only save a whole population of people, but the whole world.'

'Yes.'

'It's true?' demanded her father.

'Yes, dad. Look,' Aria said. She turned around, and, with little effort, unfurled her wings and filled the space.

'Oh, honey,' Aria's mother gushed.

Her father stood up and slowly walked towards Aria. 'Can I…' he started asking.

'Yes,' she answered, and her father brushed his fingertips against her wings.

'What happens now?' her father asked, once he'd had enough time to absorb the news.

'I… well, I have to stay,' Aria answered.

Her mother's eyes welled up, and her father grimaced.

'Mum, Dad, I have to. The Fayworld needs to be saved.'

Aria sat down on the sofa with her parents, and they engulfed her in a hug.

'You know, honey, having a chance to think about it,' her mother said a little while later, 'maybe it's a good thing you're not here anymore. It's been quite bad here.'

'What do you mean?'

'Well, the world is going crazy, I tell you.'

Aria nodded her encouragement.

'There have been earthquakes in places that have never had them before, tornados all over the place, hurricanes in winter, blizzards in autumn, and tsunamis all over the coasts.'

Aria gaped at her mother, and she wondered if this was an effect of the events going on in the Fayworld.

They had spoken about everything else after that; she told them about her adventures; how she was still practising medicine; and she told them about Lareo. They were amazed and happy for her. They were happy for her but sad at the same time; Aria had been able to find the love of her life, but he lived in a different world to them. They only accepted it because of how happy she was. Aria told them that she would try to contact them again if she could.

'Yes, your mother is right. At least you're safe there,' her father said.

She hadn't had the heart to tell her parents that she was about to set off on a dangerous quest. After spending what felt like hours talking to them, she hugged them goodbye and told them how much she loved them.

Aria stood watching as they disappeared. She could feel the pull that she knew would take her back to her body once she said the reversal spell. She commenced the spell, which she had memorised, when suddenly things started changing. The cosy room she was in, a replica of the living room of her human house, disappeared. She was suspended into nothingness; the blackness was closing in on every side.

It was like that for a few moments, and then the scene began to reform around her with the blackness turning into a bleak wasteland. It looked like the remnants of a battleground. Aria looked around confused, but there was not much to see at all. The grass was scorched as if by magic. To the left were rocks which seemed to have broken off a large cliff. A dried-out riverbed cracked the landscape. Aria saw something lying at the base of the cliff. Walking closer, she saw that it was a person, and she rushed over.

Slowly, the realisation dawned that it was Brezan! He was lying crumpled on his side. His eyes were closed, and his face wore a pained expression.

Aria started examining him. She carefully checked each part of him, first for any outward physical signs of any problems. When she could not find any, she formed the aura around him. It was easier than before, and she no longer had to concentrate so hard. The aura moved into his body and centred. It then did something strange. The ball of magic started bouncing around to all the different parts within Brezan. It couldn't find anything wrong, and Aria withdrew the magic. She then did the only other thing she could think of; she shook him to wake him up.

'Brez. Breezy? Brezan!'

# Chapter Twenty-One
## NIGHTMARES

<u>Brezan</u> ♂

Brezan groaned.

'Wake up!' Aria shook him harder, and his eyes started fluttering.

She gently shook him again. He opened his eyes and looked blearily up at her.

'Aria?' he asked, confused. 'Where are we?'

She did not answer immediately. She helped him sit up, and he leaned against the cliff-side.

'I don't know what's going on, to be honest,' Aria told Brezan. 'I was saying goodbye to my parents, and then the scene changed to this,' she said, waving to the wasteland.

At this, he looked around and frowned. 'I know this place.'

'What is it?'

'Not 'is', but 'was'. This is the same as the pictures I've seen while studying to be a Sentry. We had to study old battles,' Brezan paused and shook his head. 'This looks exactly like a picture a Wise Leader showed me. It was the aftermath of the Battle of the Aurious Castle.'

This puzzled Aria even more.

'What do you remember from before you woke up here?' she asked.

Brezan thought about it for a bit. Then he turned to her, aghast. 'I was waiting for Lareo to finish collecting his clothes and I was watching over you. I saw you were crying, so I took your hand… and then… then I woke up here.'

Aria stared at him, horrified. 'I was told that I shouldn't be touched by anyone when I cast the spell.'

'What does this mean?'

'I don't know. Let me say the spell to go back.'

Aria said the spell that she had memorised to wake her up, but nothing happened. She sank onto the ground with Brezan and buried her face in her hands.

'I'm sorry! I didn't know.'

Staying still, Aria tried to collect her thoughts.

'Why were you there?'

'The King sent me to help you,' Brezan replied, shiftily.

Aria looked at him; he was looking away from her, into the distance.

'Why did you really come?' she asked testily.

He took a deep breath, and then said, 'I came for you.'

'I love Lareo,' Aria said. 'We have a deep bond that can't be broken. We were always meant to be together. We are each other's equals in every way. We are the Air Aurious.'

'I just heard that from Lareo. I don't know much about what it means to be one?'

Aria sighed. *Rushing recklessly into this, when he didn't even know what anything meant,* she mused, perplexed. *That doesn't sound like proper Sentry behaviour.*

She said as much to Brezan, and he hung his head in shame. When he looked back up, he implored, 'I know. I was caught up thinking about you. I have been off my game since I let the Spectre escape. And when I heard that she had attacked you, I asked for solitary duty in the forest so I wouldn't run the risk of putting anyone else in danger. I had been called back for reassignment when the King asked if I wanted to accompany you. I thought this would be my chance to win you back.'

Aria nodded. She was too unsettled to reply in any other way.

'You need to be able to focus fully and do your job properly if you want to come with us,' Aria said firmly. 'What we need to do will be dangerous, and we can't afford to have to protect you the whole way.'

She looked at Brezan sternly. Then she looked around, 'If we can ever get out of here.'


#


## Lareo ♂

As Lareo walked back to Aria's room, with his packed bag slung over his shoulder, he formulated a plan of action. Aria should be nearly finished with the dream spell; she had said she wouldn't be long. They would go to Caellum's room afterwards, where they had planned to meet, and then they would leave immediately. They could not risk getting caught up in a war.

*It's foolproof*, Lareo thought happily. He was always more at ease when there was a definite plan to follow.

Walking into Aria's room, his good mood came crashing down around him. What he saw knocked the wind out of him.

Aria still lay right where he had left her. The problem was Brezan, who was sitting by the bed, holding her hand.

Besides the fact that he did not want his best friend

holding hands with (and having feelings for) the love of his life, this was perilous. Spiro had explicitly warned her that no one must have any contact. Horror washed through Lareo as he realised that he hadn't told Brezan.

The panic rapidly intensified in Lareo. Would this kill her?!

The door burst open behind him. Elvya stood in the doorway.

'What's happened?' she demanded.

Lareo couldn't fathom how she knew to be here, but he just pointed at the bed. The scene was self-explanatory. Spiro and Caellum arrived shortly after Elvya. They all stood gasping at Aria and Brezan.

'That foolish boy!' Spiro exclaimed.

'Lareo, try contacting her mentally,' Elvya suggested.

Lareo concentrated, *Aria? My love, can you hear me?* He waited.

After a couple of minutes, he felt his message coming back to him. It was as if there was no one to receive it.

He stumbled over to the chair and sat down heavily.

'It's as if the message bounced back to me.'

'You mean it was blocked?' Caellum asked, puzzled.

'No,' he sighed. 'I have had her block a message before. I felt a wall slamming between us that time. Now it was as if there was nothing there. Or rather, there was no one there to receive the message,' and he buried his face in his hands.

'I'll go and fetch the Dream Expert.'

The waiting was dreadful; it seemed as though it was an eternity. Lareo longed to hold her and comfort her, but he did not want to make a bad situation worse.

He was, therefore, surprised when he felt a hand squeeze his shoulder. He looked around and realised that it was Elvya. He saw the same distraught expression he was sure he was wearing. He had not appreciated her role before, but now he understood. She was their balancer. She cared deeply about both of them.

She didn't say anything or try to do anything, but he understood her completely. The three of them were now on the same level. They were united. They truly were the Air Aurious. After that moment of realisation, energy flowed between them. He hadn't lost the gravity of the situation, but he felt calmer. Balanced. He was thinking with a clear head and could see the possible solutions more clearly.

Eventually, the door opened again, and Spiro came through, followed by a Wise Leader who was wearing the usual yellow robes and silver belt. She was a Dreamer, as they were often called.

'No!' she gasped as she saw what had happened. 'I told you explicitly that no one was to touch her.'

'Yes, we were very clear on that. I take full responsibility for what happened.' Lareo said, stepping forward to face her.

'You?'

'Yes. I hadn't warned Brezan that he shouldn't touch her. I had underestimated his feelings for her and overestimated his duty.'

'That is beside the point,' Spiro said exasperated. 'What happened, and what can we do?'

The Dreamer took a deep breath, as if to collect her thoughts. 'Well, what happened is that when this foolish

Sentry,' she threw a look of disgust at Brezan, 'took her hand, he pulled her into his dream world. Aria is not currently in her own body.'

They gaped at her.

'She… she's dead?' Elvya asked over a sob.

'No. Not yet anyway,' the Dreamer said gravely. 'She is now trapped in the mind of Brezan – is that his name? Neither will be able to leave until she is returned to her own body. But,' she saw their hopeful faces, 'thus far no one has ever managed to do it. Countless Dreamers have died in the attempt.'

Lareo shook his head in despair. *This was not possible; I can't lose her. This can't be her end; she was prophesied to be the saviour, the one who will unite the Auriouses and defeat the Spectre Queen and thus the Spectres and Goblins. I must save her!*

'No! She must be saved! It is her destiny to be saved. What went wrong the other times?' Lareo snapped out of his self-pity.

The Dreamer was affronted. 'What makes you think you could save her, Prince?' she said tartly.

Lareo had to hold his temper at bay. 'Firstly, as your Prince, I deserve more respect from you,' he said tightly. 'Secondly, as an Aurious, I have more power than you could even begin to dream of, and I could annihilate you in a heartbeat,' he said in an icy cool demeanour that cut through everyone. The Dreamer merely stood transfixed. 'Now, you will tell me what you know.'

The Dreamer gulped and then nodded. 'We have tried t-to t-touch the f-first person dreaming b-but nothing h-happened,' she started shakily. Taking a deep breath, she continued, 'Then we tried touching the second person, and they got trapped as well. We have also tried, uh, physically severing the ties. Doing that always brought the third person back but killed the first two, no matter which connection we severed.'

Everyone blanched.

'What did the third person say?'

'They always came back saying the same thing; they were unable to find the other two. We even tried Healing them before we severed the connection, but nothing worked.'

Lareo thought about it for a moment then faced everyone, 'I'm going in after them, and I will find them!'

#

## Aria ♀

Aria and Brezan had been sitting against the cliff-side for a while. Their clothes were completely soaked through; the heat was unbearable. Up against the cliff, they had a fraction of shade, but they could barely breathe in the stifling heat. Although Aria couldn't feel anything wrong with Brezan, he seemed to be getting weaker.

She tried to keep him awake by telling him the whole story of what had happened to them after they parted ways. He was still guilt-ridden about having let the Spectre escape; he listened with awe when she told him about getting her powers and about everything that it meant to be an Aurious.

When Aria had finished, he looked at her and said shamefully, 'If I had known about the bond you two share, I would never have tried anything. I thought it was just friendly competition between us and that all I had to do was win you back like he had.'

'It's fine. I forgive you.'

Aria looked around again; she had been thinking about this for a while. The scenery just did not make any sense. She had dreamed of the room she had spent most of her life in with her family. This was such a bleak place to dream of.

'Breezy, I've been wondering, why are we here?'

'What do you mean?' he asked puzzled.

'Well, when I was dreaming of my parents, I dreamed of a room in which we had spent time together as a family. It was my last thought before I said the spell. The way I figure it, this is your dream, and you conjured this image.'

Brezan pondered about that for a bit, and then finally he said, 'I had just spoken to Lareo, who mentioned about how you are an Aurious. I was thinking about the Auriouses. I was also thinking about what he felt about you, and then I realised that I didn't stand much of a chance.'

Aria nodded. That must mean this was a result of his troubled thoughts mixed with the last picture he had had of the Aurious and the only connotation of them he knew. This, of course, did not help with their return in the slightest.

While Aria deliberated this through, she had absently picked up a stick and started digging at the earth. After a while, she looked down at what she had uncovered and saw lush green grass under the wasteland soil. It was as if the wasteland was covering up something far better underneath.

Aria had just turned to tell Brezan about her discovery when two things happened simultaneously: Brezan's eyes fluttered closed, and there was a shift of scenery.

The wasteland around them changed as abruptly as it had appeared. In its place was the Aer Forest. The air instantly cooled down. Aria was able to take a full, clear, crisp breath of fresh air. The cliff that they were leaning against had changed into a tree. She also felt another presence —it was the same feeling she had before she found Brezan in the wasteland. Aria sprang to her feet, scanning the surroundings.

*Aria?* Lareo's voice echoed through her mind.

*Lareo!* Aria replied and spun around, looking for Lareo.

*I'm coming to find you!*

She nodded to herself. Lareo would be here any moment.

Aria stood waiting for a while, but no one came. She started to feel tired; she sank against the tree next to Brezan to rest while she waited. Her eyes grew heavy, and the green trees blurred into one blob. *At least it's nice and cool here,* she thought pleasantly.

#

## Lareo ♂

Lareo found himself in the Aer Forest. He was not sure exactly why he was here, but he knew how. It had taken longer to get here than he had anticipated. Or rather, it had taken longer to get the others to stop arguing with him. They had debated for what felt like hours. The Dreamer wanted to make sure he understood the risks, and then she tried to explain the technicalities. The two Wise Leaders tried to persuade him not to go. Lareo was more surprised at Elvya's argument.

236

She had merely wanted to go with Lareo on the rescue mission. She said that it was her duty to go with him and help in any way she could. Lareo refused. He did not want anyone else risking their lives.

They had argued over him as he learnt the crucial return spell. Finally, he overruled everyone's arguments and asked the Dreamer to explain things as simply as possible.

He thought back to what she had said: 'The way we understand it, the dream takes place in either the last place you think about before you say the spell and fall asleep, or the place you think about most often which has the most sentimental meaning for you. Also, you must not stay there too long. If you can't find them within ten minutes, you must return immediately.'

'Why?' Caellum had asked.

She had turned gravely to Caellum and said, 'The intrusion of outside forces weakens the mind. The others have been in there for some time. The effort of joining that dreamscape will be significant. The longer you stay, the faster your energy will drain. Too long, and you will die.'

Lareo had been so furious about the wasted time that he had grabbed Brezan's hand and woke up in the Forest.

He did not have any time to squander pondering the whys. He immediately contacted Aria mentally.

*Aria?* Lareo called out

*Lareo!* he heard her reply.

***I'm coming to find you!*** He almost shouted out loud.

He calmed himself down and called his Tracking power.

He held a picture of Aria in his mind as he connected to their shared power. It took longer than it had last time he had done this.

At last, he sensed her. The compulsion was much weaker than when he had searched out Caellum. He grasped on to the direction the force was leading and followed it. He had thought that Tracking Aria would be much easier than a stranger doing so because of their strong bond.

As he flew through the forest at high speed, dodging trees, he felt as if he was getting nearer, but the pull was getting weaker. That did not make any sense at all.

He slowed down, feeling sure she was nearby.

*Aria?* he called out again.

He waited a few minutes, but there was no reply. There was something wrong. Frantically he flew in circles around the area where he had felt the faint compulsion.

Purple caught the corner of his eye. He spun in that direction. At last, he had found them.

The relief turned to panic when he saw them slumped against a tree with their eyes closed. Lareo flew down and threw himself at Aria.

He felt for a pulse and found a very weak one. He shook her gently, but she wouldn't wake. He tried to access the magic within her; it was faint, but still there. Frantically, he tried to focus on what he should do, and then he decided he would have to channel her Healing power into himself.

He laid her down tenderly and then placed his hands on the centre of her chest where he knew their power radiated from. He concentrated on connecting their powers. He could feel her two sources of magic: the Healing and the Aurious coinciding, the same way his did. His Aurious magic twinned with hers, and he was able to access the Healing power. He felt it running through him, and then he could direct the power back into Aria's body, Healing the weakness. He didn't really think of how he was doing it, but just let it run its course.

For a few minutes, he sent a steady stream of magic into her while listening to her breathing. It went from laboured to easy. Watching her face, he saw her eyelids start to flutter. He stopped sending magic and cradled her. He stroked her face, trying to get her to wake up.

# Chapter Twenty-Two
## THE RESCUE

<u>Aria ♀</u>

Aria could feel the warmth that had spread through her body as it chased the weakness out. Her eyes fluttered half open, and she caught sight of two bright green eyes. *I would recognise those eyes anywhere*, Aria thought, smiling. She opened her eyes fully and confirmed what she already knew.

'You came for me,' Aria whispered, lifting her hand to his face.

'I will always come for you.'

Lareo helped her sit up and then said, 'I'm sorry to have to ask, but there's no other way. You are going to have to do some Healing. First, we need to wake Brezan up.'

Aria nodded and leaned over Brezan, sending her power into him. There was nothing hurt, but she could feel the weakness, having just recovered from it. She sent strength and Healing into an aura, and then into him. Slowly he woke up.

'Great, Aria,' Lareo said, pulling her attention from Brezan. 'Now comes the most important part. You have to Heal yourself.'

Aria didn't understand. He had managed to Heal her, and although she was still weak, she felt fine.

'Not you here. You need to Heal your body so that you can return to it.'

Aria contemplated that for a moment. Then the meaning

occurred to her. She was not in her body anymore since Brezan touched her. But she had no idea how to go about doing that.

'I can still feel my body in the real world,' Lareo explained, and then looked at Brezan, who nodded.

Aria tried to feel the rest of herself, but she couldn't sense anything. She shook her head.

Lareo looked worried. He was silent for a moment, then his brow furrowed.

'Maybe you could Track it?'

'How?' This puzzled Aria. She didn't have Tracking powers or even the slightest idea about it, despite having read the book on it.

'The same way I Healed you!' Lareo said, looking purposeful.

'You did?'

'Yes! I felt the magic within you, the two parts. Then I aligned my Aurious power with yours, and then I could access your Healing power.'

Aria thought about this; it was worth a try. She nodded. Lareo lay down in front of her.

'Now place your hand on my chest. Where our source is.' Aria did as he said. 'Now close your eyes and feel my powers within me.'

She closed her eyes and felt. All she could feel was how healthy he was.

'No. Don't feel with your Healing power. Feel with your Aurious power.'

Aria called up her power from within. She felt the wind swirl around her in response. She tried to send it into his body, but she just couldn't.

'I can't get through.'

'This is important! You have to!' Lareo said, becoming angry. Aria looked at him. The anger didn't reach further than his words. His face had drained of all colour, and his eyes were wide. Lareo gripped her upper arms tightly.

Aria searched his face; she had never seen him this close to panicking. She turned back to the task, took a deep breath and concentrated. She couldn't completely get rid of the worry, but it receded as the task at hand took over. Aria called her Aurious power again and felt the air moving around her. She let the power move from its source within her into Lareo.

It was a different feeling to sensing out hurts. Instead of her Healing power seeking out anything wrong, her Aurious ability pursued his power and quickly located Lareo's source. She moved her power to his and felt it twin of its own accord. She then felt the other part of his power, the Tracking power. She accessed it as she would access her own Healing power.

Aria felt the power fill her. It was a very different feeling to her own power, but she immediately understood it. All she needed to do was focus on the person she wanted to find; in this case, herself. It was the strangest feeling ever, trying to search for herself. However, she concentrated hard.

After a few minutes, she understood what the problem was. She had lost herself in this dreamscape. The disconnection caused her entrapment. She had entered someone else's mental world, and she couldn't find her way back to her own. But through Tracking, she found the path she needed to follow to reach a portal, as it were. She now felt the cord connecting which lead her to her own body.

Aria released the Tracking power and withdrew her Aurious power. She opened her eyes. 'I know what to do.'

'Good,' said Lareo, sitting up. 'Do what you need to do. Brez and I will say the spell once you've done what you need to do.'

'I need to follow a trail. I don't know what will happen once I get to the end of it.'

Lareo paused for a moment. 'We have to try.'

With that, Aria set off. She left Lareo crouching next to Brezan, teaching him the spell.

Having Tracked the trail, she could now feel the right way to follow. She walked for what felt like ages. The feeling started getting stronger, pulling her in the right direction like a magnet.

When the pull reached a peak, Aria saw the end of the trail. She walked toward it but couldn't go any further: she had come across a barrier.

Aria put her hands against it to feel a gap. But instead of an opening, she felt something else. It was as if she was sensing a body she was trying to Heal. She could feel the lungs breathing, the neurons firing, and the heart pumping. Only the pumping felt strained and as though it was slowing down.

With a jolt, Aria realised that she was feeling her own body. She could feel what was going on, but she couldn't cross over to get back.

She did not know what to do. Aria thought frantically. *Should I try Healing myself?*

She moved her hand along the barrier and felt her way

around. She tried sending Healing magic through, but it wouldn't penetrate. Lareo had been wrong; it wasn't about Healing herself.

Aria could feel the heart's feeble pumping. She could feel that her grasp on life had become just as feeble. She had no way of getting through the barrier.

She sank to the ground; she couldn't keep her eyes open any more.

*What will happen to Brezan if I can't get out?* Aria wondered, dazed. He would be saying the spell, but nothing would happen. She felt dizzy despite her eyes being closed and lying down. Aria drifted into numbness.

*The spell!*

The words reverberated through her mind, and she sat up, horrified that she had almost given up. I need the spell to get back!

Aria jumped to her feet, ignoring the dizziness. She pressed her hands back against the barrier and said the spell and kept saying it over and over. The barrier was giving way.

Aria kept saying it and walked through.

#

## Lareo ♂

Lareo had taught the spell to Brezan and then said it himself. He returned to his body, waking up, and he looked around the room at the expectant crowd. The sun had come up, refreshing the room, but everyone looked exhausted. They looked partly relieved to see him waking up. He just nodded his assurances to the others and went to sit next to Aria.

He was careful not to touch her and start the mess all over again. He watched her closely, and he caught the decrease in her breathing. She appeared to be slowly slipping away. He glanced up at Brezan, who looked the opposite. His breathing was normal. His eyes were fluttering as if he was trying to wake up but just couldn't.

Lareo slowly put the two conditions together. His stomach dropped as he realised that Aria was holding Brezan back, and she couldn't get back either.

*The spell!* He shouted in his head, trying to communicate mentally.

He didn't know if it had worked. He put his head on the bed and started sobbing. He was going to lose the love of his life to something as foolish as this one simple mistake.

He felt a hand on his shoulder, which he shrugged off. No one could comfort him now. The hand returned to his cheek, and Lareo caught his breath and looked up.

He found Aria's bright turquoise eyes. He grabbed her in a tight embrace that she returned weakly. He let her go and looked at her properly.

'What's wrong?'

'Tired,' she breathed.

Lareo looked up at Spiro and said, 'Please get a Treater.'

Spiro was getting up when the Dreamer said, 'I'll fetch one. I need to get back and tell everyone what happened. But first, can you tell me what happened?' she asked the three of them.

Lareo looked at Brezan for the first time. He seemed fine, a bit weary but in good health, unlike Aria. Lareo waited for

Brezan to explain his part.

'I took her hand, and everything went black. I woke up with Aria shaking me. We were in a wasteland of some kind, and I recognised the old ruined Aurious castle. We figured out it was a combination of my last conscious thoughts. I had heard about the Auriouses and my desperation over my unrequited feelings,' he said. Brezan was embarrassed and couldn't bring himself to look at everyone. He cleared his throat and looked back, 'That's all I remember until Lareo was there.'

Lareo nodded. 'When I got in, there was no wasteland. I was in the Aer forest. I tried calling Aria, and she replied. I tried Tracking her, but it felt wrong; I could only feel a faint trail. I flew in the vague direction I felt and spotted her wings among the trees. When I got to them, they were both unconscious. I felt for Aria's powers and then directed it back into her to Heal her. She then healed Brezan. We then did the same with my powers; she channelled my power to find her way back. She left, and I taught Brezan the spell and said it myself. Then I was back here.'

When he finished, he looked around to see everyone staring at him, transfixed.

'What?' he asked Elvya. 'Is that not a normal Aurious power?'

'Swapping powers? No. I've never heard of that,' she said, looking at Caellum who shook his head. She continued, 'I don't even understand what you said.'

Perplexed, Lareo recalled the dream world. 'Aria needed Healing, but she was the only one powerful enough to do it. So, I thought maybe if I could access her power, I could use it.

I put my hands over the centre of her chest, where our powers are. I felt her two sources that were just like mine. I could feel the two parts; the Aurious and the Treater powers. My Aurious power was absorbed – no, that wasn't it – they seemed to join as if they were a part of a whole. When that happened, I could access her Treater powers and direct it back into her to Heal her. But then when she did it with my power, it was the same thing. But it took longer.'

'Why did it take longer?' Caellum asked, pausing from writing everything down.

Lareo thought about it again. 'She couldn't feel my powers until I yelled at her. Maybe… maybe it only works when we're in a crisis?'

'Could be why no one has ever heard of it. Maybe the past Auriouses were never in a big crisis,' Caellum suggested.

'One more thing, you said when you Healed her it went straight into her body? Without an aura?'

'Er… yes?' he answered uncertainly.

'How remarkable,' Caellum's awed expression reflected everyone else's, including Aria's.

'Maybe because you sent the magic from within the body already?' Caellum muttered off while writing.

There was a moment of silence and then, 'Now will you get someone?' Lareo snapped. The Dreamer jumped and nodded her head. She left quickly, wishing everyone good luck and good health on the way out.

# Chapter Twenty-Three
## PREPARATION

The Treater came in and looked at both Aria and Brezan. He couldn't find anything wrong with them other than tiredness. He gave them a herbal mixture to help restore their strength.

Lareo stayed by Aria's side. Brezan regained his strength quicker than Aria. No one was exactly sure why, but they suspected it was because she had been the first in the dream world and had stayed there the longest. As Lareo wouldn't leave Aria's side, they all spent time in her room during the day.

Spiro had gone off in search of lunch and to find some information about the Spectre army. Caellum had left during the morning to put his notes together. Lareo would not leave Aria's bedside even while she slept. Brezan, still rather weak, sat in the armchair he had been in all night, with Elvya sitting by him to keep him company. Lareo paid them no attention as they spoke.

It was an uneasy truce, but it was slowly getting better. Elvya, while relieved that everyone had returned, was angry at Brezan for causing the crisis. When she had woken up to eat, Aria had asked Elvya to be nice to him. Elvya reluctantly agreed.

Brezan bounced back faster than Aria. Elvya noticed a change in him; not only did he look much better, there was something else different. Before last night, he'd had a haunted look in his eyes, as if he was carrying a considerable weight on his shoulders, but when he woke up, he seemed to be less guilty. He certainly looked horrified every time he looked at Aria or Lareo, which Elvya was secretly pleased about. But, generally, he looked happier than he had before.

They spoke for ages about their pasts and things they enjoyed doing. They found they had many common interests, much to Elvya's surprise. Slowly, as Brezan's colour and strength returned, so did his good humour. Elvya had heard Aria talking about him being a witty and charming person, but until now she had not seen that side of him. She reluctantly came to see what Aria had meant and why she had been so saddened to lose his company.

Slowly, as the days went by, Aria began to get better. But with her improvement came a growing sense of unease. They were only two days away from the estimated day of attack from the Spectres. They needed to get out of the Faydom and down the mountain before the incoming army was anywhere close to them. If they did not leave soon, there would be no chance of escape.

Everyone could barely contain their impatience, and they tried to curb their restlessness, but they couldn't move on yet. Lareo would not dream of moving Aria before she was fully better, but they were running out of time. He tried hard not to pace, not wanting to show her his worry, which he tried to keep hidden as much as possible. He had to leave occasionally to get things organised, and he used this time to vent his frustrations.

He tried out all the weapons they were planning to use to make sure they were in working order. It helped to be active and doing something productive. He should be leading the Sentry and getting them ready, but he understood that what they were doing was of greater importance.

Brezan followed Lareo as he went to test the weapons. He had tried to talk to Lareo several times since he and Aria had come back from the dream world, but Lareo ignored him.

'Larey,' Brezan pleaded.

'What?' Lareo snapped.

'I'm sorry. Please. You must forgive me. You're like my brother.'

'You have been trying to steal my mate, the love of my life! And then you nearly killed her! You honestly want me to forgive you?!' Lareo yelled at Brezan.

'I was saying goodbye. I thought she was just sleeping.'

Lareo started walking away, but Brezan caught his arm.

'She's yours, and she's alive. What more can I do to make it up to you?'

Lareo shrugged away from Brezan's grasp and stalked off.

#

'Aria? How are you feeling?' Lareo asked gently. He had been asking this question every morning and had always got the standard reply of 'a bit better'.

Today, however, she replied, 'Much better. We have to leave, don't we?' She read the mood in the room correctly.

'Yes, my love. I'm afraid if we don't leave now, we won't get a clean break. We're all prepared. We have organised a carriage for you to use.'

At this, she glanced at Brezan, assessing him. She seemed to think he was fit for travel because she turned back to Lareo and said sceptically, 'A carriage?'

'Not like the one my parents sent us, a simpler one. You aren't strong enough to travel on foot yet.' She nodded.

And the preparations continued. Although they were all packed and ready to go, the carriage had needed supplies. Spiro had organised a few weeks' supply of food and cooking utensils. Lareo, ever the General, had prepared weapons for all of them – despite their powers, he felt better with a couple of bows and quivers, and a few swords. Caellum gathered his books and writing equipment.

'That's quite a lot of stuff to fit in one small carriage,' Aria mentioned. They all chuckled at her joke, which puzzled her.

Lareo came back into the room, carrying some weapons. He handed a sword in its scabbard to Brezan and then turned to Elvya. He didn't try handing her a sword, but instead gave her a bow. Aria was surprised that she took it without questions or complaints. She was even more amazed when he turned to her and handed her a knife the size of her forearm. She, unlike Elvya, complained about this.

'I know you don't want to carry one but it's just as a precaution. We can't be caught powerless like last time.'

She sighed and let him strap the knife to her shin. Lareo helped her to get up – more out of habit from the past few days than real need on Aria's part. She was much better and stronger.

They walked out of the room, subdued. This had been a real home for Aria, Lareo, and Elvya, something none of them had experienced in a while. They were reluctant to give up the comfort and safety of the tower, but they knew that they had an essential duty lying ahead of them.

#

## Aria ♀

Lareo had his arm around Aria. It was pleasant, even though she didn't need to lean against him. They made their way down the passage. She glanced out of the window as they passed and gulped down her fear of leaving the tower. She knew that there was an army on the way, and she was worried that they might be trapped. The incoming army also made her feel guilty. They were escaping the threat of war, when countless soldiers would be preparing to fight, and so many families will probably lose loved ones. She didn't say any of this out loud so as not to make Lareo feel worse, but the thoughts kept playing on repeat.

They reached the vertical passage. Lareo looked around, confused. He usually took Elvya down, but now he had Aria to worry about. Aria tried flapping her wings, but she was still too weak for them to hold her up. Aria turned to Brezan. He also tried his wings and seemed to be more successful. His wings were beating hard enough to lift him.

He turned to Elvya and held out his hands, and she smiled tentatively and walked over to him. He picked her up and walked to the gate. They were soon out of sight.

Lareo did the same thing to Aria, and she laughed for the first time in days. He scooped her up and held her tightly. It felt warm and safe in his arms. Aria could feel his shoulders move slightly with his wings, and then he landed next to Elvya and Brezan.

They walked out to the entrance. The Wise Leaders looked at them encouragingly, and some even patted them on the back or shoulder. It appeared that word had spread about them and their quest.

When they got outside, Aria saw the carriage waiting. It was a basic carriage made of plain wood, unlike the extravagant shiny wood of the royal carriage. The windows had white cloth curtains covering them instead of colourful silk. As Aria got closer, she could see through the door; the seating wasn't going to be comfortable. It was made of solid wood.

Elvya and Brezan stood together on one side of the door as Aria and Lareo joined them. Lareo stepped back as two Sentries approached. They were levitating a crate each and were followed by Spiro and Caellum, who also had a box each.

'Last minute supplies,' Spiro explained as he reached the carriage.

Aria looked around the carriage. Although it was bigger than the royal carriage, she had her doubts. There was no room for anything at all; the two benches - which had six spacious seats - took up all the available space. There was no way those crates were going to fit. Aria was about to say so when Spiro and Caellum closed their eyes.

Puzzled, Aria watched closely. They were standing over the crates with their hands open above them. As she watched, Aria could almost see the power radiating out of their hands, as she felt a surge of air flowing towards them. Then, to her surprise, the crates started shrinking. When the crates were about the size of a hand, they stopped and looked up.

Reading Aria's expression, Caellum handed her the crate that he had just shrank. Aria looked at it and saw the tiny latch. Carefully she opened it and saw minuscule colourful objects that she took to be food. Caellum took it back and put it under the one bench. Aria then saw rows and rows of little crates in perfectly fitted cubicles. Caellum selected another crate and handed it to her, smiling.

Opening this one, Aria saw the tiny coloured objects in orderly lines. 'Books?'

Caellum nodded with a delighted expression to match Aria's. 'About half of these under this bench are my books or writing equipment. You never know when something may be useful!' He went back to help shrink and pack the other crates.

'Spiro, I want you to have this,' Lareo said, holding out his Tracking tools.

Spiro frowned, 'No, they are yours.'

'You were the best mentor I could ever have hoped for. Give them to your next pupil.'

Spiro reluctantly took the tools, and then he and Lareo hugged in farewell.

Caellum shook Spiro's hand fondly as he said, 'Thank you.'

Spiro turned to them, and Aria saw that he looked sad. Aria had a lump in her throat as she watched.

Brezan shook his hand. Elvya threw her arms around his neck and whispered, 'You've been like a father. Thank you for giving me hope and safety.'

He then turned to Aria, who hugged him fiercely. 'Thank

you for saving me and everyone,' she gasped.

Aria climbed in and sat down. Brezan and Elvya sat on the bench across from her. To Aria's surprise, Brezan had his arms around Elvya, who was crying. That reminded Aria of something she discovered in the dream, although now wasn't the time to mention it.

Lareo came in and sat next to Aria. He wiped her cheek, and only then did she realise that her tears were streaming as liberally as Elvya's. Lareo held Aria as she shook in silent sobs. Caellum brought up the rear. He closed the door and settled into a seat by the door next to Elvya. They were all sitting with enough space, even if the seating wasn't ideal.

#

## Lareo ♂

They took a slight detour on the way to the Southern Perimeter to try to find Abelia's spell book. They stopped in Rose Clearing where Aria had landed. *And where I had first met her*, Lareo thought and beamed at her. She returned the grin. They each knew the other was thinking the same thing.

They all got out and stood, staring around. There were many rose bushes, hence the name, which could be problematic. But Caellum seemed to have a plan.

'We need a rose bush that looks slightly different to the rest. So, an unusual colour, or shape, or something like that.'

They nodded and spread out to search. Lareo stayed near Aria.

They always kept in contact with each other, even if it was

only their wing tips.

When Aria felt Lareo's wings brush hers, she turned to look at them, and remembered that she had noticed something odd. She did something strange; she encased herself in her wings.

When they opened again, she said, 'Our wings have changed.'

Lareo studied her wings for a moment. He remembered every detail of their first day.

'The yellow is brighter and a deeper shade,' he said slowly. 'And...' he gasped and stared in awe, '... the yellow has... a pattern that is different from those in the colour.'

He moved closer and saw that there was a spiral repeated throughout the yellow outline. He checked his own wings and found the same yellow shape and identical spirals.

'We are the Air Aurious,' he beamed at Aria and grabbed her in a tight hug and spun her around.

After that, he seemed more interested in trying to pull her behind a tree to kiss her than doing any actual work. She kept giggling every time he tried, which only made him want to do it more.

It wasn't that Lareo thought what they were doing was a waste of time, but rather the fact that he had come so close to losing her, which made him want to spend every second with her. To add to it was the fact that she was outside and not bedridden. Every time he had seen her in bed, he remembered that she had almost died.

She belonged here in the forest, especially in Rose Clearing; it was where both of them belonged. He could feel it now. The air around them was re-energising them, and the plants were the source of that air. It made perfect sense that they felt at home in the forest.

Brezan cut through Lareo's thoughts and fun by calling for them to come over.

He was standing in front of a rose bush that did indeed look different. There was a combination of rose colours, which was impossible on its own. But, in addition to that, the roses were shaped differently. They were the round shape of a natural rose, but the inside looked unusual.

Caellum had a piece of parchment out and a quill. He was drawing something. When he finished, he looked up, smiling delightedly. 'It's the symbol for air,' he said, as he showed them the drawing.

There was a spiral inside the circle. Lareo looked back at the roses. Now that Lareo knew what to look for, he could see it. He had not noticed it before because the swirls of the rose petals disguised it. But looking closely, he could see the faintest hint of tiny little spirals in a yellow that matched their wings. Lareo and Aria exchanged a meaningful glance.

'We've seen that pattern before,' he explained.

He turned around, showing his wings clearly. Aria followed his example.

Everyone looked closely at their wings.

'It is the same spiral,' said Elvya, as the two turned back around. She was the only one unsurprised.

Aria's expression turned into delighted surprise. She burst out laughing.

She felt around in a small pouch at her waist – she had

never lost her Treater habits. She pulled out a coin that Lareo had never seen before. It was dark grey, like the necklace Aria always wore.

Grinning, she handed it around to show all of them.

'Elvya made this for me when we were in the forest. It has the same spiral. I thought it was simply an interesting design.'

'It has both our names?' Lareo whispered, unable to believe what he was seeing. 'You knew then already?'

'I had suspected it. Of course, I didn't know for sure until you both displayed your powers.'

'So, we have the official symbol for the Air Aurious. This makes it final and binding,' said Caellum happily.

Caellum called Lareo forward and asked the rest of them to stand back.

'What is he doing?' Lareo heard Aria whisper to Brezan.

'Lareo needs to Trace the book,' he whispered back. 'Everything we touch leaves a Trace. It is usually too faint for normal Trackers to find it. But I'm guessing Lareo is powerful enough to do it.'

Brezan was right. Lareo did not even need to concentrate. He knew Aria's Trace as if it was his own. He could sense the Trace behind him, where she stood. And the path she had walked to and from the bush.

Further down from that, he felt the faintest Trace. It was slightly different to what he knew so well. He went to that spot and gently pushed the soil away. Not too far in, he found what he was looking for. He pulled it out and gave it to Caellum. The two of them stared at the book in puzzlement until the others came over.

Aria quickly understood the confusion and explained, 'It's plastic. It's something the humans make. It's actually very harmful to the environment, but as you can see, it's durable and protects things.'

Everyone just stared dumbfounded at her. Lareo did register one thing with pleasure; she had referred to them as humans. She was entirely a Fairy now.

Aria took the book and opened the thing she called plastic and showed it to them. It was thin like parchment but see-through. Lareo eyed it with interest but didn't touch it. Caellum took it gingerly and promised to hide it so that it would never fall into the wrong hands.

They didn't have time to linger and were soon back inside the carriage and on their way.

# Chapter Twenty-Four
## SURPRISE
## ENCOUNTERS

<u>Aria</u> ♀

They had been travelling for two days. Aria remembered the start of their journey.

'Can we do something to keep the book safe?' Aria had asked when they left the clearing.

Caellum had contemplated it, and then said, 'We could shrink it, and make it so that only we can grow it and then read it.'

'How?'

'Well, we could…' he thought for a second, '… or maybe… Elvya could try to use Lareo's Tracing ability and imbue it into a sort of cover, which we could then fuse into the book.'

Everyone looked overwhelmed at the request. It was powerfully advanced magic they were trying to do. Nonetheless, they tried.

Lareo had to sit for a while, concentrating. Then he held their hands in turn. Finally, he held his hands up in the air, and in the space between them, there was the faintest shimmering.

'I think this is all of our Traces. I would never have thought it possible to make a copy, as it were, of them. Elvya, you need to take this essence somehow and make it real.'

Now it was Elvya's turn to think long and hard about it.

Cautiously, she stuck out a finger and poked the shimmering essence. Slowly, she withdrew her finger and touched it to the other. The shimmering took a more substantial form, but not like the normal material she worked with. She traced out a shape and then grabbed it out of the air.

'I think that's it. I took the Trace essence and used it as I would any other material. The problem, however, was getting it to be more substantial,' she explained. 'I combined it with a tiny drop of my elf-material but not enough to change the composition or to make it look too dark. If you'll please pass the book,' she asked, holding out her hand.

When she had the book, she floated it in front of her along with the cover. She eased the book open and placed it within the barely visible cover. She closed her eyes for a moment, then closed the book and looked up.

'I think it's fused together.'

'We must take turns holding it and trying to read it,' Caellum prompted.

They passed the book around; everyone could open and read it.

'Of course, we won't know for sure if it has worked until a stranger tries it. However, I think that it is safe to say we have achieved extraordinary magic today!'

They had each taken turns to look at the book. It meant nothing to Brezan; to Lareo, Elvya, and Aria, it was interesting. A lot of it was about past events, but it didn't have anything that could help them fight. However, it meant everything to Caellum. He had read through it several times.

The part that Aria found interesting was the family history.

Abelia had written a bit about her parents and her life as an Aurious.

Her parents were called Breeze and Zephyr – very air appropriate names. Their Light-Keeper was called Paxy.

Abelia had just started developing her Aurious powers when the war began. But she explained that that was not always the case. Often the children of the Aurious are not the next generation of Aurious. It was an individual trait that could manifest in whoever would be the right person.

Her mate was not an Aurious, for example. The other Air Aurious had not developed his power before they fled, and so they never knew who he was.

There were a few spells that made sense only to Caellum.

'There is a spell that could take you back if you want to,' he had told Aria. 'But… I don't know if you would be able to return.'

'No thanks. Please destroy it or hide it away so that no one can access it.'

'Really?' Caellum asked.

Aria nodded.

Aria refused it without a second thought. Mostly because there was no way she would leave Lareo. She hadn't found her true love in the human world, and now she knew why. The fact that she had discovered him here made her certain that this was the right place to be.

The other reason was that Aria knew she had to do the right thing by everyone. She had been chosen for a reason, and she had a duty to both worlds to save them. She had to stay and follow her destiny.

\#

Now they were taking a break. Everyone was staring around in boredom. Tense boredom.

The strain within the carriage mounted as they had descended the mountain. Today was the day that reports predicted the arrival of the Spectre Army. Everyone was feeling worried and guilty. Although they all knew that what they were doing was vitally important and that it would help in the future, it was still tough to flee the battle instead of helping.

They had travelled through the forest, south of the tower. The forest there was thicker and less used; the path was overgrown. The carriage magically pushed through anything in its way. When they got to the Southern Perimeter, they stopped for the night. They knew it was a vulnerable point of entry and everyone else took turns to stand guard, but they all insisted that Aria should get as much rest as possible.

When they left the perimeter, the trees had thinned out, and Aria could now see the view down the mountain; it was magical. She could not see the other Faydoms, but she had seen coloured, hazy bubbles that looked like jelly in the distance.

'Caellum, what are the coloured bubbles over there?' Aria asked while pointing them out.

'I don't know what you mean.'

Aria looked around, feeling puzzled.

'I can see them too,' Lareo spoke up, while everyone else shrugged.

'What does it look like?' asked Caellum.

'That one to the left is red, the one on the right is green, and the one in the far distance straight ahead… is,' Aria squinted.

'It's blue,' finished Lareo. 'It's hard to see against the sky, but it's a darker shade.'

Aria nodded. She turned back to where they came from and said, 'That is yellow.'

'You can see the colours of the Faydoms. Fascinating!' said Brezan.

'Yes, that is very interesting,' agreed Caellum.

The carriage shook and brought Aria out of her brooding. It was now mid-morning. They were not due to stop for another couple of hours. Suddenly, she lost her composure. The tension was so great it was almost stifling.

'Stop!' Aria shouted, and the carriage stopped. 'Everyone out! I can't take it anymore.'

Puzzled, they followed her lead and stepped out.

'What's wrong?' Lareo asked, concerned.

'I need fresh air,' Aria said simply. The others nodded with understanding.

Aria tried to think of the best way to encourage them. The others were looking around where they had stopped. Aria focused on the distance to gather her thoughts and spotted something strange. Aria was looking at the three colourful hazes, when another one appeared; it had no colour, nor was it fixed, but rather it moved in the sky in their direction!

'What is that?!' Aria asked uncertainly.

The others all spun round to look in the direction to which

Aria was pointing.

'Birds?' Elvya suggested.

*They can see it also*, Aria thought. *That means that the bubble isn't a magical Faydom related thing. Uh-oh!*

'No. They're too big... they are...' Caellum trailed off, squinting into the distance.

'They are Mort-Spectres,' said a deep voice behind them.

There was immediate action: Elvya and Brezan drew their weapons, Caellum's hands were glowing, and Lareo and Aria had drawn the wind to them. All within a split second as they spun around.

'Wha-' Aria squeaked as she looked up at the thing. It was a huge bird. Only... it was not a bird. Slowly scanning the creature, she saw that it had the head, wings, and front claws of an eagle, and the body, hind legs, and tail of a lion. It was taller than them; Aria came three-quarters of the way up its shoulder. She was staring up into the eyes of a-

'Griffin,' Caellum stated.

'And you are not allowed on our land, Fairy,' spat the Griffin.

'We are just passing through,' Caellum replied tightly. 'We don't mean any trouble.'

'You always bring trouble, even if you do not mean it,' he growled, looking into the distance.

'Please!' Aria cried. 'Please let us pass. Please let us through before they find us.'

'It is too late. They have already found you.'

'What?!' exclaimed Lareo.

The Griffin sighed as if he were talking to a young creature who did not understand basic things. 'Your power can be felt radiating from you for miles around,' he said, looking at Lareo and Aria. 'Those creatures can sense it, as do we and all other magical creatures.'

They were stunned. They had thought that by escaping the Faydom before the army arrived, they would be safe. What did this Griffin mean? They all looked at Caellum, who looked aghast.

'I did not know that was possible,' he whispered.

'Yes, Fairy, it is possible. And now, thanks to your ignorance, we are all in danger.'

'Can you fight those things?' Lareo asked, snapping into his old role.

'No, not entirely. They are too strong for us to defeat them.'

'And if you had help?'

'You mean you?' the Griffin asked sceptically.

'Well, yes. You said it yourself; you can feel our power. Then you must know that we are more than normal Fairies.'

'Yes, it is true that I can sense your magic. But what is it that you think you can help us with?'

'We control the air,' Lareo stated simply.

The Griffin considered this for a few minutes. 'Fine, we will go back to our forest,' he said, indicating over his shoulder with his head.

He led the way. All of them, except Lareo, followed in the carriage. Lareo walked next to the Griffin, apparently discussing strategies. The carriage stopped after a few minutes travel, and they got out.

The trees ahead of them thickened and seemed to grow.

They were twice the size of the largest tree Aria had ever seen. Looking up into the branches, she breathed a soft 'oh'. Amongst the sturdiest branches there were huge nests, ten times the size of an ordinary bird's nest.

As they walked through, bird heads popped out of the nests. Some of them flew down and stood on their hind legs, brandishing their claws and flapping their wings.

Aria gulped. They held their ground, watching their guide.

Aria distracted herself from the sharp claws by focusing on the rest of the Griffins. Their colouring varied from blacks to greys, shades of brown and gold, and white. Some of those on the ground were demanding an explanation from the Griffin leading them.

They were led to the centre of the forest. As they followed, Aria could not help but think that they were being delivered to their deaths. While she worried, she was taking in her surroundings. It was not until she felt something unusual that she realised she was using both her powers and her senses to survey her surroundings. What Aria felt was great pain and a body slowly failing; it was unlike any other dying body she had felt.

Aria unconsciously started moving toward the source. Three Griffins, including the one who had been leading them, sprang in front of her. The Griffins slashed their claws at Aria. She stopped abruptly and backed away.

'I just wanted to help. I'm a Treater.'

'You cannot help us, Fairy,' one of them roared.

Lareo came over and pulled her back, apologising. The Griffin in charge of them returned to his original position and continued leading.

Brezan came over to her and whispered, 'He's right, Aria. You can't help them. Treaters can't Heal creatures as it makes them worse.'

Aria nodded. She had not known that. But now, even with that knowledge, her instincts were pulling her back there to help. She had to dismiss it and focus on what was happening.

When they reached the centre, they saw a massive tree. On the thickest branch was the biggest nest they had yet seen. The Griffin called up to the nest with a combination of words Aria did not recognise, and whistles. Without warning, another Griffin landed in front of them. He was quite different from the guide. His head was as white as the moon, which contrasted with the black of their guide's feathers, although his wings were also black. He looked bigger and brawnier than all the others they had seen.

'Yes, Fyn?'

'Sorry to disturb you,' he said bowing. 'We are about to be attacked.'

'By Fairies?' the bigger Griffin scoffed, pointing over Fyn's shoulder.

'No, of course not. By Mort-Spectres!' His words received a startled reaction.

'So, you brought the Fairies here?!'

'Yes. They wish to help.'

'How?' the leader exclaimed.

Before Fyn could answer, Lareo had drawn his power. He threw a gale-force wind at the leader. Only his good reflexes and sturdy body prevented him from being blown and smashed into a tree. His hind legs braced him, and his claws dug deep into the ground, but the wind still pushed him back several feet. Both Fyn and the leader looked at Lareo with astonishment when he pulled his power in causing the wind to die down.

The leader stepped forward and said, 'Very well, Fairy. We accept your help. Is it just you who possesses this power?'

'No. My partner also does,' Lareo said, pointing at Aria who stepped forward hesitantly.

'Good. Both of you will ride with two of my warriors. Fyn, gather the troops.'

Fyn let out a screech. Within minutes, all the Griffins who had sprung to defend their nests surrounded them.

The leader gave the orders briefly, 'We are about to be attacked by Mort-Spectres. Two Fairies will help us. Rifina, stay behind. The rest of you get ready.' They all departed except one.

This Griffin had grey feathers, and on its head were extra feathers standing up, like a crest. It looked smaller than either of the other two. Aria guessed that this one was female; her guess was confirmed when the Griffin spoke.

'Yes, Great One?' She bowed.

'You are to carry a Fairy in the battle.'

She looked outraged. 'No! I will not.'

'This is not a request,' he boomed.

'Fine.' She begrudgingly lowered her forelegs.

Aria looked at the leader, who indicated that she should climb up. The Griffin was a bit shorter than Fyn; Aria was as tall as her shoulder. She flapped her wings, which were almost back to their full strength, flew up and sat gently astride the Griffin's back. She was unsure where to hold on, so she gripped firmly with her knees and placed her hands on the Griffin's neck. Lareo had done the same with Fyn when he had come back from gathering the troops.

Once she was sitting firmly, they took off. It was a strange experience. It was not the movement that bothered Aria; she experienced the same jarring motions when she flew by herself. It was the strength of the wings around her and the body beneath her that was curious. They followed Fyn through the trees and out above the forest.

From this position, they could see that the black cloud had nearly reached the colony. Fyn and Rifina landed on two strong branches high up, so they still had a clear view of the incoming threat.

'It looks as if the whole colony of the Mort-Spectres is coming,' Fyn said to Rifina, looking worried. She just nodded in reply. Lareo was confused and asked him to explain.

'There are not many of them, but they are powerful. They cannot be killed easily. We outnumber them, but we can never win against them. We do not threaten them, and so they do not attack us. Until now.'

As they sat waiting, Aria heard leaves rustling and branches creaking. A look around confirmed that the rest of the Griffins had taken their places among the trees. They all had an air of grim determination; they did not expect to survive this battle. *What have we sentenced these creatures to?* Aria thought.

**Don't think about it. Just concentrate on bringing down as many as you can.**

Aria was startled at how well Lareo knew her. She just nodded. She formulated her battle plan. They are flying creatures, so they need air to support them; if they no longer have air around them, then they wouldn't be able fly.

*Plan A: create a vacuum. If that fails, Plan B: use a gale to smash them together,* Aria thought to Lareo. He turned around, startled.

*That's a brilliant idea, love.*

Aria barely had a chance to feel confident about her plan, when the cloud fragmented into individual flying creatures before her eyes.

# Chapter Twenty-Five
## BATTLE

Aria tightened her grip on Rifina, who didn't notice at all as she had tensed her whole body in anticipation. Ahead of them, Fyn had also tensed, ready to pounce.

The creatures got closer; close enough for Aria to make out their general detail. They were completely black, and there was an ethereal quality to them. They were like ghosts that were somehow also powerful and substantial. They had large red eyes, a long snout full of razor-sharp teeth, big bodies that were black, which somehow strangely shimmered like a pond at night, creating the illusion of insubstantial ghostliness, and reptilian wings. The Griffins sprang into action, with Fyn in the lead. They flew out to meet them, clear of the forest.

Aria concentrated on the air around her and didn't pay too much attention to the others' actions. Aria called the air to her effortlessly, as it was now second nature. Through the air, she could sense everyone, including Lareo who felt as though he was the air itself.

There was a difference between the Griffins and the Mort-Spectres. The Griffins felt as though they worked with the air. They used the air to hold them up, but at the same time also drew from their own strength. The Mort-Spectres, on the other hand, felt like intruders. They were forcing themselves through the air. This made picking them out easy.

Aria went for the closest one to her and Rifina, which was

coming in to attack. She created a bubble of turbulence around it, and then sucked the air out. It died instantly. Aria felt Rifina rearing and snatching at another with her claws. She got it around the neck, and it fell from the sky.

Soon Mort-Spectres were falling like hailstones; Aria kept sucking the air out of their lungs. While Aria was creating a vacuum around one of them, she saw two more about to attack them. Aria could feel Rifina thrashing underneath her; she was busy. Aria kept the bubble creating the vacuum going and turned to the incoming threat. She felt the air around them but could not make a second vacuum.

Instead, Aria called forth a gale, confining it to the two attackers. It slowed them down but, as they didn't use the air to fly, this had little impact on them. Aria felt the vacuum suck the last of the air out of the first Mort-Spectre and it collapsed, but she could not swing the vacuum around to the other two. The air couldn't move them, but maybe it could hold them.

The air this high up in the mountain was cool but not freezing. If I could alter the temperature and make it colder, it should stop them. This thought popped into Aria's head, and without a second to consider it, she implemented it.

#

## Lareo ♂

Lareo was in the middle of sucking the air out from two Mort-Spectres, when he felt the change in the air. He had been using the air around him to warn him of incoming threats. He had also discovered the difference between the Griffins and the

Mort-Spectres and was intrigued by it.

What he felt now was incredible power. The two Mort-Spectres fell from the sky, and Lareo had a moment to spin around and see the disturbance. He both saw and felt what was happening; Aria was facing two incoming Mort-Spectres. Lareo could feel the freezing cold air coming from that direction. He felt the air particles being forced together and the temperature dropping to sub-zero.

He couldn't believe what saw. Aria had frozen her attackers in place. But they were not frozen because of the temperature – it didn't seem to have affected them at all. Instead, it was the fact that, despite their ability to force their way through the air, the air was now so thick and dense, it held them in place.

Lareo snapped back into action. This allowed for so much more; he could now kill and freeze different attackers at the same time. Unsure on how many he had killed, he just kept on going without pausing. Fyn was doing the same. The fighting continued this way for several minutes.

There was a break in immediate attacks. Lareo took that opportunity to look around at his fellow warriors. Everyone seemed to be handling themselves well. He did notice that their numbers had diminished, but not to the same extent as the Mort-Spectres, which was encouraging. He turned to find his next target, when he caught sight of Aria and realised that she was in danger.

She was holding two Mort-Spectres in a bubble of air slowly being vacuumed to her right-hand side, and in front of her, she was combining particles to freeze two more Mort-Spectres. What she had failed to notice was that a Mort-

Spectre hurtled towards her from behind. This one looked as if it was the leader; it certainly was the biggest and most aggressive of the lot. It had clearly marked Aria as the biggest threat and was about to attack her.

Lareo yelled for Fyn and directed him towards her. Fyn had just ripped a Mort-Spectre to pieces and turned to look. He understood immediately and set off. Lareo was glad he had not launched himself into the air; there was so much turbulence from the flapping of so many giant creatures.

As they neared Aria, Lareo's heart plummeted. The Mort-Spectre was going to reach her before they did. Lareo didn't know whether his power could extend to cover the distance, but he had to try, anyway. He employed both tactics at the same time; he created a bubble and thickened the air; although this was not enough to kill, it did slow it down.

As Lareo came closer, he sucked the air out of the bubble so powerfully that the surrounding air reverberated and knocked everyone slightly. The Griffins were able to withstand the ripple, but the Mort-Spectres could not. This tipped the odds in the Griffins' favour, and they could now finish off their attackers.

#

## Aria ♀

Aria had just brought down four Mort-Spectres when the air rippled from right behind her. Rifina spun around in alarm. Aria saw a Mort-Spectre falling from the sky. It looked as if it had been a mere hand-span away from Rifina's hind legs. Aria looked around bewildered and saw the rest being ripped apart in the confusion of the blow. Then she found Lareo and their eyes locked.

*What happened?!* Aria thought to him, panicked.

*One of them was about to kill you from behind while you were concentrating on those others.*

Aria's ears began to ring as all the Griffins shouted in jubilation. They turned around and headed back into the forest. Aria slowly regained her composure and started celebrating the victory. They landed and took stock.

There were a significant number of Griffins still standing. But of those numbers, a lot were injured. Aria looked at Fyn and saw that he was sporting a broken back paw and his tail hung limply. Aria slid down Rifina and examined her. She was in bad shape. The talons on one claw were bleeding, and her wing looked injured, possibly broken. Aria hadn't realised that she had been injured while they were flying. Aria was amazed at her courage and determination and ability to keep flying and fighting, and she asked how Rifina had managed it.

'It was all because of you actually,' Rifina said, gratefully. Aria looked at her, perplexed. 'With you on my back, I was not flying through the air, but rather I was being held by it.'

Aria had no idea what that meant; she would need to talk to the others about it later. In the meantime, she was concerned with all the injuries Rifina had sustained.

'You're injured,' Aria stated.

'Yes, I will Heal in time,' Rifina replied, moving gingerly.

'Please let me try?'

Rifina heaved a sigh, which turned into a wince. 'Fine. But

you are wasting your time.'

Aria first examined each part that she thought was injured and then did a thorough inspection of each other area, just to get an idea before starting. There was a lot more to the injuries than she'd thought. In addition to the bleeding talons and broken wing, there was also a lot of bruising.

Instinctively, the magic came without being called on. It flowed from Aria's hands and formed an aura. It took longer to be completely full as Rifina was larger than anyone else she had ever Healed before. Once created, the aura seeped into Rifina and formed the centre. The magic moved its way through the body. Because of the number of injuries, Aria was holding the stream of magic for longer than she expected.

Luckily there was no internal bleeding. Aria started from the inside. The magic slowly Healed the veins causing the bruises and eased out the sprains and aches. She slowly edged the magic all the way out to the paw; it stopped the bleeding and encouraged the talons to grow. Then Aria finally pushed the magic to Rifina's wing. It was the most difficult bit to Heal. The bones had to be fused back together carefully to ensure they set properly.

When Aria had finished, she withdrew her power but did not open her eyes straight away. She took a few deep breaths of air, using it to recharge herself. She opened her eyes and was startled by what she saw. It was pitch-black now. It had taken all afternoon to Heal Rifina, but it had not felt that long. Aria looked around and saw that they had been moved back into the forest somehow. The entire colony had gathered around, staring at Aria, who looked up at Rifina.

'I am completely Healed,' Rifina announced to the colony.

The leader came forwards and looked intently at Aria. 'You Healed her with your magic?'

'Yes,' Aria said meekly.

'Over the years, we have had a few Fairies passing through our land,' he explained. 'Some of them were Treaters. They tried to Heal our sick or injured but only made things worse. Their magic combined with ours in a deadly way.'

Aria stared at him, puzzled. She turned to Rifina, who answered with a look that said she had trusted Aria either way. Aria nodded in understanding.

'Fyn told me how you tried to get into one of the nests with a sick Griffin in it. How did you know?'

'I... I felt the sick Griffin.' Aria turned in desperation, searching for Lareo or the others. A couple of Griffins parted to reveal Lareo standing next to Fyn, with the others behind them.

'Can you do that again?' he asked, indicating Rifina.

Aria turned to the leader, once more puzzled.

'That Griffin you felt is my daughter. Her egg was damaged right before she hatched, and she has had a broken wing ever since.'

'I can try,' Aria answered uncertainly.

'Follow me,' he said as he launched himself into the air and flew towards the nest Aria had sensed earlier.

He landed in it and Aria followed suit. Her jaw dropped, and she gasped. The nest was big enough to fit three grown Griffins. There was one area that had leftover bones and some pieces of meat. On the opposite side was a small Griffin about half the size of Rifina. She had dark feathers. Her eyes were yellow and wide open in shock. Her one wing opened as she stood up, but the other did not.

'Father?'

'Do not worry, my child. She is here to help you.'

'But she is a Fairy.' Aria sighed at this remark.

Her father, however, said soothingly, 'Yes, she is. But she is more than a mere Fairy. She has lots of power.'

She looked worried. 'If you think she can help…'

The leader turned to Aria and nodded. She edged forward until she was standing in front of the young Griffin.

'Make yourself comfortable. I don't know how long it will take.'

# Chapter Twenty-Six
## AFTERMATH

<u>Lareo</u> ♂

Lareo had spent all afternoon going over every detail of the battle for the others, mainly so that Caellum could make notes of it. They were amazed at the things they had done. Lareo was even more shocked at what happened after the battle; no Fairy Treater had ever been able to Heal other creatures besides Elves, who were similar to Fairies.

They watched the Griffins closely. They became more and more restless as the time passed and news of what Aria was doing spread. Fyn came over to them and explained what had happened the previous times a Fairy tried. But he was quick to assure them that Rifina had agreed to it.

Lareo and the others sat at a distance, watching what Aria was doing. It was quite amazing. She had her eyes closed and didn't seem bothered by all the noise around her. She moved strategically, placing her hands on each part of Rifina's body. In some places, she lingered for a longer time than others; clearly, these were the more damaged parts.

As for Rifina, she also had her eyes closed. As Aria moved to new parts, Rifina's face contorted and then slowly changed to relief. This happened every time Aria placed her hands, whether she lingered or moved on quickly.

Eventually, as the sky grew completely dark, Aria finished. There was a moment of uncertainty until Rifina announced that she was Healed. The leader walked over and started having a conversation with Aria. Lareo edged forward to get a better view of what was going on and locked eyes with Aria. He was about to ask her, mentally, what was going on, when the leader took flight, and she followed.

Rifina came over and explained where they were going. This would probably take even longer than it had taken with Rifina. Fyn suggested they get some food, and he offered them an empty nest, which they accepted. Brezan and Elvya went back to the carriage to get some supplies and blankets for the night, and they flew up into the nest and made themselves comfortable.

Despite being completely drained from the battle, Lareo could not sleep. He tossed and turned in the nest. Eventually he flew down and went in search of the nest where Aria was. He asked a few guards along the way who pointed him to the right nest. He flew up and landed gently.

In the nest, the leader sat staring with beady eyes, and flapped his wings occasionally. He watched his daughter, who looked as though she was sleeping peacefully, while Aria held her wing, concentrating with her eyes moving rapidly under her closed eyelids. Lareo took the blanket he had brought with him and draped it over her shoulders. He settled down against the edge of the nest with the other blanket.

After a long while of silence, Lareo and the leader started talking. Lareo explained their whole story and how they had ended up outside the protection of the Faydom.

The leader was amazed at what they had done and what they were planning to do. He slipped into silence, while pondering everything Lareo had said. Despite fighting against it, sleep overcame Lareo. He was restless but managed to get enough rest to recover his strength. He was stirred awake by a gentle rustling in the nest.

#

Lareo squinted into the bright sunlight. When his eyes had adjusted, he saw that it was Fyn and Caellum who had landed in the nest, carrying food. They were uncertain whether they should try to feed Aria and the Griffin, or whether that would disturb them. They settled on trying to give them some juice to keep them hydrated and provide them with some strength; both of them took it as a reflex.

Caellum and Fyn settled into the nest to keep them company; it was now a tight squeeze in the nest with three grown Griffins. Fyn asked Caellum question after question about their journey. He looked absolutely enthralled. He then turned to Lareo, and they started discussing what happened during the battle and how the Aurious power had helped immensely. Lareo enjoyed talking to a warrior leader; they shared tactics and strategy.

The sun had set before there was any movement. First, the Griffin stirred, followed by Aria. Lareo bolted to Aria to catch her before her knees gave way. She looked slightly dazed and confused. She blinked slowly, and comprehension dawned. She leaned over to the Griffin, who opened her eyes as Aria stroked her cheek.

'Let me check you,' whispered Aria and she closed her eyes

again while her hands touched either side of the Griffin's face.

She nodded every now and then. Finally, she seemed satisfied and released her hold.

'She is better. I had to grow and mend the bones,' Aria explained. 'The outer structure with the feathers, which develops after hatching, grew normally as she aged. It was the bones inside her wing, which were damaged before hatching, that were the problem. How long was I busy?'

'A whole day. It is now the night after you started,' Caellum answered.

'Love, you need food and rest,' Lareo told her. He turned to the Griffin leader. 'So does your daughter.'

He nodded and said, 'Yes. Thank you both. You have done my colony and me a great service. Please stay one more night so that we may talk again tomorrow?'

Lareo agreed. He picked Aria up and flew her down, followed by Caellum and Fyn. Fyn bowed and wished them a good night. Lareo and Caellum flew back to the nest they were using. Brezan and Elvya had food waiting for them, and they were relieved to see their friends return. Aria had some food, laid down and was asleep in an instant.

Although exhausted and not fully recovered from the battle, Lareo stayed up to explain. Caellum wrote feverishly with a look of awe on his face. Brezan was utterly stunned; it had always been an impossible feat. Only Elvya didn't look as surprised. 'I could always feel her power. As I can yours.' She nodded to Lareo. 'Nothing you two do will ever surprise me.'

When Caellum's quill had stopped scratching on the paper, they decided to sleep. Caellum was itching to know more, but as the only one who could answer his questions was sleeping deeply, he decided he may as well join her. Two of the four fell asleep. The other two stayed up.

# Chapter Twenty-Seven
## BEGINNINGS AND ENDINGS

<u>Elvya</u>

The friendship had been a strange development. Elvya had been so furious at Brezan for putting everyone in danger in the dream world, especially Aria, who had become like a sister to Elvya. However, when she was tasked with the duty of looking after him, her hatred began to wane. From there, they had progressed into friendship. When Aria and Lareo were fighting, they had comforted each other. Caellum was too absorbed in his books to notice much. They had clung to each other until they heard the warriors flying back amidst victory cries and went to investigate. They had hugged each other in happiness.

Elvya smiled as she thought of what had happened next; they had stepped back from each other, and she had felt something other than relief. She realised that she felt a deep affection for Brezan. He had gently stroked her cheek and lifted her chin. Just as gently, he kissed her.

Now they lay together in the nest, exhausted after the emotional and physical turmoil of the past few days. She snuggled closer to Brezan.

As she looked out at the predawn darkness, she mused about her life. The darkness used to frighten her and force her to relive all the sorrows of her past. But not now. No, last night she had been as far from her past as the sun was from the moon. Sunrise no longer meant relief that she had survived through the horrors of the night. It showed that she had faced them and overcome them. As his arms tightened around her, the happiness and effervescence bubbled inside her from the love she felt. He had appeared in her life so suddenly, and yet he fit in perfectly. They were each other's equal match. This was her bliss; staring at the sunrise through the dewdrop-covered twigs of the nest, wrapped in his warm embrace. She knew she could face anything with him at her side.

She had an uncontrollable urge to giggle now. She looked at Brezan and smiled. He beamed back at her. They moved closer, and together they settled down and fell asleep.

#

## Aria ♀

Before Aria was fully conscious, she could smell the trees around her. She was warm and cosy, cuddled next to Lareo. Aria opened her eyes and saw that he was fast asleep. She stared at him for a few minutes. *I was fortunate to have found him*, Aria thought happily. *And to have survived everything together*, she added. She gingerly slid out from under his arm and sat up.

It was not long after dawn. The sun, although starting to shine brightly, had not warmed everything up yet. Aria looked around at her friends. She was just thinking how grateful she was to have them all, when a strange sight made her smile.

Elvya was sleeping on Brezan's chest, and he was holding her tightly.

As Aria watched, Elvya stirred. She looked around warily and jumped when she saw Aria watching her with glee. Aria went to sit down next to her as Brezan woke up. He looked sheepish as he saw Aria.

Before they could explain, Aria said, 'I knew already.'

They looked stumped. 'How?' Elvya asked.

'Well, when we were trapped in the wasteland, I was digging at the earth to occupy myself. Under the dirt, not too far down, I discovered lush green grass. Since we returned from the dream, I have been thinking, and I realised that it meant that you were genuinely in love. The wasteland was your mind, your subconscious. I think that you have been feeling that love for a while and you thought it was directed toward me and therefore you felt conflicted, which created the wasteland and covered the happiness.'

'Wow!' they said together.

'You are the most well-rounded Treater that there has ever been,' came Caellum's voice from behind.

Aria turned to see that both Caellum and Lareo had woken up and were listening with rapt attention. She smiled and said, 'Did you hear all of that?'

'Yes,' Caellum replied, and Lareo nodded.

Lareo walked over to Brezan and held out his hand. Brezan took it, and Lareo wished him congratulations. They finished off the food that they had brought last night. Aria sat with Elvya, and she explained everything that had happened that led to them being together. She was overjoyed with happiness.

\#

They were all in excellent moods when they had finished breakfast. They flew down to meet Fyn and Rifina on their way to talk to the Leader as they had promised. The Griffins led them to the biggest tree.

'This is where the leader and the army leader meet to discuss strategy,' Fyn explained.

They all flew up with Brezan helping Elvya; Aria was back to full strength. Landing in the nest, they saw the leader waiting with two other older-looking Griffins. Fyn and Rifina bowed. The leader greeted Aria and Lareo as old friends and invited all of them to sit.

'So young warriors, what is your next course of action?'

Aria looked to Lareo, who said, 'We are planning on going to Fiamme.'

'And then?' the leader asked sceptically.

'And then... we look for the next Auriouses and their Light-Keeper.'

The leader just looked at them and blinked. Aria understood what he meant; it was not much of a plan.

'We are going to try to find the fire Light-Keeper first. Elvya will be able to sense them as we near them, so we'll be able to identify him or her. After that, the Light-Keeper will be able to help lead us to their Auriouses, as it is their job.'

'That sounds better,' he said, nodding. 'I do not want my two best fighters going off on a fruitless journey.'

Aria exchanged a puzzled glance with Lareo, who mirrored

her confusion. He obviously was not privy to this information either. Aria looked at Rifina, who looked completely at ease and not surprised at all.

'What?' Aria asked the leader.

'They came to me this morning and asked if they could join you on your journey and be of any assistance. They said they felt a bond with you and could not imagine leaving you to go out on your own.'

Aria gaped at him. She had felt the same reluctance to leave Rifina. But she had never imagined that the Griffins would join them.

'It will be a perilous journey. It does not end in Fiamme. We have to go all the way to the Aurious castle and reclaim it,' Lareo explained carefully to the two Griffins.

They smiled and nodded. 'Yes, we had expected something like that. Even amongst us, the prophecy is known,' Fyn answered.

Although they tried, there was no way to persuade the Griffins otherwise. In the end, Aria and Lareo accepted their help gratefully. They all agreed that it was best to leave straight away. They thanked the Griffin leader profusely, only to have his thanks returned in equal measure. They went to gather everything from their borrowed nest and repacked the carriage with extra food and supplies that the Griffins had gathered.

There was nothing left to do but say goodbye. All the Griffins had come out in full force to send them on their way. The leader's daughter stepped forward.

'I want you to have this,' she said, holding out a bracelet, 'as a token of my thanks.'

Aria took the bracelet gently. It was made of strong plants woven together, with a stone hanging from it. It was an average-size stone, dyed with mud and plants in varying shades of colour, and had been polished to a shine. There was a hole through the middle, through which it was attached to the weaving. Next to the weaving through the hole was a small feather held in tightly.

Aria looked up and asked in awe, 'Did you make this?'

'Yes,' she said humbly. 'Before you healed me, that was all I could do with my time.'

'Thank you, it is beautiful,' Aria said as she hugged her.

It was a very teary goodbye after that. They got into the carriage, and Lareo wrapped an arm around Aria's shoulders. The two Griffins walked on either side as the carriage set off on its own.

They were setting out into the unknown. Seven friends ready for the journey ahead.

*~THE END OF BOOK 1~*

# How reviews help our authors.

Readers choose books based on recommendations. Leaving an Amazon review is like telling your friends how much you enjoyed your latest read…

After 20-25 reviews, Amazon includes the author's books in 'also bought' and 'you might like' lists. This increases its visibility on the site and helps boost sales.

After 50-70 reviews, Amazon highlights the book for spotlight positions and its newsletter. A HUGE boost for an author.

Reviews help authors sell more books.

Leave your review here.

*Music is a journey, and they're lost in the lyrics.*

When musicians Matty and Sandy crack open a dusty old book of folk songs, they hope to escape into the whimsical stylings of the past. They don't expect to actually be taken there.

Yet just a few notes sung from its cursed pages whisks them away to the world of Old England and all its hey-nonny-nonnies, myths and magic. In a dire twist of fate, Sandy is taken prisoner by the heartbroken Lord Donald who seeks to sacrifice her in the hope of resurrecting his lost love.

Knowing he must find Sandy and stop the murderous Lord before May Day, Matty needs allies now more than ever. Can a lustful witch and a plucky swordswoman guide him through the musically-induced mayhem of this strange - yet oddly familiar - world? Or is Sandy well and truly folked?

Drake Banks is a 12-year-old boy who is used to moving from one army camp to another. After the death of his father, Drake and his mother have to get used to living a normal life in the town where she grew up. This proves challenging for Drake as he misses the army life. Drake finds an old arcade in his new town. He loves video games! One day, after arriving at the arcade, Drake discovers a new game called Death Trap. He did not know how his life was about to drastically change. After pressing Start, Drake is sucked into the video game.

Upon entering this new world, Drake has to face a series of dangerous challenges and survive if he wants to get back home. But he soon realises that he is not alone. There are two other competitors, Scott Vent and Crystal Moon, who are computer programmes. The race is on! However, it isn't long before they realise that they cannot face these challenges alone. Can they put their differences aside and work together?

Cosmo knows he's crazy, his homicidal squirrel tells him so every day. Not that Bandit has to, he just likes reminding him of the facts of the situation. After living at Wellspring Hospital for the last two years not much has changed for Cosmo. His pills are still rainbow coloured, therapy is still a bore, and above all he isn't getting better. Bandit's trying to help too, but the dead body he brought in seems to be causing problems. In an attempt to understand what's going on behind the secure walls a band of misfits come together in the search for a murderer. However, it's easier said than done when you don't know what's real. Maybe it's easier? Maybe, just maybe, the only people who can find the truth are those that have to question everything.

Whatever happened to all those Classical gods and goddesses after those pesky mortals tossed them by the wayside? They didn't just vanish; you know.

Goddesses of The Light such as Athena and Freya, continue waging a never-ending war against the Anubis-led Darkness as they vie for a portal controlling time and space. Not being one to trifle with such tedium, Apollo sips nectar and chases togas with his friend Bacchus, in the VIP section of Heaven's hotel bar.

But life turns on a dime when Apollo finds himself trapped on modern-day Earth. A wonderful "New Earth" filled with electric guitars and street tacos and a morally flexible tour guide named Coyote. But Apollo soon learns he's lost his powers and immortality and, to make matters worse, he's being stalked to feed an ancient Sumerian demon who grows stronger each time it consumes a god's essence.

When the war in Heaven takes an unexpected turn, more gods are exiled to Earth. They must overcome their distrust of one another to get return tickets to Heaven – even if means saving humanity to do so.